The SISTERHOOD of Unlikely FRIENDS

Books by Sara Brunsvold

The Extraordinary Deaths of Mrs. Kip

The Divine Proverb of Streusel

The Atlas of Untold Stories

The Sisterhood of Unlikely Friends

The Sisterhood of Unlikely Friends

SARA BRUNSVOLD

Revell
a division of Baker Publishing Group
Grand Rapids, Michigan

Published by Revell
a division of Baker Publishing Group
Grand Rapids, Michigan
RevellBooks.com

Printed in the United States of America

Library of Congress Cataloging-in-Publication Data
Names: Brunsvold, Sara, 1979- author
Title: The sisterhood of unlikely friends / Sara Brunsvold.
Description: Grand Rapids, Michigan : Revell, a division of Baker Publishing Group, 2026.
Identifiers: LCCN 2025053845 | ISBN 9780800746131 (paperback) | ISBN 9781493455515 (ebook)
Subjects: LCGFT: Christian fiction | Novels
Classification: LCC PS3602.R865 S57 2026
LC record available at https://lccn.loc.gov/2025053845

Cover illustration by Lauren Mortimer
Cover design by Laura Klynstra

Published in association with Books & Such Literary Management, www.booksandsuch.com.

Baker Publishing Group publications use paper produced from sustainable forestry practices and postconsumer waste whenever possible.

26 27 28 29 30 31 32 7 6 5 4 3 2 1

For the women I walk with
shoulder to shoulder,
toward Home.
May you see your influence
in these pages.

PART 1

ALONE

1

MID-AUGUST BAKED the Flint Hills. It fired into my skin once more as I lumbered sideways down the front steps of my childhood home with a dining chair at each amply padded hip. A dry Kansas breeze carried the chaff of little bluestem grass from the vacant lot behind the house to new destinations and kicked the leaves of the cottonwood towering above the limestone-sided cottage into a chorus of goodbye waves. My Chevy truck rested in the pool of shade on the lawn that Thursday, all of my slowly replenished possessions arranged like a jigsaw puzzle in the bed. The grip of heat stirred up a vague tingle in my left hand, a stubborn remnant of an injury I don't remember sustaining. Since turning forty-two, I had trouble pinpointing the origins of most of my musculoskeletal tweaks.

Behind me, Dad hobbled out the front door, the steady click of his cane measuring his steps. "Sure did pick the finest day to move," he muttered.

"I have a track record of stellar decision-making, Dad."

"Hmmmpf." It was the most he had said in one stretch the whole time we'd worked to load the truck over his lunch break.

I reached the front walk and bowed my head in an attempt to avoid the sun burning holes into my retinas. My shirt clung to my chest with the same sticky sweat that pulled my makeup off in cloudy drops and dribbled down my neck. My hair, which never laid the way it was instructed to anyway, flopped against my ears. Some of the strands caught in the murky rivers of perspiration and stuck to my skin.

I reached the open tailgate and set down the chairs, then paused a moment to stretch my back. Middle age did not play nicely with lugging furniture in the heat, or really anything else.

Dad arrived next to me and held up the yellow Dollar General sack he had carried from the kitchen. "Where you want this, Jess?"

"Floorboards by my plants would be great. Thank you."

He glanced down at the sack. Peanut butter, tortillas, and applesauce. "You sure you don't want to take more?"

"Whatever I'm leaving is all yours. I can get more. Supposedly there's a grocery store right in my neighborhood, walking distance."

He set his mouth in a straight line, the most common answer he gave when I started talking about my two-hour move to Kansas City. He would stay silent when I told him about my remote data entry job with the law firm, had spent all of thirty seconds reviewing the photos of my rental house, and would veer to talk of Woodfield High football if I mentioned anything about said house having room for both of us.

He couldn't see the potential. Somehow, I would get him to see, to believe as strongly as I did that Woodfield was not where we were meant to thrive. Especially not me, the one who had only her seventy-two-year-old father to help her pack.

He click-stepped toward the passenger door to deliver the sack. Sweat had moistened the back of his work shirt along his spine, cutting through "Becker Automotive" across his shoulder blades. His tin-colored Dickies pants retained the old oil stains that I had been unable to release no matter how many times I washed them. He needed to get back to the shop before long.

I wiped my forehead with the back of my hand and dried it on the waistband of my cotton shorts. The chairs were the last things to tie in. I heaved myself into a seated position on the tailgate, then eased up onto my feet. My knees crackled with the movement. A bit of space remained on the driver's side of the bed, between the foot of the twin-size mattress and the sidewall. The bed frame, a folded futon, a nightstand, and a dresser held up the mattress on the passenger side, and a small square dining table, TV stand, and folding table on the other. My bedroom in Dad's house, the place I never thought I'd ever have to live in again, had steadily filled to the gills over the past two years as each item found its way into my possession. I lifted the first chair from the ground by its back and wedged it into the space.

Dad returned from the cab, rested his cane against the tailgate, then held up the second chair to me. I tucked it seat to seat on top of its partner.

"Be sure to tie those down extra tight," he said. "Don't want them flyin' out on the interstate."

"On it." I grabbed the bungee cord already anchored to the sidewall and began the tie-down process. As I crisscrossed the mound of my meager belongings, Dad instructed me where to direct the cords and which parts needed more than one. He was good for such practical advice, but not the kind that would have kept his only child from chasing things—people—she was never meant to hold and going down paths that eventually led only to turned backs and half-true rumors. My choices were my choices, though, and at least I had made one that was right.

Across the street and a block over, the steeple of my Sunday morning home for the past two years rose above the tree line. In that little church, I had chosen the only One who did not view me as a pariah or a pawn in small-town games.

Last cord secured, I eased to the ground again. Dad looped around the truck, tugging on each cord to ensure its security.

"All good," he said at last and reached for the old-school tire pressure gauge he kept as a permanent accessory in his shirt pocket. "Let me check your air real quick."

"I did that already, Dad."

"What about the oil? Fluids?"

I patted the tailgate. "I take care of Hank, and he takes care of me." Some dads taught their kids math or how to throw a ball. Kevin Becker taught car maintenance. I had amassed more facts about carburetors than about my own late mother. He was the reason I had known that Hank, despite his age and all his hard farm miles before I purchased him, was a good bet.

Dad repinned the gauge to his pocket, then scratched the side of his head, mussing the hair above his ear. The back stood up like a mangled rooster tail, thanks to his philosophy of "If I can't see it, why bother?" The skin on the backs of his hands was dried and cracked around the knuckles, the natural consequence of his lack of urgency in personal care or partaking in medical care of any kind. In Kansas City, I could ensure he went to the doctor, ensure he actually enjoyed his golden years, maybe even take him to watch the Chiefs at Arrowhead. The 2023–24 season promised lots of home games, according to the team's website. He could be the happiest he'd ever been. We could be the happiest, together.

I had been too young to do anything to help my mom tend to her diabetes, but I was far old enough and almost together enough to take care of him. If only he would let me.

He dropped his hand to his side. "Guess that's that, then." His pale gray eyes lifted to mine. The lenses of his glasses needed a good clean, his shock of white eyebrows a good trim. A dozen different versions of him flashed one after the other on his form. The dad of my youngest years, standing in my bedroom door asking if I was ready for school. The dad of my teen years, rousing in his recliner as I attempted to sneak in well past my curfew, asking where I'd been. The dad of those seven years I lived with Mick, never asking either of us why rings were not exchanged.

The dad who opened his front door after the breakup two years ago when I had nowhere else to go, and who never asked for any rent. The dad with a furrowed brow, standing in the kitchen one summer Sunday shortly after that, when I had come home and declared my life was different from that point forward.

All the versions of him I ever remembered had the heady scent of automotive fluids and the stained hands of a working man. All of them launched an urge within me to throw myself into his arms and insist he stuff himself in with my plants. But we Beckers didn't hug. We certainly didn't cry in front of each other.

The backs of my eyes burned. I blinked against the sensation. "Guess that's it," I echoed. Words ballooned within me. All I could get out was, "Stay out of trouble."

He nodded at my words, spoken and unspoken, and pointed at Hank. "Keep an eye on that oil. You know how he gulps it."

Hidden among the words were the "I love you" I had never stopped longing for. I nearly broke. Instead, as he would expect of his offspring, I swallowed down the rise of bare honesty, climbed into my truck, and turned the key.

We nodded to each other, and then I drove away.

His was the only farewell I received from the town of a thousand, and his would be the only hello I craved to hear again soon.

I cried for the first one hundred miles.

2

"THE TRICK IN FORGETTING what lays behind is believing in what lays ahead," the pastor at the Woodfield church once said.

As I-35 pulled me into the outskirts of the Kansas City metro, belief grew. Every exit thrummed with activity. People with objectives going here and there. The roads were smooth and wide, overpasses pristine and modern, the stores and businesses more numerous and diverse than seemingly the rest of Kansas combined. The tears forgot to come, my eyes forgot to burn. The place was alive with possibility and promise. In a metro of two million people, I could be who I wanted to be. No one knew Mick or understood the influence of his Shuckers Bar and Grill or what it meant to be shunned out of the employment and company of both.

The interstate crossed into Missouri within a mile of the downtown high-rise buildings and the four signature pylons of Bartle Hall convention center. As the highway curved to take aim directly at them, it dipped sharply and slid under the dense city core. It emerged again on the other side, then swept north toward the Missouri River and the suburbs beyond. I held tightly to Hank's wheel, guiding him through the crush of vehicles and big rigs all competing for space in the multiple lanes of traffic. Belief bloomed in my chest and sent rays of anticipation through me and down to my fingertips. The sensation usurped the vague tingle in my left hand.

Twenty minutes later, I pulled into my new neighborhood off North Oak Trafficway. The bustle of the thoroughfare quieted the farther I followed the street down the row of houses. It narrowed to barely wider than two car widths before winding into a long, sloping curve.

Then, finally, there it was—the house that before then was only an image on my phone screen. The narrow, cream-colored bungalow, all nine hundred square feet of it, was the runt amid the sprawling ranches and split-levels all around it.

I eased Hank into the driveway and stopped adjacent to the front yard on my right. The asphalt slanted downward on a gentle grade along the side of the house and spilled into a paved pad at the back. The covered front porch was a little longer than Hank's bed, and the outdated windows and worn siding spoke of their vigilant fight to stave off the elements. A long, wide, empty lot of freshly trimmed grass stretched between my driveway and the Dutch Boy blue ranch next door. Full, mature trees stood sentinel along the back property line, the shadows of the canopies not quite reaching my roof.

"It's adorable." Nicer than any home I had ever had, far better than the single-wide Mick and I had shared. And it was all mine. The new life I had dreamed of for so long was about to begin.

I checked my phone. Five minutes until two o'clock, the appointed time for me to meet my landlord, Seymour Bove. Until that point, he had been only a voice on the other end of the phone line, saying he lived near downtown and didn't come to my neighborhood much but would drive up to meet me on move-in day. So far, though, Hank was the only vehicle at the house.

With the skill Dad had taught me before I could legally drive, I arranged Hank so that his tailgate was mere feet from the porch steps. While I waited for Seymour, I could at least start untying my load.

As I cut the engine, a glint across the empty lot caught my eye. An older man stepped through the glass storm door of the blue ranch. He hooded his face with his hand, his attention full bore on me.

"Already got myself an audience." I lifted my hand from the steering wheel in my best country-girl wave.

In response, the man launched into a brisk march, aimed squarely my direction.

"Oh, all right." Quickly, I gathered my keys and pushed open my door. With my phone at the ready in case I needed proof I belonged there, I stepped around to Hank's front grille. Waves of heat from the long drive puffed against my bare forearm, carrying with them the aroma of motor oil.

The man was halfway across the lot, his strides as rigid as his sinewy arms at his side. His military-straight posture tracked with his blue T-shirt with "Navy" in gold letters across his chest. He wore it tucked neatly into his cargo shorts. The first person I was to meet in Kansas City stared me down as if I were a threat to all he held dear.

I smiled, assuring him I came in peace. "Hi there. I'm—"

"Jessica Becker?"

I reared back. "Uh, yes?"

"Ron Torres, property manager. Seymour asked me to meet you. He got called away to something else." Ron stopped on the opposite side of the driveway. His salt-and-pepper eyebrows, more pepper than salt, accentuated the undertones of his golden-oak complexion.

"Sorry," I said. "I didn't realize there was a property manager. You live next door?"

"Seymour likes to have a trusted eye on his properties at all times." He settled his hands on his hips and looked me over, then Hank. The below-market rent Seymour charged probably did warrant the extra vigilance.

"Nice to meet you, Ron. Please, call me Jess."

"You can come to me if you have any issues. I also take care of the mowing." The cut lines in the grass of the lot between our houses were almost as perfect as his undercut hairstyle. "Just you, right?" he asked.

"Just me, and my dreams."

His expression remained unchanged. I took it as a sign of mild amusement.

At the far end of the lot, in the shade of the mature trees, lazed a regulation-size soccer goal. The net hung like loose skin from the crossbar. I nodded toward it. "Neighborhood kids play in this lot?"

"My granddaughter. She lives with me."

He had a granddaughter. There was even more potential he had a softer side socked away. "How old is she?" I asked.

"Fourteen. Started high school this week." He craned his neck to peer over my shoulder at the haul in Hank's bed. "Got somebody to help you unload?"

Clearly we were moving on to other topics. I followed his lead. "I don't have much stuff. I can probably get it."

"I can help once we're done with the walk-through."

The softer side emerged. I nodded. "That would be nice."

"Ready to see the place?" He started for the front door before I could answer.

Perfunctory and efficient. Two of Dad's favorite things.

Two short steps led up to the porch. The treads needed a coat or two of paint.

"Are you a Navy man?" I asked, clunking up to the porch behind him.

"I am. My daughter's in the service now. Kyla's mom. She's on the *Roosevelt*, underway in the Mediterranean."

"Sounds exotic."

He pulled his keys from his pocket without a reply.

I tucked my hair behind my ear and waited for him to unlock the front door, which bore the same Dutch Boy blue as his house and a large, gold-trimmed oval of frosted glass. I folded my hands at my waist. In a matter of seconds, I would be standing in the house that had occupied my thoughts every minute of my extra shifts at the Red Rooster gas station.

The dead bolt clacked open under Ron's command. The hinges whined as he pushed open the door. He stood aside. "After you."

I held my breath, then stepped inside. The pictures from the rental listing burst into life. Hardwood floors throughout. Sunlight streaming through the bare windows, highlighting the brush marks on the khaki-colored plaster walls. From the front door, the entire length of the house was visible. The living room ended about ten paces from the door, the boundary marked on the right by a pass-through window into the kitchen and on the left by a knockout bay window. The square table would fit perfectly in the nook.

I crossed the living room, gathering whiffs of fresh paint. "This is nice," I said.

The bay window overlooked the lot and the soccer goal at the end. I turned right, through the arched doorway framing the galley kitchen.

"Fridge is new," Ron said. "The back right burner of the stove doesn't work, but I can't find parts for it."

"I don't really cook anything more difficult than canned ravioli anyway." I opened every cabinet and drawer. They offered minimal storage space, but that was more than enough for me. I turned around and joined Ron in the hall.

He pointed at the door next to the kitchen entrance. "Basement. Runs under the back half of the house. Your laundry's up here, though, just across from the bedrooms there." He indicated a set of accordion doors next to the nook on the left.

After the basement door came the bathroom, the only one in the house. The pastel-pink tile and aqua-colored tub were straight off the set of *The Golden Girls*. But the toilet was new, all the grout was intact, and the tub faucet lacked calcified hard-water buildup. In that regard, it far surpassed the bathroom in Dad's house back in Woodfield.

Next came the smaller of the two bedrooms, barely large enough for a twin bed and a dresser. The only window faced east.

I stepped into the room and spun slowly around to see it from all angles.

"Previous renter had bunk beds for her kids in there," Ron said. "Bigger than it looks."

"Big enough for a desk, and that's all I need. I work from home. Data entry for Henson-Miden Law Firm. First job I've ever had where I didn't need to be on my feet all day." I stopped and looked at him. "Not sure why I felt you needed to know that, but there it is."

He shrugged one shoulder. "Good to know you're employed."

That I was. Employed, and gainfully so. Much more than Red Rooster or burger flipping at Shuckers ever offered. Yet more proof that Woodfield was not where I was meant to thrive.

He moved us on to the laundry closet. The accordion doors screeched on their tracks. Behind them hid two ancient Kenmores, the kind with clicky dials and metal buttons.

"They're old but still work," Ron said.

"I know the feeling," I quipped.

It drew the slightest uptick in his lips before he continued. "This used to be a closet, so you've lost some storage space."

Capping off the hallway was the door to the second bedroom. Though double the size of the first one and possessing two side-by-side windows with a view of the backyard, it was still only large enough for a queen-size bed, a dresser, a nightstand, and maybe a bookcase. I had only two of those things, but I vowed to someday have them all. And someday was bound to come soon enough.

Last on the tour, the basement. Ron led me down the stairs, the angle of which was not as sharp as I expected for the age of the house. They pivoted at a landing halfway down and finished against the east wall somewhere under the first bedroom.

Ron reached the bottom and switched on the main light.

A single open room ran the length and width of the back half of the house. The spaces between the exposed floor joists overhead were stuffed with insulation, draped with wires, and partially filled by air ducts. At the opposite end was an insulated outside door flanked on each side by a window. Tucked under the upper flight of stairs were the HVAC system and water heater, along with a closet. The cinder-block walls were painted white to pull in as much light as possible, but the concrete floor remained its natural steely hue.

"Previous renter used it as a rec room for her kids," Ron said. "Even had a mini fridge and high-top table. She put down rugs to keep the floor warmer, though it stays pretty comfortable down here."

Instead of playthings, though, my imagination drew a twin bed against the wall. Dad's TV, his recliner. Some freestanding cabinets I might find on clearance at the home improvement store. If the landlord was up for me paying for the renovation, maybe I could convert the closet to a half bath with a toilet and a pedestal sink. It could be Dad's own space, private and cozy, with a separate door for all the coming and going he cared to do, maybe to ask Ron to have a beer. It could all be his. It could be amazing. After all I had squandered, all the years wasted waiting on someone else to get himself in gear so I could follow along, God had given me a chance to lead, to create more good in life than I ever thought possible. I wasn't about to screw it up.

My chin trembled. I covered it with my hand.

"How's everything look?" Ron asked.

I shook my head, took a steadying breath. "I think it's better than I could have asked for."

3

WITH RON'S HELP, it didn't take long to get my furniture moved in and set up. The little square dining table indeed fit into the nook across from the kitchen as if that spot was its destiny. Off to the side of the bay window, within arm's length of the table, I set up my one-year-old, pink-striped rubber tree plants, Shania and Mariah, on their wire stands. It was the perfect spot for "the divas" to bask in the indirect sunlight. They had each grown to over a foot tall, and their new environment would surely keep them vivacious.

As I cleaned the road dust from Mariah's waxy leaves with a wet paper towel, Ron tromped into the house carrying the last box. "Got any more furniture coming?" he asked.

"Nope, that's it."

"Really?" He set the box on the table and looked around at the sparseness. The futon and television on its stand made the compact living room seem twice as large. "Did you come from a studio apartment or something?"

"Or something," I said, starting on Shania's bath.

He didn't dig into that answer. Instead, he told me about the "pretty good" thrift store in the same shopping center as the grocer. His allowance for my personal stuff to remain personal was a clear sign he'd do nicely as a neighbor. As was his quick exit thereafter to "let you get settled."

When the latch clicked behind him, I paused to soak in the moment. My first solo moment on my first day in my first house. *My.* That had a nice ring to it. In the hug of the bay window, I closed my eyes and gathered in as much air as my lungs could hold. A soft prayer wove into my exhale. "Thank you, God."

The rest of the afternoon blazed by with all the tiny to-dos that creating a nest entails. Clothes to be put away. DVDs to stack in the TV stand. Dishware to be organized. Shower curtain to be hung. Bath rug to be unfurled and placed just so.

A little before four o'clock, a Henson-Miden Law courier arrived with my tech equipment, along with an IT quick-start guide and the direct number of my HML boss, Paul. According to the note that human resources had included with the delivery, I was to log in for orientation at eight o'clock the next morning. The recruiter had told me during the offer call that they didn't typically start people on a Friday, but I had insisted I didn't want to wait around any longer than I had to.

I placed my new laptop and monitor on a folding table in the small bedroom, scooted a camping chair into place, and stood back to admire the small beginning of a big adventure.

Such a beautiful sight, that little setup. I was big time. In the city, with a real, respectable job, one with real benefits and a predictable income. I could support the Jess Becker of that moment and the Jess Becker a year from then, and still have enough left over for Dad. Me.

I chuckled. The sound bounced off the empty walls. "Who would've thought, Jess?"

Certainly not Mick, or any of the "friends" I had until our breakup. As soon as he turned his back on me, he ensured they all did too.

With the house in order, I roused up Hank for our next great first: city grocery shopping.

Cost Cutter was five times bigger than anything near Woodfield, and far more opulent. Its sleek roofline was held aloft two stories from the ground by steel-framed glass. Large chrome letters spelled out its name between the two sets of sliding doors. Winging out from the grocer were nearly two dozen businesses. A gym, a clothes resale shop, two banks, a coffee shop, a dollar store, several fast-food joints, and the thrift store Ron endorsed. All within a mile of my house. Sweet Hank with his rusty wheel wells and oil cologne offered a perfect socioeconomic bookend to the Mercedes sedan I parked next to.

I picked my way through the lot on my way to the entrance. Ahead of me, a woman in a dinky tank top that could double as swimwear strolled with graceful confidence and a designer handbag slung over her forearm. Her ribs showed under her skin as she walked.

I turned my head to the right, not needing another reminder of how far from skeletal my sagging body had become.

In the distance, across the busy street on the south side of the shopping center, a sizable brick church crowned a hill. Its massive, snowy steeple jutted straight into the atmosphere. Ten copies of the church I attended back in Woodfield would have fit inside. No one there would know about my ex, my dirt, or the butterfly tattoo on my shoulder that had seemed like such a wise choice when I was twenty-four. Maybe that brick church on the hill was where I needed to be, able to choose whether I was seen or not.

Twenty minutes later, I returned to Hank with four plastic bags of generic-brand staples suspended from my hands and not a single hello exchanged with anyone who was not paid to greet the customers. Anonymity was refreshingly easy to come by in the city.

Hank and I rattled our way back to our little home on the narrow street. A stiffness crept into my joints in the most pleasant way. It wasn't from standing for hours ringing up bottles of sodas and packs of cigarettes for earth-splattered customers, to earn pennies that someday, maybe, Lord willing, would fund a way out. It was from completing the foundation upon which all that came next would be built.

Who would have thought it?

I pulled into my driveway with a grin and visions of what the next weeks would bring, the freedoms to be enjoyed, the paths to be carved. But when I started looping the sack handles around my wrists, a different kind of sensation took over. Someone was watching me.

I sat up straight, dragging the sacks and my purse across the seat. On the other end of the grassy lot, a teenage girl stood with one foot on a soccer ball and her gaze fixed my direction. Both her complexion and her studious stance hearkened to Ron's. She stayed put the whole time I pulled myself and my possessions from my truck and shut the door.

I waved with my least burdened hand. The gesture was met by absolute stillness.

"Definitely takes after her grandfather," I mumbled and headed to the porch.

The girl returned to her practice before I reached my front walk.

Such, then, would be our relationship—me waving from a distance and her stoically entertaining the notion about reciprocating. She was a teen, after all, and I was the sweaty, non-skeletal tenant next door. No need to push it further than that tenuous social balance.

So why did I come to a stop on the porch steps?

I sighed. We weren't strangers passing in the grocery store aisle. We lived one grassy lot apart. The whack of her foot against the ball reached me there on the porch. The refrain of her play would likely bleed through the windows too. I couldn't just gloss by that forever.

I gritted my teeth and set the sacks and my purse on the top step. Then I turned around and headed toward my next chance to be awkward.

The girl had her back to me, her ponytail of thick, dark hair swinging as she worked through a semicircle of balls she had arranged in front of the goal. After checking the alignment of one ball near the top of the arc, she backed up several paces, launched into a running start, and sailed it into the net with a force the placekickers at Woodfield R-1 High would have envied.

I whistled softly to myself and continued my trek through the grass.

The next ball. *Whack*. Sail. Net!

"Wow, you're pretty good at that," I called.

She jerked around to face me, her expression somewhere between shock and mortification. I would have had the same reaction at her age had any unknown adult dared to enter or be near my personal space.

I stopped several yards away, giving us both a buffer. "Wanted to introduce myself. I'm Jess Becker, your new neighbor. You must be Ron's granddaughter. Kyla, right?"

She crossed her arms and nodded.

"Your grandpa told me you were a soccer player."

She only nodded again, which was fair because I wasn't giving her much to work with.

I folded my hands and tapped my thumbs together, willing the action to somehow jar loose an engaging next line. "So," I said, "do you play for a team?"

Her voice was quiet. "Hoping to play for my school."

"Right. High school. You're a freshman?"

Another nod. She eyed the next ball a few feet away.

"Seems weird I know all this about you and you've never met me, doesn't it?" I chuckled. It sounded weird and forced, and like something I should never do again.

"Is high school as delightful as I remember it?" I asked. "And by delightful I mean the worst thing ever invented?"

We progressed to a shrug.

"Math was always my worst subject," I said. "Or chemistry. PE wasn't all that great either. English was probably my favorite." Rambling was not helping my cause by any means, but to my utter shock, she tilted her head as if receiving every word.

After a brief pause, she nodded toward my driveway. "I like your truck."

"Thank you. That's Hank. He's a good truck."

Her eyebrows pushed together. "You named your truck?"

"Sure. In my family, it's tradition. I mean, I started the tradition, but still. I've named every vehicle I've ever had."

A grin played on her lips. "Nice."

A teenager thought something I had said was nice. That was my signal to quit while I was ahead. "It was great to meet you, Kyla. Thanks for letting me interrupt your practice. Hope it goes well."

She nodded a thanks and then, breakthrough of all breakthroughs, waved.

My first day in the city, in this new life I had secured, would end on a high note.

I headed back to my groceries, swishing my shoes against the grass the way I used to on my way to right field for my high school softball games.

Whack. The next soccer ball was on its way to the net. It had been a long, long time since I had challenged myself in any kind of athletic endeavor, or been anywhere close to Kyla's age. She seemed far more determined than I had been to make it as an athlete. The only thing I had been that fixated on as a freshman was learning from the older girls how to have the same kind of draw over our male peers as those women in the girlie calendars hanging in my dad's shop had over his crew. Because trying to fill a hole I was too young to name was my real favorite subject. Unfortunately, I was a good student.

4

BY THE END of my orientation for HML on Friday morning, two things had become clear. One, the remote job was a blessed fit for someone with a preference for elastic waistbands and not ending the day smelling like gas station pizza. Two, I would be hard-pressed to find meaningful conversation with anyone at HML.

The day began with a virtual meeting with an HR trainer who led me through the employee handbook and benefits package with an efficient deftness. The only thing I starred on my yellow legal pad (because how appropriate) was the fact my benefits kicked in September 1. I bookmarked the link to the enrollment site she sent me over Slack.

Then came Paul, my supervisor, senior paralegal, and Jeff Goldblum lookalike who was nothing like his famous, goofy doppelgänger. He jumped right into business, forgoing any kind of warm-up breeze shooting. He rattled off what application to go to for my project assignments, which one to use to track my time for each case I worked on, and how to fill out each client's spreadsheet of data that the attorneys would use as an exhibit for demand letters and in mediation.

"We work primarily with the PI team," he said, "but occasionally you might be asked to fill in for the business clients."

PI was personal injury. Exhibit meant attachment. Demand letters were what the attorney sent to the defense to prove the injured party deserved the requested funds. I already felt like a legal insider.

"We'll have weekly calls to go over your assignments for the week," he told me. "Outside of that, you can use Slack to chat me any questions."

Lunch break rolled around, and I spent it standing in the nook with a peanut butter sandwich and my newsfeed. My lack of posting much of anything in the two years since Mick said I was no longer "what he needed" meant that the algorithm fed me far more perimenopausal weight-loss trends and 1990s entertainment trivia than was healthy. But in the midst of the suggested content was an update from someone I actually knew. Jill Norman had been a mutual friend of mine and Mick's. Her post contained a handful of pictures from someone's birthday party at Shuckers. Mick was in three of the pictures, with his latest woman hanging on him in all of them. She was younger than me, skinnier, with hair that stayed where she styled it. In the last picture, her left hand was draped over his shoulder. A gold ring glinted on her finger.

Seven years. That was how long I had lived with Mick. Had dated him for a decade prior to that. Not once had we talked about rings or anything with gravity other than who was paying which bill and where the party would be after closing time on Saturday.

I exited out of my feed, but the smiling faces and frozen laughs clung. It had been my world for so long. I still knew all the regulars' orders by heart. I could still predict with some accuracy how much each would drop on a Friday night at Shuckers, and which of them would spend far more on drinks than they should with kids at home. I knew which ones were most likely to break out in song and which were most likely to attempt to hustle a newcomer at darts. I could hear every picture in that post.

It's a weird feeling knowing a people and place well enough to name every color in every memory but wishing those years had never been part of your existence. It was a feeling no one else in my life understood.

I tossed the mostly eaten sandwich on the table and switched to something more productive: calling Dad.

The rat-a-tat-tat of an impact wrench competed with his voice. "Hello?"

"Hey there. How's your day?"

"Fine."

"Not 'better than average'?" It was his signature reply to any customer who asked him how he was.

"I said I was fine." The background noise quieted, an indication he had moved into his office at the back of the shop.

I stepped over to the divas on their stands. Their pink stripes were extra bright on the clear day. I stroked Shania's large top leaf, soothing myself with the dichotomy of smooth top and fuzzy bottom. "Don't know if you checked the deep freeze," I said, "but I left some burger patties and chicken tenders in there."

"Why'd you do that?"

"I wanted to."

He harrumphed. "I can take care of myself. Who do you think did all that cookin' and cleanin' when you were growin' up?"

His memory and mine of those years after Mom died when I was eleven had always been drastically different. Making sure bologna was in the fridge did not equate to cooking any more than stocking the toilet paper counted as cleaning. I stopped trying to fill the gaps by the time my first boyfriend came along my sophomore year. Dad hadn't noticed.

I let go of the leaf. "Yes, you can cook for yourself. I was only trying to save you a trip to the store, is all."

Instead of words, the creak of an office chair seeped through the speaker. It wasn't hard to picture him leaning back, free arm crossed defiantly over his rounded belly.

"Busy at the shop today?" I asked.

"Every minute. Got someone coming in now, looks like. Good thing I'm here today. Two of my regulars called about their repairs going sideways and they need to bring in their vehicles again. I swear these boys don't have a lick of sense sometimes."

He said that a lot, his dogged campaign to prove the shop couldn't survive without him. He would never retire, never sell, never admit he grew weaker each year. The "boys," who were men with families and mortgages of their own, could at least lower themselves onto a creeper to inspect the underside of a Ford.

"Sounds like a full day," I said.

"Mmm," he replied.

The end of my lunch break ticked closer. He would hole up in his office only so long too. "Just wanted to check in with you, Dad, and let you know my first day on the job is going well. I've got a nice little setup in my spare bedroom. They gave me my own laptop. Did you know I can write off a portion of my internet and utilities since I work at home?"

"Weird job you got there," he said.

"Maybe, but it pays nearly twice as much as I was making. Plus benefits and a retirement plan."

Silence. He was stubborn in his refusal to show any interest, despite the fact my job was better than ninety-five percent of all jobs in Woodfield. And I had learned only an hour prior that part of the benefits package was a tuition reimbursement clause. HML would pay for me to earn my paralegal certification. That was the cherry on the sundae for me. For him, it would be noise.

I tapped the side of my thigh. "My house is comfortable. Got two bedrooms now, and a nice bay window." My better judgment told me to stop there, but I had so little practice listening to it. "The basement has a ton of potential. It's big enough to be a studio with a half bath. Has its own entrance too."

He saw right through me. "I'm not moving to Kansas City, Jess."

"Never say never," I said.

"I can and I did. I'm not moving!" He used a couple more colorful words in those statements. Until I stopped using profanity, I had never noticed how much he relied on it.

I bit my lip. Sinking people often reject the lifeline right in front of them. For so many years, I had done the same thing. Then all my poor judgments collided, leaving me to salvage what clothes and personal effects I could from the trailer's front lawn in the middle of a downpour. Tillie Watts later found me soaked and sobbing in my truck in the gravel lot of her church. Why I ended up there, I never put together. But it happened to be choir practice night, and she had stopped on her way inside to knock on my window. She stood in the torrent, under the shield of her umbrella, and asked with a serenity I envied if I wanted shelter from every storm. She'd passed away two weeks before I was baptized.

Her offer was the one I was determined to give to Dad—a shelter from every storm.

I switched the phone to my other ear and moved us on to neutral topics. I asked him what he was working on. He told me about the Johnston boy's stock car engine, new tires for Mrs. Woolworth, an alternator replacement for the Munsuns' farm truck. All the things he thought proved that his life was full and worthy right where he was.

When at last we said our goodbyes, I stood in the quiet with my fingertips resting on the table. The empty table, in a house that suddenly seemed bigger than necessary.

5

RON WAS RIGHT about the thrift store. Pennies from Heaven offered a wide range of furniture, all shoved into a mosh pit of no discernible order between a sea of clothes racks and shelves of toys and sporting goods that had barely been cleaned after years of languishing in attics and garages. Even with my hairline budget, it took me five trips to my truck to load up my scores after a shopping spree on Saturday: a coffee table that sagged ever so slightly in the middle, a somewhat wobbly armchair for the living room, and two dining chairs that were neither the same wood finish nor the same height but had four functioning legs. The best find, though, was the high-backed pleather office chair that swiveled as smooth as butter on a four-wheel chrome base. Despite the peeling arm pads that left little black flakes on my forearms, it had a corner-office vibe. Not to mention lumbar support.

Before I left the shopping center, I stopped in at Cost Cutter and opened a customer loyalty account. It came with a "welcome bonus" of half off an entrée at their Chinese food station, which I took them up on immediately. Taking a new way home, I stumbled upon the local branch of the library. Compared to the one room in the back of the courthouse that served the Woodfield community, the branch was a cathedral of education. It was replete with private study cubicles, conference rooms, and row after row of DVDs. I came out with a library card and the first full season of *Boy Meets World*, a welcome reminder of my innocent childhood days.

Piece by little piece, I built upon the foundation of my new life.

The daytime hours had nearly ended by the time I pulled into my driveway, but the sun acted like it didn't know. It threw down its oppressive rays as fiercely as if it were midday. Yet there was Kyla, trundling from her garage with soccer shoes strapped on and a mesh bag of balls and orange cones slung over her shoulder.

I slid out of my truck with the food and DVD in hand and shut the door. The thud roused her attention. To my surprise, she waved with her free hand. We were for sure making progress as neighbors.

"You're practicing in this heat?" I called.

She shrugged. "It's in the shade."

That much was true. The shadows of the trees at the property line stretched beyond where she had arranged her semicircle the day before. "Still," I said. "I'm sweating just watching you think about playing."

A giggle—an unmistakable giggle—bubbled from her.

It really wasn't all that funny, but I'd take it, and the invitation it represented. I headed across the lot. "It's Saturday night, Kyla. Why aren't you going out with your friends to see a movie or get into some shenanigans?"

She entered the pool of shade and swung the bag around to her front. "Is that what you're doing tonight?"

I held up the food and library loan. "This is all the shenanigans I can handle. Cheap Chinese food and iconic nineties entertainment."

She smirked and loosened the bag's cinch closure. "Guess I'm just as lame."

"Hey now."

Her almond-colored eyes danced above her smile. As I joined her in the shade, sack of food bumping against my leg, she turned the bag upside down and let the contents tumble out. The cones landed in one stacked pile. The balls bounced against the ground or each other and rolled over the grass. One came close to me, and I tapped it back toward her.

"Any of your friends play soccer?" I asked.

"Not really. Not anymore, I mean." She picked up the stack of cones and held them in both hands. "They're into other things now."

"Things you're not into?" I asked.

She nodded, zoned in on the objects in her grasp. The bright smile faded. Different was the worst thing a teenager could be. It wasn't that great for adults either. My difference, though, was self-imposed. The girl in front of me obviously understood what it meant to be left out of group chats and sleepover invitations. She and I were an entire mindset and half a life removed, yet we had overlapping experiences.

"You know, Kyla," I said, "I'm not all that familiar with soccer, which is to say I only understand that the ball goes in the net and everyone cheers. But if you ever get tired of practicing alone, I'm game."

Kyla narrowed her brow and looked up at me. "You'd play soccer?"

"'Play' is a strong word. How about we leave it at 'I will help in some way.'"

Her continuous frown indicated her struggle to believe such a promise from someone who wore oversized shirts in a futile attempt to mask a bulging middle.

"Believe it or not," I said, "I was mildly athletic when I was your age. Emphasis on the mild. I could probably figure out how to kick the ball with you or help you do whatever those are for." I gestured at the stack of cones.

"Footwork drills."

"Right. Yes. I can ensure your feet are worked."

The frown loosened into a look of mulling. She glanced at the goal, then back at me. "Would you be goalie?"

"Goalie?" The whack her kick had produced had resounded over the entire neighborhood. What would it sound like inches from my face? "Wouldn't I need a suit of armor or something?"

Her grin smacked of cockiness. "Don't worry. You won't come close to the ball."

I arched an eyebrow. "Just for that . . ." I set my stuff aside and marched toward the goal. "Let's do this, Beckham."

She laughed. "You don't know soccer but you know who David Beckham is?"

"Only because he married a Spice Girl." I took up residence in the middle of the goal, feet wider than hip width and arms straight up and out like points of a star. "Ready." I beckoned.

She shook her head, which told me that was not how goalies stood, but at least she was smiling again.

Kyla toed a ball away from the others and brought it to a stop directly in front of me about fifteen yards back. As soon as she backpedaled, I regretted every choice I had made for the past two minutes. My muscles froze. She quick-stepped toward the ball, swung her leg back, and *whack*.

The ball sailed into the top right corner of the net. *Swish*. Perfectly placed. I hadn't moved an inch.

"Lucky shot," I said.

Kyla pulled another ball from the mix. "Here comes the next one." Set, backpedal, quick-step, *whack*.

I squeezed my eyes shut and shuffled blindly left as I waved my arms above my head.

Swish.

"Was I close?" I asked, opening my eyes.

"Not even."

"But I'm getting better?"

Kyla laughed and lined up for the third shot.

Right as her foot swung back, I shouted, "It's going right!"

Nope. It whizzed into the middle left. She pumped her fists in the air.

Fourth shot, top left.

"These things sound like missiles," I said, returning to the center.

"I'm not even kicking that hard. Watch this." She toed the fifth ball into place and backed up a few more paces than before. She sprinted forward, flung her leg back higher, and *whack*.

I moved my arms in a faux-serious attempt to block what whistled toward the goal. Like all the others, it was supposed to go by me, supposed to fling the net back taut with the emphasis of five exclamation points. Instead, it plowed right into my stomach.

"Ooopf!" Down I went, thudding like a cinder block.

"Jess!"

I curled onto my side, knees to my chest and arms clenched tight to my screaming midsection.

Kyla knelt next to me. "I'm so sorry! Are you okay?"

Talking seemed like a burden in that moment. I sucked in air. "Fine," I managed.

"I caught my toe wrong on that. It was supposed to bend right. I'm so, so sorry."

I clutched my abdomen as I lifted onto my knees. "It's okay." Every word made me wince. "All . . . part of . . . the game."

"I promise I won't ever kick that hard with you again. Do you want an ice pack?"

Traction sounded better. But despite the pain, that part about "with you again" stood out. She wanted to involve me again, and that was no small thing. I met Kyla's gaze. "I only need you"—wince—"to admit defeat."

She frowned.

I jutted my chin toward the ball. "Didn't go in."

Kyla turned. The ball, brutely blocked by my spleen, lay a good foot shy of the goal.

The light eased back into her expression. By the time she looked at me, she was laughing.

I laughed too, and immediately whimpered. But goodness, it was worth it. So very worth it.

6

MY ALARM WOKE ME in plenty of time to get myself together for the big church on the hill. The second of their three services started at ten, and I had every intention of going—and arriving in the middle of the music and sitting as far to the back as possible. Maybe I'd stop at the coffee shop by Cost Cutter on the way for a little caffeine reinforcement, and to have something to do with my hands. Nothing made an uncomfortable situation a thousand times more uncomfortable than empty hands with nothing to do.

I peeled off the covers and swung my feet onto the lumpy rag rug at my bedside. The moment I attempted to sit up, the ache of my bruised abdomen announced itself with vigor. I moaned and clutched my belly. Gingerly, I rose from the bed, then lifted my Diet Coke–themed pajama shirt above the injured area. No sign of injury, though a little internal bleeding didn't seem entirely out of the question.

One hand on my injury, I dragged myself into the bathroom for the immediate morning needs. My first Sunday in Kansas City had begun, and I was about to be in the same room with more people than the whole of Woodfield. Judging by my reflection in the bathroom mirror, I'd need a good thirty minutes of fluff and spackle to be ready for full visibility by other humans. But first, breakfast.

Despite promising myself a tasty beverage from the drive-through, I started a cup brewing with my single-serve coffee maker. That was my one splurge for my move, and I had big dreams for that pricey little machine. It would not sit dormant, by golly.

The aromatic, midnight-colored liquid filled my Becker's Automotive mug. I splashed in some milk, pulled the box of generic cornflakes from the cabinet, then plopped on the futon to watch another episode of *Boy Meets World* as I ate. I set my breakfast on the new-to-me coffee table and pressed play on the remote. My favorite fictional Philadelphia schoolboy and his band of family and friends were far more corny than my childhood memories claimed, but I was no traitor to my generation. I had binged the first ten episodes the night before, well on my way to the goal of finishing the season that weekend. In between handfuls of dry flakes straight from the box, I sipped on the milky coffee and tried not to be bitter toward Cory for complaining about his dad wanting him to play in the father-son softball game. Some kids would have done anything to have their dad *want* to play softball with them at all.

Three knocks startled me away from the screen. It was not even eight thirty on a Sunday, and a visitor was at my door. I brushed the crumbs from my shirt and pulled myself up from the futon. At the door, someone a little shorter than me waited on the other side of the frosted glass.

I unlatched the dead bolt and pulled open the door.

Kyla stood on my porch, fully dressed, hair styled in an adorable straight fashion.

"Wow," I said, "I didn't know teenagers got up this early on the weekends."

She brushed my comment aside. "Can you give me a ride?"

"A ride where?"

"I promised to meet this girl from school. She texted me last night. Pop was supposed to take me, but he got called to fix something at another house."

"You mean take you right now?" I asked.

"Yes. I'm supposed to meet her by nine."

My hair still had a loose nest in the back. I tried to smooth it with my palm, to no avail. "Okay. Where are you meeting her?"

"Trinity Community Church."

I blinked. *Kyla* had church plans too? "I didn't know you were a churchgoer."

"I'm not. Not really, anyway. But this girl from school invited me, so . . ."

So help me make a friend, her pleading look said. Who was I to deny her that, or church attendance?

"Uh, sure, of course." I ushered her inside. "Let me go freshen up and we'll be on our way."

"Trinity is, like, fifteen minutes from here." Kyla woke her phone to check the time. Twenty minutes to nine. "But you don't have to change or anything. You're just dropping me off."

All she saw were the T-shirt and shorts. She didn't discern the lack of undergarments, which were typically encouraged when visiting the house of the Lord.

"I'll be gazelle fast," I promised, already on my way. "Five minutes, tops. Just hang tight. Have some cornflakes if you want."

I rushed back to my bedroom. Fortunately, after many late nights ahead of an early shift, I had become quite adept at getting myself out the door in the space of minutes. It was all about prioritizing. Brushing teeth and applying deodorant were musts. Makeup optional. Uncooperative hair could be flung back into a messy bun. I followed my well-honed guidelines, opting for khaki shorts that covered most of my dimply thighs, an unwrinkled T-shirt (over undergarments), and flip-flops. Voilà! Ready for drop-off duty.

I hustled back to her and declared, "Under three minutes!"

The drive also took less time than we'd estimated. We pulled up to the single-story brick building with five minutes to spare. People were still walking in, some in jeans and others in Sunday best. One woman noshed on a breakfast sandwich as she glided next to her family.

I pulled Hank up to the curb near the entrance. "Is your friend able to give you a ride home if needed?"

"I don't know." Kyla's head was on a swivel, turning every which way except toward me. She jiggled one leg. "I don't see Wren."

"Maybe she's waiting in the lobby."

"What if she's not?"

"Only one way to find out."

She jiggled her leg harder, looking from the doors to the lot and back to the doors. Finally, she turned to me. "Will you go in with me?"

"Go inside?" I glanced down at my rushed outfit more appropriate for a morning on a fishing boat than in a church. A few strands had already loosened from my sloppy updo and brushed against my cheeks. "Oh, Kyla, I'm a little too unfiltered for church at the moment."

"Please, Jess? I don't know anybody in there."

"You know what's-her-name. Wren."

She bit her lip and looked at the church entrance, as if judging whether whatever was on the other side was truly what she wanted. She beseeched me with a simple, profound "I'm scared."

She wasn't a churchgoing girl. The odds were good she rarely if ever set foot in a church. And she had come to me for help.

The rearview mirror showed the dark circles under my eyes. No time to slather them with concealer or attempt to bring out my essentially nonexistent lashes with a good shellacking of mascara. And my pale, flabby legs would be out there for all creation to gawk at.

Hank's idle rattled through me, like he, too, attempted to shake me loose. I only needed to walk Kyla to the doors.

I sighed. "Okay."

Relief flooded her expression.

I moved Hank over to a front parking spot marked Visitor and strapped on my purse. Kyla led the way to the doors. As we stepped under the long awning stretching to the curb, I reminded myself that she might see her friend through the glass as soon as we got close enough, and I could scurry back to my truck without having to go inside.

It's been said that the best way to make God laugh is to tell him your plans. When a woman with a name tag strung on a lanyard stepped through the door and pinned me with her gaze, I gained full confidence that God had plenty to chuckle about.

7

THE WOMAN SWOOPED toward us, her clay-red maxi dress fluttering with her steps and turquoise oval earrings swaying beside her earth-toned cheeks. "Good morning."

Kyla glanced back at me with a question in her eyes. I nodded that it was safe to proceed, though I did linger another step behind her. We met the woman halfway up the front walk. Her straight, dark strands fell gracefully against her shoulders, with white streaks streaming from her middle part. Her still, restful expression emanated a warmth, like a sandy riverbank toasted by the sun.

"Is this your first Sunday with us?" she asked.

Before I could answer, a girl with wavy blond locks burst through the door. "Kyla! You made it!"

My young charge turned to me, one foot already stepping toward her hostess. "See you after."

"Wait," I said, "does that mean I need to—"

But she was gone, enfolded into the chatter of her fellow teen, who shuttled her into the lobby. Funny enough, the first part of my plan had worked. My feet were still on concrete, many paces from the entrance, when Kyla and her friend connected. But that's about where God said, "And now my turn." The woman standing sentinel over the scene had no one but me to unleash her attention upon. She folded her hands under her name tag, which bore the name Reva Nez-Acardi.

"Your daughter seems to have settled in," she said.

Only a complete stranger would assume I had the chops to be a parent. "She's my neighbor, actually. She needed a ride, so I did my neighborly duty." My laugh sounded more like a forced cough than the breezy nonchalance I aimed for. It made my flip-flops and shorts seem all the more embarrassing as well. I crossed my arms, and my extra-large T-shirt bunched over them.

"Are you looking for a church?" she asked.

"You mean right this second?"

She stared at me for a beat. "Sure." Her stoicism made it hard to determine if she was amused or annoyed.

Either way, I couldn't lie on God's front step. "Kind of. I mean, I planned to go to one by my house later this morning."

She shrugged. "But you're here. Might as well stay."

I pinched my arms. Behind me, Hank waited. An older couple came up the front walk. They nodded a hello to me, then greeted Reva by name as they passed.

"Sunday school is starting soon," Reva said when we were alone once more. "My husband leads our class. We'd love to have you."

I was surely leaving marks on my arms, as hard as I squeezed the flesh. "I'm not exactly dressed for Sunday school—or for being in public, quite honestly. I had only planned to drop off Kyla and go."

She looked me up and down. "I see nothing wrong with how you look."

I guffawed. "That's super generous of you. But really, I'm a mess."

In that deadpan way, she countered, "Just because someone's dolled up doesn't make them less of a mess."

That Reva was one solid string of valid points. Her certain, straight posture proclaimed she was in control of all her senses, and perhaps a few of mine. I ached to make a dash for Hank, but did it really make sense to leave? If Kyla needed a ride home, I would miss the big church on the hill's service anyway.

I curled my toes against the soles of my flip-flops, and for the second time in the span of thirty minutes, I agreed to do the thing every ounce of self-will told me not to.

"Okay," I said.

My decision brought out the shine in Reva's eyes. She moved her hands to her sides and nodded toward the door. "Follow me. My name is Reva Nez-Acardi, by the way."

Her name sang, like the whistle of the wind slipping through tallgrass. Mine, meanwhile, sounded like a cow flumping against a metal gate. "Jess Becker."

Reva was a head shorter than me. I walked on her left side, close enough for a scar across her cheekbone to jump out. A chunk of flesh had been torn away, leaving an oblong pock about an inch in length.

We walked into the mostly empty foyer. A man in a suit waved to us from his position in the middle of the open space before resuming his monitor of the entrance. Behind him were two sets of open double doors that led into the back of the sanctuary. Several men set up microphones and instruments on the stage. A young woman scurried by the doors, holding a little girl's hand. They headed for the hallway to the left, past the church office. They had come from the hallway to the right, which Reva directed me toward.

"The youth wing is down that way," she said, pointing to the mom and daughter's destination. "The adult wing is over here."

We turned the corner. The hallway was short, with restrooms on the right followed by two more doors. The entire building would take maybe five minutes to tour, end to end.

"Our church has about a hundred and fifty people," Reva said. "We have two adult Sunday school classes, one for the older adults and one for the young adults. My husband and I lead the young adults."

"You're taking me to a young adults class?" I asked. "I haven't been called a young adult in at least a decade."

"Me either." Reva glanced up at me. Her eyes spoke mirth, but her stick-straight lips refused to give anything more away. The mysterious woman had a depth that promised to keep things interesting.

We stopped outside the first classroom. "This is the older adults class," she said.

Inside, three round tables hosted people in various levels of engagement with those around them. One man simply stared at a spot on the table. Everyone had white hair and thick glasses. A few had walking aids stowed near their chairs. All strikingly similar to the congregation I'd sat among in Woodfield.

"Guess I am a young adult," I said.

Reva tweaked an eyebrow. She led me on to the next classroom. A sign affixed to the wall outside the door read "Allelon, Sundays, 9:00 a.m." Underneath was a Scripture reference: Romans 12:10.

"What is Al . . . All . . ." I gave up and pointed at the word.

Reva pronounced it slowly. "Ah-LAY-loan. It's what we call our class," she said. "It's Greek for 'one another,' as in the New Testament 'one anothers.'"

I nodded without a single clue as to what that meant. "Cool."

She studied me, probably seeing through my response, then held out her arm in an "after you" gesture. She wanted me to dive into the belly of that rectangular room abuzz with multiple conversations I might or might not be able to add a single drop of relevance to. Rarely did anyone at the Woodfield church ever discuss things with me other than how my dad was or which potato casserole I liked better at the potlucks. Aside from Tillie Watts, who unfailingly asked me what I thought of the sermon, most had kept me at a distance, let me listen to the pastor's teaching in peace, and we all went about our days. I had nothing in common with the strangers in this classroom except for Jesus (assumedly) and the fact we were still roughly in the front half of our natural lives. But there was no turning back. I shoved my hands into my shorts pockets and stepped inside.

The people carried on without noticing me. They huddled in pairs and trios among the cushioned burgundy chairs, which were arranged in two columns of three rows each, running perpendicular to the door. A few people milled about a folding table by the windows on the opposite side of the room, where open boxes of donuts lay side by side. At the front of the room, a tall man in a blue dress shirt looked up from his Bible splayed across the top of a skinny lectern. Goose-gray hair feathered back from his slender face. Upon spotting us in the doorway, he broke into a smile and strode over.

"Welcome." He extended his hand to me. "Gio Acardi."

"Jess Becker."

"So glad you're here, Jess." He towered over me. His hand was twice as large as mine, but his clasp was tender. His pale complexion made Reva's appear more bronze. The two seemed so opposite in every way, but side by side, they fit like contrasting puzzle pieces made to snap together.

"This is quite a day, Reva," he said. "We have *two* visitors."

"A great day," she said, then motioned for me to follow her down the aisle closest to the door.

Gio returned to the lectern. The other people ranged in age from young and wrinkle-free to couples who were probably elbow deep in their kids' after-school activities. Aside from the Acardis, I was the oldest among them.

The woman from the lobby entered the room and started down the aisle after me. I smiled at her. Her gaze traveled down my outfit—hooked on my naked legs. She lifted an eyebrow behind her blue horn-rimmed glasses.

My smile faded, and I quickly turned away. Was that a look?

She veered into the middle row and chose a seat next to a man and another couple about her age.

Reva led me onward to the very last row, where a young woman sat alone. She couldn't have been that far out of high school. Small, fake rhinestones glinted along the front collar of her black tank top. The straps of her bright-pink bra peeked out. She wore her shoulder-length brown hair neatly parted down the middle, creating a tidy, pale river from her snowy forehead straight back to her crown. Thick eyeliner tried fruitlessly to camouflage under-eye circles. She angled her striking blue eyes our way, mouth in a tight line, arms crossed.

Reva stopped at the end of the row and motioned for me to enter first.

I turned sideways and scooted down the row that was a little too narrow for my unnarrow hips. I managed to avoid disturbing the quartet in front of us, though Horned Rims did throw a glance over her shoulder.

When I was close enough to the young woman, I stuck out my hand. "Hello," I said.

Her handshake was as limp and quick as her "Hi." One knee stuck out of the large hole in her faded jeans. She, too, wore flip-flops.

Reva leaned around me. "Austie Russell, this is Jess Becker. She's visiting with us as well."

The people in front of us turned partially around to observe. Their curiosity didn't last long, though. Horned Rims leaned in and whispered something, drawing them all into a huddle. I had to fight to disbelieve it had anything to do with me or my marshmallow-like legs.

I sat next to Austie and smiled. "Nice to meet you."

She politely parroted my greeting, then glanced at the quartet. Her alert system seemed to be as high as mine.

I turned to thank Reva, but our hostess was already shuffling out of the row, leaving me in the company of a woman half my age. I tucked my hands between my knees. The clock above Gio's head showed straight-up nine o'clock. Even so, he and Reva began a quiet conference between them.

"So, Austie," I said, searching for the words even as they tumbled out. "First time here too, huh?"

Austie nodded, eyes on her lap. Her legs stretched out into a long, thin line that ended with her feet crossed under the chair in front of her. Her guardedness was not so unlike a certain fourteen-year-old's when I first met her.

"I bet you at least planned to come today," I said. "You clearly had time to brush your hair, anyway."

She looked at me, brow puckered. "Didn't you?"

"The hair or the planning?"

She shrugged. "Both."

"Yeah, no. To both." I freed my hands and rubbed them down my thighs. "I'm only here because my neighbor girl needed a ride."

"Then how'd you end up in Sunday school?"

"That would be her doing." I pointed to my escort. "Reva extended an invitation. Actually, it was more like she hammered an insistence."

Up front, the mismatched couple pored over a paper in Gio's hand.

Austie watched Reva. The frown melted into a crooked grin. "Sounds like her."

Interesting reaction. And a telltale sign that we had broached a comfortable topic. I could work with that. I started to face her more fully, but Gio chose that moment to call over the din.

"Let's get started," he said. "Only four minutes late this time."

Laughter bubbled throughout the room, and conversations quieted. All attention rested on the leader as his wife wrote something on the whiteboard behind him. But I could only half listen to his opening salvo of housekeeping items. Too many questions started to ping inside my head.

How did Austie know Reva? Their age difference was even greater. Reva was old enough to be her mother. How had Austie come to have so much admiration for her? How did she end up in a room of people she obviously felt so little connection to?

And what had happened in Austie's life to make her as suspicious of Horned Rims as I was?

8

HAVING EXHAUSTED all the announcements, Gio set the list down. He moved to the side of the whiteboard, where Reva's crisp handwriting was easily legible from the back of the room.

"On to the meat of why we are here," he said. "It is time, ladies and gentlemen, for our weekly check-in. Reva has our references on the board. Thank you, my dear."

From her chair in the front row, his wife nodded.

"You all did your memorizing, yes?" He looked from person to person, eliciting mumbled affirmatives. He pointed to the left side of the board, where Reva had written in blue dry-erase marker, "Last Week: Colossians 3:16."

"Who wants to recite this verse for us?" Gio asked.

For all the confident yeses among them, the participants let the uncomfortable silence linger. Finally, a singsong voice arose. It belonged to Horned Rims. "'Let the word of Christ dwell in you richly, teaching and admonishing one another in all wisdom, singing psalms and hymns and spiritual songs, with thankfulness in your hearts to God.'"

Gio grinned. "Beautifully shared, as always, Thea."

The man next to her draped his arm across the back of her

chair. "You'd think my wife was a Bible Quizzing coach or something."

Several people chuckled, including Gio.

I leaned to Austie and whispered, "What's Bible Quizzing?"

She shrugged, clearly as uninitiated as I was.

Whatever it was, it apparently was a big deal because Thea's husband reported that her team was headed to regionals in Iowa in two weeks. Amid the wave of admiring looks and congratulations, Thea dipped her head. The last time I had received such group praise was when I put fried pickle spears on a cheeseburger for a regular's birthday ten summers ago. Shuckers still served the Pickle Patty, without credit to me, of course.

I started to quietly applaud along with the others when Thea lifted her head. There was an air to her smile—I couldn't quite name it—and a lack of blush in her cheeks. Maybe it was nothing, but maybe it was everything I needed to know about her.

Gio pulled everyone's attention back to the check-in. "Now for the more challenging weekly question. Who has an example from the week of how they lived out Colossians 3:16 or witnessed someone else living it out?" He leaned on the lectern and grazed his eyes over the class.

In the silence, Reva rose from her chair with papers in her hand. She started down the center aisle, straight toward Austie.

From somewhere on the other side of the room, a woman said, "My nephew had a big test this week, and I gave him a Psalms verse to carry with him."

Reva stopped at our row and handed Austie two sheets of paper. "One for each of you," she whispered.

"Thank you, Joan," Gio said. "Who else has an example?"

Another person spoke up as Reva returned to her seat. Austie handed me one of the papers. The Trinity Community Church logo was centered at the bottom. Across the top was the heading "Daily Allelon," accompanied by a short, introductory statement: "The New Testament has more than fifty 'one another' verses that guide us in our relationships with fellow believers as we walk the narrow road together. Keep this somewhere you can be reminded daily."

I pulled the paper closer to read the smaller print flowing down two columns. My reading glasses were among the many things I would have brought with me had I known I'd end up in a Sunday school class. My Bible being another. Each column contained key snippets of twenty-five verses along with their references.

Be at peace with one another.

Forgive one another.

Pray for one another.

Be hospitable to one another.

Spur one another on.

Outdo one another in showing honor.

There was the Colossians one about teaching and admonishing, of course. Then others about serving, being kind, speaking truthfully, bearing one another's burdens, being devoted to each other. They were the rules of social engagement for Christians. I exhaled slowly. Believing was apparently the easy part of "the Jesus stuff," as Dad so eloquently called it. Living as a Christian required a whole lot of extroverting I wasn't positive I had in me.

One particular Daily Allelon verse toward the middle of the second column caught my attention: "Clothe yourselves . . . with humility toward one another." I grimaced and angled myself a bit to my left, away from Thea.

Gio welcomed the last of the examples from the class, encouraging each person with a "Well done" or "Wonderful." When everyone who wanted to share had taken the opportunity, he pointed at the right side of the whiteboard and the verse Reva had labeled "This Week."

"Let's talk about our focus for the next seven days," he said. "Someone please read 1 Thessalonians 5:15 for us."

"I will," said a man in the front row. Though he alone agreed, his classmates also began to flip through the thin pages of their

Bibles, creating a symphony of crackling. Spurred by their action, Austie bent over and pulled a Bible from the backpack on the other side of her legs.

"Mind if I share?" I whispered.

She nodded and opened her Bible to a random page. The spine creaked from the movement, the pages perfectly smooth and crisp. She glanced around. Others had already arrived at the verse and cradled their Bibles with both hands in preparation for the reading. She turned pages—in the wrong direction—then glanced at me. Her panic was clear.

If only she knew how much I understood what that was like. I smiled at her and gestured to the open book. "May I?"

She dipped her chin and handed over her Bible.

If only she knew.

Using the children's song the Woodfield pastor had referenced in one of his sermons (which I later had to look up on YouTube), I flipped to the middle of the New Testament and landed at the correct spot right as the man finished reading. The rest of the class moved on, but I traced my fingertip under the words as Austie leaned in to follow along.

See that no one repays anyone evil for evil, but always seek to do good to one another and to everyone.

"But this is a different kind of 'one another,'" Gio was saying. "It includes both fellow Christians as well as 'everyone,' or 'all,' as some translations may say. And notice it says 'always.' It's an active, ongoing pursuit to everyone around us, even those we'd rather not cross paths with too often. That unfriendly coworker or that surly HOA president—not that I would know anything about that."

Laughter.

"It's everyone, always," he reiterated, to multiple nods of agreement. "And the good could be as simple as a kind word or holding the door for someone. It could be acknowledging someone who may feel sidelined." His eyes seemed to travel ever so briefly to Austie and me.

Warmth gathered in my face, but Austie kept her gaze aimed at the words on the page.

"In speech, in attitude, in action," Gio said, "we actively seek ways to do good to others. Why? Because God has been so good to us. We love because he first loved us. Amen?"

Agreements rolled through the room. One person raised a hallelujah.

Beside me, though, in that back, overlooked row, Austie tucked in on herself. She pulled her slender legs closer, propped her left elbow on her knee, and rested her cheek against her fist. She didn't look up the rest of the hour. That alone provided a deeper read on the young woman: She was overwhelmed.

If only she knew how much I understood that too.

9

AS SOON AS Gio started the closing prayer, Austie placed both feet flat on the floor, as if ready to sprint. She reached down with her left arm to stuff her Bible in her backpack. From that new angle, the tattoo on the inside of her left bicep flashed. It was a small profile of a lion head. A universal symbol of power, and a biblical symbol connected to Jesus. Did she know about the latter?

The amen came, the din arose once more, and Austie was on her feet. I started to rise, reaching out my hand to touch her arm, but then Reva appeared in the center aisle.

"Austie, before you go," she said, "there's someone who's been wanting to meet you." She whisked my young counterpart away to the other side of the room.

I was halfway up from my chair at that point. Without enough leverage to lift myself all the way, I sank back down.

"Hi there." The sweet-honeyed voice came from the row in front of me. It belonged to the other woman of the quartet.

Through a series of highly ungraceful movements, I made it to a standing position to match hers and smiled. "Hello."

"My name's Ellen Walthum." She held out her dainty hand.

I shook it. "Jess Becker."

Her gaze never strayed from mine, never evaluated my hairstyle or questionably reverent attire or lack of Bible in hand. "Is this your first time at Trinity?"

"It is."

The two husbands, still deep in conversation, stood and scooted around Thea, who watched my exchange with Ellen like a criminal profiler assessing the scene.

My pulse quickened. "I'm, uh, I'm new to town. Reva invited me."

"She's good about that," Ellen said.

"So I hear." Reva was another person I had loads of questions about.

Ellen hooked her left thumb around the straps of her tote bag. A simple solitaire gleamed from her ring finger. "Where'd you move from?" she asked.

"It's called Woodfield. It's a small town near Emporia."

"Is that near the Tallgrass Prairie Preserve?"

"It is. You know it?"

"I know the Preserve. I went there on a class trip in high school." Her smile smacked of someone who would offer ice cream to her own kidnapper. "Did you come here for a job, then?" she asked.

"I did. I work at Henson-Miden Law Firm."

Thea cut in. "Are you a lawyer?" Unlike her friend, who wrapped her questions in gentle curiosity, Thea leveled questions like arrows zipped from a bow.

"No," I said. "I'm on the support staff at the firm."

"A paralegal?" she asked.

I shifted my weight from one foot to the other. "No."

"Admin or office manager?" The woman was relentless.

I pulled in a breath, chasing away the unkind thoughts rushing to my brain that said women like her only asked personal questions for one reason: to find what to use against you. I would clothe myself with humility at my own peril.

"I'm a data entry specialist," I said.

"Oh" was her only response.

I refocused on Ellen. "What do you do?"

"She's a mom," Thea said, refusing to be shut out.

"That's noble work," I said to Ellen.

Fortunately, her chill vibe did not waver. "I also work as a weekend nurse at a nursing home."

"A nurse. Great. Maybe you could tell me what to do about carpal tunnel." I lifted my unruly left hand in a mock offer to have her examine it.

"That can be so painful," she said with a slight wrinkle of her nose. "Have you had it long?"

"I mean, I haven't been diagnosed with it, but I do get this tingling in my hand sometimes." I opened and closed my hand like a claw, the way I would the two times the fizzle had lit under my skin.

Ellen tipped up her chin in that tell-me-more posture. "You get tingling?"

"That's not normal," Thea said.

Both stared at me, waiting. Heat crept into my cheeks. I backtracked. "I'm probably making it sound worse than it is. My luck, it's just one of those middle-age body failures, you know? If I sneeze wrong these days, I'll snap a rib." I chuckled, but both ladies were far too young to relate to my woes.

"Yeah, you need to get that checked out." Thea shook her head and gathered her belongings.

The nurse was less alarmist. "Maybe mention it next time you see your doctor."

Four minutes of small talk and two strangers had imminent concern for my well-being. I was killing it with the extroverting.

"I will," I told her. "But like I said, I'm probably making it sound worse." All the same, I stuffed my hand into my front pocket, fully out of sight.

While Thea abruptly left the conversation, Ellen made a

polite exit, saying she needed to go pick up her boys. "It was lovely meeting you, Jess."

"Yes, you too."

As Ellen made her way down the row toward the door, Reva returned in the center aisle. "Met some of the other ladies, I see. Are you staying for service?"

"I wish I could, but I need to go find Kyla and take her home."

"Maybe next Sunday, then."

"Yeah, maybe." Before Reva could squirrel me into committing, I scanned the room. "Did Austie leave already?"

"She did. Her ride was here earlier than she expected."

Which probably explained why she was so eager to jet from the room. That, and being overwhelmed.

"She should be back next week," Reva said, dangling the carrot.

I smiled, but I still didn't commit.

"Before you head out," she said, "I wanted to see what you're doing for lunch today. Gio and I would love to host you. Are you available to come to our house at 12:30?"

I blinked. A lunch invitation? From someone I'd met an hour prior? What kind of church was Trinity?

Her deep-shaded eyes lingered on me. My gut instinct about Reva was that she would fight a bear if need be and not break a sweat doing it. And I very well may have been that bear.

"We're having carnitas," she added. "Gluten- and dairy-free, if that's a consideration for you."

It never had been and, Lord willing, never needed to be. "That's very kind of you. I wouldn't want to impose."

"It's not an imposition if you're invited."

The intensity of her expectation lasered through any notion of swathing myself on the futon and eating leftover Chinese while finishing out *Boy Meets World*. "I'd love to," I said.

Within a minute, I had Reva's number in my phone and a link to her address in my text messages.

10

THE ACARDIS' STREET eased gently between colonial-style houses and wide sidewalks under mature trees. Their house was the third from the end of the block. Three dormer windows popped up from the high roof, and a row of tidy box shrubs skirted the white-brick front. If houses could match the owners' personality, the Acardis' matched theirs with flawless accuracy. Trim and prim, everything perfectly fitted, and worlds above anything I had ever lived in. It was the kind of house that reminded me how very, very far away I was from a put-together life.

After carting Kyla home, I had changed into my best capris and a floral-print top. And brushed my hair. And put on concealer and mascara. But outward adornment covered only so much.

I parked behind a sparkling-clean Acura in the driveway as invited/instructed by Reva. For several moments, I sat with my head bowed, a knot blooming in my stomach. "Do I really want to be here?" If only I had a drop of Kyla's excitement when she'd found me in the lobby after Sunday school. She'd insisted we return the following Sunday, which would have been music to Reva's ears.

I filled my lungs and exhaled slowly. "All right. You can do this."

I gathered my purse and my shaky courage and headed up the front walk.

Reva arrived at the door at almost exactly the same second the doorbell stopped chiming, as if she had been watching for me. "Glad you could come, Jess."

"Thank you again for inviting me."

She swept her arm toward the interior. "Please come in."

Though my feet hesitated, I pushed them forward, into the nucleus of Reva's world. The inside was as proper as the outside. A sleek, modern couch and matching loveseat rested upon an authentic-looking oriental rug. Sprigs of fresh flowers adorned a side table, bringing a pop of pale pink to the neutral-toned room. Secured to the wall opposite the large picture window was a collection of black-framed photos of various sizes arranged to form a rectangle. They captured the faces and moments at various points in the Acardi family history, from the reddish Kodak colors of the 1980s to present day.

Reva closed the door behind us. "Did you have any trouble finding our house?"

"No trouble at all. I do feel bad showing up empty-handed."

"Don't worry about that. I asked you at the last minute."

Silverware jangled from beyond the wall of photos. Gio hummed a vaguely familiar tune. The wonderful noise carried through the passageway between the living room and kitchen.

Reva stepped around me and glided toward the kitchen. "We're getting everything set up. Come on through."

I fell in behind her, the soft taps of my footfalls on the polished wood floors blending in with hers. As we neared the wall of photos, one image hooked me. I stopped and leaned toward it. A young-looking Reva held preschool-aged girls on either hip. Both children boasted the same sleek, dark strands as their mother. All around that picture were others of those two girls growing up. "This must be your family."

Reva turned and met me in the middle of the memories. She

scanned the photos, a subtle lift to her lips. "Our children and grandchildren. We have two daughters, one in San Antonio and one in Chicago. Both are married with two children of their own."

A few of the older photos could have been taken right there in that living room, based on the similarity of the picture window in the background. Two little girls in front of a Christmas tree. A teenager in a marching band uniform. A young woman in a cap and gown on the lawn of a college. Two preschoolers with chocolate-smeared faces. Reva in a hospital rocking chair holding a swaddled bundle.

She reached out and wiped away an invisible spot of dust from one of the frames. "We see them a few times a year. Everyone comes to stay with us when they're in town. Our basement is one big family suite."

The frame she tidied wrapped around a photo of a younger Reva standing with one of her daughters on a majestic precipice somewhere, their hair blown sideways and suspended in air. Reva's hand rested on her daughter's shoulder. The girl wore a Congress Middle School Cougars hoodie. Her daughter had been on a precipice of a different kind at that age, one that separated childhood from adulthood and came with a tidal wave of challenges even in normal circumstances, let alone if a parent has died.

Did Reva's girl know how blessed she was to still have her mom at her side at that age? To have a photo like that to look back on and remember? My memories of Mom had started to fade into snatches of things here and there by the time I graduated high school. A vague memory of her voice calling me awake for school. A struggle to remember how long she fried the bologna for Dad's sandwiches. The way she hushed me when I ran into the house for water during her soap operas on a summer day. If there were photos of me with Mom, Dad kept them stashed away.

Reva pointed at the photo. "That's my youngest and me in New

Mexico. We took the girls to the Navajo Nation reservation to show them their roots."

Quick calculations buzzed through my brain. "You're Navajo?"

"I am. I was born on the reservation. I lived there until I was ten, before my parents moved us to Texas. That picture was taken about a year before my dad passed. My mom was already gone by then."

Having grown up in southern Kansas, a state named for the Kansa people, and in such close proximity to the mix of nations in Oklahoma, I had heard plenty of stories about reservation life. But I had never had a chance to ask someone who actually lived it. "Do you remember anything about growing up on the reservation? What was it like?"

Her eyes stayed on the photo, the only one in the mix that appeared to have been taken on tribal land. "There's so much beauty in that community, so much I've always wanted my girls to know. I remember gatherings with friends and family. I remember the games us kids used to play and the sunsets so big they practically engulfed you. I remember endless trails we'd explore for hours on the weekends. But we didn't have indoor plumbing for most of my childhood there, and meals were not always guaranteed. Income opportunities were limited. Those challenges led to the types of things a parent wants to keep their children away from."

She dusted the frame again. The photo hinted at the enamoring landscape with deep horizons and ancient soil that bore little in the way of crops but contained the blood and sweat of those to whom it belonged. "It's a strange thing, Jess, to have your heart so entwined with a place where you can't practically stay."

In that single statement, I gained the words to express how it really felt to leave Woodfield. Though my experience was different from hers, we both understood what it was to have a torn love for our first homes.

"So true," I replied softly.

Reva locked her gaze onto me. I had said only two simple

words, but for someone like her, studious and intuitive, I had shared entire pages of my biography. She nodded, as if understanding the resonance between us as well as I did. Then she led me into the kitchen.

Over our lunch of carnitas and street corn, Gio's easy laugh and unambiguous grin complemented Reva's more unchanging but no less graceful demeanor.

"Reva, this is absolutely delicious," Gio said as he scooped a bite of corn from his plate. "I'd say you've perfected this carnitas recipe."

"Not that you're biased," Reva said.

"Objective as a court justice." Gio winked at me.

It was easy to be relaxed around them. As relaxed as a screwup could be in the presence of people who had obviously found their way much earlier in life.

"It really is delicious," I said. "I haven't had carnitas much. I think the Mexican restaurant one town over from Woodfield had a burrito with it, but I usually went with a good old taco salad."

"Woodfield, Kansas?" Gio asked. "Is that where you're from?"

"Do you know it?"

"Outside Emporia. Had a big flood back in the nineties when Wood River overflowed its banks."

"Wow, you really do know it."

"Gio was in the Corps of Engineers back then," Reva said. "He worked that flood."

He chased his food with a sip of water, then set his glass on the table. "I remember a steak place on Main that was pretty good. Is that still there?"

"Morty's. Yep, still there."

"I'll be." He turned to his wife. "We'll have to take a road trip sometime, Reva. I'll get you a good Kansas steak."

"How delightful," she quipped and lifted her taco to her mouth.

Gio's hearty laugh poured over the table. "Reva's not much of a steak person. Me, I can't get enough. Beef in all forms, I say."

"He nearly had it printed on a T-shirt." Reva's deadpan humor played impeccably against Gio's more overt style.

I laughed right along with them. "You sound like my dad, Gio." I didn't think anything of the peek into my personal life, until Reva tilted her head to the side.

She swallowed before speaking. "That's the first time you've mentioned your dad."

My amusement dried up. More questions were bound to follow, and then more, and those answers would point to things parents tried to protect their kids from. I quickly gathered a bite, preparing to stuff my mouth.

But Reva was quicker. "Do your parents live in Woodfield?"

I pushed my corn kernels together with my fork. "It's just my dad now." I calculated how much to say, pushed the last kernel into the outer rim of the mound. "I'm actually trying to get him to move up here with me, since I have the room in my rental house. But, you know, he's set in his ways."

Reva watched me. The follow-up questions practically flashed in her expression. About what happened with my mom. About why I left Dad behind, left Woodfield behind. About what had happened between those two mile markers of my life.

I pulled on a fresh smile. "So," I said, "how did you two meet?"

Gio took the diversion in an instant, playfully jutting his fork at me. "Now that's a story!"

Off he went, regaling us with the tale of how their paths first intersected in Lawrence, Kansas, where he worked at Clinton Lake for the corps and Reva was a student at Haskell Indian Nations University. There was a situation involving a trio of adventurous college girls captained by one strong-willed senior named Reva Nez and an old canoe that wasn't exactly seaworthy.

I laughed in all the right places, prodded them both for more details to paint a complete picture. I relished the natural progression of their story into their first years of marriage, Gio's new job as a civil engineer in Kansas City, and the birth of their first daughter.

But throughout it all, Reva would frame me with her piercing gaze, the questions sharpening. Because no one left a home they loved without good cause.

11

THE DAY WAS BARELY half over and already I had revealed far more than I ever intended to, and to far more people than I ever thought possible. Still, I caved when Reva promised there would be chocolate cake if I hung tight.

Gio insisted on doing the dishes alone. He gave us refilled glasses of iced lemonade and shooed us out to the screened porch off the back of the house. Reva led me to a square patio table surrounded by four cushioned chairs.

"Have a seat," she said.

My glass began to sweat in my hand before I could set it on the ceramic tabletop. The temperature had climbed noticeably, and the humidity gathered like a wool blanket against my skin.

I chose a seat across the table from my hostess and took a long, cool drink before settling against the cushions. A robin pecked at a bird feeder on the outer rim of the porch roof. Other than that hungry little creature, we were alone.

Reva rested her elbows on the arms of her chair, her hands draped over the front ends. "I appreciate you coming to have lunch with us today."

I set my glass on the table. The heavy bottom clinked against the ceramic. "You both are wonderful. I've enjoyed myself."

"Sorry if we dominated the conversation."

I wiped my hand on my pant leg. "Not at all. I enjoyed learning more about you."

"That is the best part of sharing a meal with someone, isn't it? Getting to know them." Her gaze held mine.

I resisted the urge to bite my lip. I'd given far too many tells already.

When I didn't answer, she pivoted her forearms inward and folded her hands. "You don't like talking about yourself, do you?"

That bottom lip of mine had a mind of its own sometimes. It retreated between my teeth. Forcing it out again, I replied, "Not really, I suppose."

"Why is that?"

"Just private, I guess." Droplets of condensation trailed down my glass. Sweat began to do the same on the hidden part of my chest. She had been so open with her life, so willing to invite me in. I should be able to do the same, should be able to tell her one important thing about my past.

"It's okay, Jess."

I met her eyes.

She nodded, assuring me I had heard her right. "It takes wisdom to know what to share and with whom."

Once again, she could hear everything I had left unsaid. How did she do that? She had given me permission to share on my own terms. Still, it seemed only fair to give her some kind of insight.

She was the one to break the silence, however. "May I ask you something?"

I nodded.

"Did you feel uncomfortable in class today?"

I fiddled with the hem of my blouse. "A little."

"Why?" Compassion coated her inquiry.

I reached for my glass, because full hands made awkward situations a tad easier. The cold seeped through my skin, up my hand. My words were halting. "All of this is still kind of new to me."

"What is?"

"Church. Christianhood, or whatever the term is." I traced my fingertips through the condensation the way windshield wipers cleared away the rain. "It's not as natural as breathing for me as it is for you all. Yet, anyway. I hope."

One side of Reva's mouth tipped up. "If it's any consolation, it will never be natural."

"That's not much of a consolation, no."

She laughed softly, her lips not moving any higher, then she turned to watch the robin.

In the pause, I sipped my lemonade. The coolness slipped down my throat, attempting to soothe the tension coiled there.

The bird darted away from the feeder and into the oak shading the backyard. Staring after it, Reva said, "I've come to observe that those who find faith later in life understand the cost in a more nuanced way than those who grew up in the church. Not good or bad, just is." She centered her gaze on me. "I came to faith in my early thirties, after my kids had been born, and right around the time Gio and I separated the second time."

I righted. "You separated?"

She took a long drink. Nothing was rushed about her. "We married young and had our first child not long after. Neither of us were mature enough to handle the stresses of it all. I made a lot of mistakes in that time. Mistakes that hurt my kids, dishonored my husband. Mistakes that gave me a reputation in the world that I was actually proud of back then. I was a fighter, and not in the good way." She gestured at her cheek, at that pocked scar, and the inference behind it. "But deep down, in places I didn't want to admit existed, I was worn and tired, begging for someone to see the real me and love me anyway."

Tightness clenched my chest. I drew my hand away from my glass and let it fall into my lap. The first time that tingling had presented in my left hand was the same day I was forced to pick up my sopping clothes from the grass and stuff them into my truck—no boxes or bags or suitcases at my disposal, but plenty of heavy storm clouds crowding out the evening light and wielding even more damage upon my shattered life. I had been tired, worn, used, and tossed. Begging for someone to see me and love me anyway.

Reva's tender voice reached into the aching memory. "The someone I found, as you know, Jess, was Jesus. And if it hadn't been for a coworker who was brave enough to talk to me about him, I may not have discovered the lover of my scarred and beaten soul at the moment I needed him most. I suspect you know exactly how that feels."

My favorite pair of jeans had landed in a pile of dog excrement made soggy again by the rain. I had to surrender them, and all my electronics and furniture ruined by the rain. But as my clothes dripped onto the floorboards of my truck, Tillie Watts sat me in the front pew and led her choirmates in hymns that soaked me in things no one had ever taught me. Things about an unrestrained heavenly love that waited for me to receive it.

My reply to Reva came softly, squeezing through my clenched throat. "I do."

"I thought you might." She sat forward and leaned her arms against the edge of the table. For a moment, she looked off to the side.

I sniffed back the tears blurring my vision and folded my hands.

Finally, she turned to me. "I want to talk to you about Austie—and ask you to consider something."

An hour later, I climbed into Hank with a container of leftover carnitas, Austie's number added to my phone, and Reva's suggestion rattling my nerves. Jesus stuff really did require a kind of extroverting I wasn't convinced I was ready—or right—for.

12

THE NEXT SATURDAY, as afternoon whittled down to evening, I stood in my freshly cleaned kitchen, phone in hand, thumbs poised over a new message to Austie. Nearly a week had passed since my lunch at Reva's, and at least three times before, I had landed in that very pose, face bent toward the screen, cursor blinking. And like every time before, words failed to materialize.

I dropped my hands to my side with a sigh. "You don't have to do this, Jess."

It was true, I didn't have to do it. Reva had asked me to invite Austie out for coffee or something, but I didn't owe her that. In fact, I never had to see Reva or Austie or anyone from Allelon again if I didn't want to. It was a fluke I ended up at Trinity anyway.

But the self-consolation did not fade out the image of Austie hiding her face in the back row. It didn't overwrite the story Reva shared with me about meeting Austie at a ministry for young women in danger of burning down their lives—just like I had, and Reva. Unlike me, though, Reva wasn't still trying to heal the singed parts. She had gained plenty of life wisdom and training to redirect a twenty-one-year-old attempting to break from boys and booze and a brush with petty theft.

I left my phone on the counter and wandered to the refrigerator for a cold can of diet soda. The updraft of the door opening flitted the Daily Allelon sheet held to the freezer by a sunflower magnet. The week's verse, which I had penciled a star next to, practically shouted at me.

Strive to do what is good.

Sometimes, though, what was good was not stepping into places I didn't belong. Who was I to save a burning life when the embers of my own still smoldered? Austie needed someone better equipped, better prepared. She needed someone who was not me.

I grabbed a can and shut the door.

For supper, I ordered a pizza and splurged on delivery, the first time I had ever had the thrill of a restaurant bringing food to my door. Half an hour after I placed the order, footfalls thumped outside my door. Three short knocks followed. Kyla was there, pizza box in hand and a grin on her face.

"Delivery," she said.

"Did they deliver to the wrong address?" I asked.

"Happens sometimes." She handed me the box. "Pop took care of the tip."

"He didn't have to do that."

She shrugged one shoulder. "He said it was the least he could do after you took me to church last Sunday. Pizza smells good. What kind is it?"

"The kind I can't eat without consequence."

"Sounds amazing," she said, oblivious to my meaning. She stared at the box with such longing that drool was bound to dribble off her lip and onto my floorboards.

"Have you had dinner?" I asked.

"Pop's making hot dogs again. I'm sick of hot dogs." She looked up at me with those pleading eyes.

"I wouldn't want you to get in trouble with him."

She shook her head. "He won't care."

The pizza box was still warm. Grease oozed through the bottom and slicked my hand. I held far more than I needed to eat, and a teenage girl stood in front of me with an empty stomach and an emptier social calendar. Even I at that age would have taken a neighbor woman with pizza over a grandfather with hot dogs.

I stepped aside. "Let's fix you a plate."

She bounded past me into the living room. Following my directions, she gathered plates and napkins while I stuffed layers of paper towels under the box before laying it in the middle of the table.

When we had the table set, she glanced back at the kitchen. "Got any soda?" she asked.

"Diet. In the fridge." I followed her into the kitchen and grabbed two apples from the fruit basket on the counter for a semblance of a balanced meal.

"What's this?" she asked, pointing at the sheet tacked to the freezer.

"That's from the Sunday school class I was in."

"At Wren's church?"

I nodded.

She pulled a can from the refrigerator and shut the door. "You going back?"

"Depends. Do you need another ride?"

"Not tomorrow. Wren's going to be out of town again. Her dad travels a lot for work, and sometimes he takes them with him."

We returned to the table. I settled into my usual chair overlooking the front door and placed an apple on each of our plates.

Kyla sat to my left, in one of the random chairs I had found at the thrift store. "Sometimes I wish my mom would take me on her tours too, but she said we'd be separated anyway when she had to sail."

"Do you get to see your mom much?"

Kyla opened her can of soda, the clack and pop breaking up the momentary quiet. "On video calls, when she can. She comes back next summer."

"Long time to wait."

"I'm used to it." She lifted the can to her lips and drank. Only a teenager could chug the way she did. I would have spilled half my drink down my front, then produced a belch that scattered birds from the trees. She downed her last mouthful and set the can on the table.

I had no reason to doubt Kyla was used to a lot of things. But being used to something didn't mean she wasn't affected by it. At forty-two, I still longed to talk to Mom one more time. "Think you'll ever get to go visit her?" I asked.

She tucked her hands into her lap and fixed her gaze on mine. "Jess?"

I leaned forward, ready to receive any vulnerability that might come. "Yes?"

"I'm hungry."

That was the best thing about Kyla—how uncomplicated she was. I didn't need any special training to know how to talk to her, only a pizza, an extra chair, and a spleen that healed quickly.

"Right," I said. "Let's dig in."

I threw back the box lid and nodded for Kyla to make her selection. I should have prayed first, but praying in front of people was like having a bright, hot spotlight an inch from my face. As an alternative, as Kyla pulled her first meat-laden piece onto her plate, I offered a silent prayer of thanks for the hands that had prepared the food, a kind neighbor who picked up the tip, and more friends who would enfold Kyla the way Wren had at the church doors.

Then we ate. We stuffed ourselves with unhealthy amounts of cholesterol and carbonated beverages. We compared notes on how we entertained ourselves growing up. She told me about her favorite YouTubers, a pair of sisters who were apparently a big deal. I told her about *Boy Meets World*, which she judged to be "so basic, bro"—big talk from someone who wore crew socks with sandals. The conversation meandered to the point I ended up digging out the card deck from the junk drawer and teaching her the only card game Dad ever taught me: blackjack. I'd spent hours playing it solo on Friday nights as a kid while he watched sports. Kyla turned out to be a natural.

Soon the sun toed the horizon. I wrapped a slice of pizza in aluminum foil and sent it with Kyla back to her house. I waved goodbye from my porch as she crossed the lot, then stepped back inside and shut the door. On the table lay the pile of playing cards and spent napkins wadded on grease-splotched plates, evidence of an unexpected evening of unexpected companionship, of indulgence and laughter. Of me doing good.

But in the stillness rose that same image of Austie hiding her face.

13

CERTAIN DECISIONS made at night often had consequences the next morning. Meat-heavy pizza was one of them. The amount of acid that broiled in my stomach on Sunday morning could have fueled a volcano. I moaned my way from the bed to the bathroom, clutching my midsection. No amount of hunching eased the burn flaming up my esophagus. My reflection in the bathroom mirror confirmed that the misery inside showed clear as the morning sky in my expression. If Mount Saint Helens had had a face before its landmark eruption, it would have looked like that.

"Never again, Jess," I groaned. I opened the cabinet and rummaged for the bottle of Pepto. On the bright side, the debate about whether to return to Trinity and the Allelon class was settled. I had a solid excuse to stay home, to take another week to figure out a more permanent answer.

The pink bottle was on the bottom shelf behind the box of bandages. I took it out, tossed the measuring cup on top onto the counter, and guzzled three long gulps. The chalky liquid slid down easily, calming the fire to a tolerable ache in a near instant, just like the old TV commercials illustrated. Able to right my posture a touch more, I tucked the bottle to my side and plodded back into the hall. My bed, the pink relief, and reclining at an elevated angle would be my best friends that morning.

I hadn't yet made it to my room when someone knocked on my door. Only Kyla had ever come to my house at eight in the morning on a Sunday, but the figure on the other side of the frosted glass was bigger than hers, with a wide-brimmed hat perched on their head. Whoever it was couldn't see me through the glass, which meant I could have ducked into my room and pretended like I didn't hear. Instead, I turned and made my way to the visitor. By the time I reached the door, I had smoothed my hair as best I could and straightened as much as the ache would allow.

Ron stood on the other side, hat shading his entire face and his "Navy Dad" T-shirt tucked into his khaki cargo pants. "Sorry to bother you so early," he said. Though he looked from my hair to my pajamas, he kindly refrained from commenting on the sad state of my appearance or the bottle in my hand, which I quickly moved behind my back. "Wanted to let you know I'm getting ready to mow your yard, before it gets hot. Didn't want to startle you."

"Wonderful. Thanks for letting me know."

He nodded, patted his thigh with his palm, drumming up more words. "I also owe you a thanks. For everything you're doing for Kyla."

I waved him off with my empty hand. "I'm not doing much of anything."

"Doesn't take much." His eyes held fast to mine, a reaction that indicated he was approaching his max capacity for sentiment.

I adjusted my grip on the bottle. "She's a good kid. She makes it easy."

He rested his hands on his hips and looked off to the side. An invisible weight slanted his aged shoulders. "She'd hate that I'm telling you this, but she's been having a hard time. With high school, I mean. I guess some of the girls aren't . . ."

I nodded, fully understanding the rest of the sentence.

"And with her mom not here . . ." He lifted one hand and rolled it in the air, unwinding the words he couldn't speak.

"Must be hard for you both," I said.

He resettled his hand on his hip and kept his eyes turned toward his mower parked next to my driveway, toward the invisible images that must have plagued him of a granddaughter he couldn't shield from everything, no matter how hard he tried. His shoulders weren't broad enough, strong enough, capable enough. Without meaning to, I had become the reinforcement, the thing I'd missed out on at Kyla's age. I was the adult who noticed the motherless young girl who desperately wanted someone she trusted to tell her she possessed goodness to give. Someone who would welcome her into their day. Someone to be a windbreak to shelter behind.

Warmth of a different kind swelled in my chest.

Ron shifted his weight from one foot to the other. "Anyway," he said with a sigh. "Thank you."

The sensation spread into my cheeks. "Of course."

He gestured toward his mower. "Better get to work."

"Have a good morning, Ron."

"You too, Jess." He headed for the steps. Before he descended, he paused and turned halfway around. "By the way, Pepcid works better."

I grinned. "Noted."

A final nod, then he clomped down the steps and on toward his duty. He was the kind of man who took care of his responsibilities not for his own glory but for the good of others. He provided stability and a home for his granddaughter, assurance for his daughter, a mowed yard and a degree of safety for me. He did it all with a quiet heroism built on small, daily acts. Not the grand gestures highlighted on the evening news; rather, the simple things. Like an offer of a slice of pizza, an open door, a willingness to take a ball to the gut.

Small, everyday acts created the strongest stitches between one life and another.

The image of Austie returned. But this time, she peeked up at me from around the veil of her hair.

I shut the door and quick-stepped to my room. My alarm clock told me I had forty minutes. Forty minutes to loosen the snarl in my stomach and to come up with some way to convince Austie I was moderately cool to hang out with.

14

I TOOK A FINAL SWIG of the Pepto, then lay the near-empty bottle in the middle seat of my truck. The visual clue would remind me to pick up a new bottle on the way home. A quick check in the rearview mirror confirmed I had applied my makeup and coiffed my hair well, all things considered. My mascara had not yet smeared upon my tender under-eye skin, its absolute favorite place to gather despite all my proactive measures to prevent it. The old women at the Woodfield church—those who still had eyelashes—always seemed to have raccoon eyes, and I never understood why until my mascara volunteered to teach me.

Satisfied, I pushed open my door with my Bible in hand and a mental list of reasons why Austie should join me for coffee that afternoon (or a milkshake if the Pepto didn't completely do its job). Hank and I had landed in a spot toward the back of the lot, in a row that ran perpendicular to the main entrance. I started across the lot. Up ahead, Thea and her family disembarked from a white SUV. It didn't take them long to assemble at the rear, as if they practiced drills at home on how to speedily get into the church.

Her husband led the pack toward the church doors, with Thea a step or two behind. She was robed in a long-sleeve khaki dress paired with dark-brown shoes. Her two small girls bopped along behind her with prairie-dog energy and animal-face backpacks jiggling from their little shoulders. Their hair was pulled tight into French braids that matched their mother's, all roots held in place by gel. No amount of play or tussling would jar a single hair loose from perfection. Thea walked with ramrod-straight posture, shoulders back, the posture of a matriarch with a self-made crown.

My cheeks burned. I covered the uncharitable attitude churning in my heart with my Bible.

An older man held open the door for the family, then, a dozen beats or so later, for me. I returned his "Good morning" and stepped into the lobby. Thea and her brood angled toward the youth wing.

Another man strode toward them and stuck out his hand to Thea's husband. "Morning, Todd. I see they let you back in."

"Seems so," Todd said with a laugh, veering away from his family to return the shake.

The two fell into animated conversation. Thea stopped and stared after her husband. Their two girls skipped in circles, singing something about "Father Abraham" and his many sons. The frames of Thea's glasses could not camouflage her deep frown aimed at Todd's back.

I slowed my pace, unwilling to step into her line of sight.

With her husband seemingly oblivious to the joyful noise reverberating through the lobby, Thea tore her gaze away from him and focused on the girls. "Let's go. Abigail, walk forward. Evie, now, please." The giggling girls rounded one last spin and, as if well practiced in immediate obedience too, trotted alongside her. They soon folded into the stream of congregants headed to the youth wing. Todd didn't seem to notice.

I arched an eyebrow in his direction on my trek to the adult wing. He didn't notice that either.

The Allelon classroom buzzed with conversations, which took

place in the rows and by the donuts near the windows. Reva stood on the other side of the room, her back to the door, nodding along to whatever the woman in front of her said. The woman looked familiar. Most of the people did. Gio was there, munching a donut next to two other men by the treat table. So was Ellen's husband. But the back row was empty.

I slipped in unnoticed, sat in the same spot as the week before, and laid my Bible on the chair next to me. The minute hand on the clock above the lectern hovered a good six ticks away from the hour mark. An eternity of time when sitting alone. Another couple entered the room. Then Todd. Then Ellen, who went straight for her husband in the front row. Still no Austie.

Four minutes to go. One reliable relief to awkward waiting-alone situations was an escape to the restroom. I rose and slipped out of the room as easily as I had slipped in.

The restroom walls were festooned with loud floral wallpaper. A small, lace-covered table in the corner boasted a vase of fake dahlias. A ceramic bowl of dusty potpourri sat between the two sinks, long past its ability to emanate the scent the decor evoked. Bless its heart, the restroom tried its best to be Victorian amid the otherwise twentieth-century building.

I pulled up to the mirror above the sinks. My mascara still behaved, and the cowlick at the far end of my part had yet to pivot to the side and create a glade at my crown. I fluffed the strands around my face as much as possible, smoothed my red-and-white-striped blouse, decided horizontal stripes made me look wider than necessary, then turned for the stall closest to the entrance. Right as I lifted my hand to push open the partition door, Thea breezed into the room.

Our eyes met. I froze. Her brow pinched.

I dropped my hand to my side. "Hello."

"Hi," she mumbled, then bustled around me, stick straight, to the stall at the end. The metal door smacked shut, sending a jolt through the whole structure. She clicked the lock into place.

Silence lingered. So did I, in the same spot, unsure of my next step. My time-passing hideout was no longer a peaceful place to seek cover. I didn't really have to answer nature's call, nor did I care to be present for anyone else doing so. I turned for the exit. With any luck, the four eternal minutes had passed or Austie had arrived.

The din of conversation had subsided by the time I approached the classroom. Gio's voice floated out the open door. He called the class to order. I paused in the hallway, just out of view, and craned my neck for a better angle of the back row. Nothing but empty seats.

Maybe returning to Trinity wasn't the best idea after all.

Reva popped around the threshold, nearly crashing into me. She startled. "Jess. Didn't see you there." She dropped to a whisper as Gio cycled through the housekeeping items of the week. "You came back."

"I did," I whispered. "I was hoping Austie would be here too."

"She couldn't make it today. Were you able to get ahold of her this week?"

I could have lied. I chose to fudge, and only by omission. "No."

"Doesn't surprise me you had trouble."

I could have corrected the misinterpretation, but pressed in the direction Reva took us. "Is everything okay with her?"

"Long story," she said. "Let's talk after."

Before I could wrap my mind around the implication, Reva shooed me into the room and shut the door behind us.

I huddled in the back row with my Bible, low enough for Gio not to be tempted to call on me. Though my ears hooked onto his words, my eyes kept drifting to the empty chair next to me, and my mind to the striking blue irises of the young woman I first met there.

15

THEA JOINED THE CLASS a solid seven minutes in, amid Gio collecting reports of how people had lived out the "Do good to one another" verse of the week. Ellen, the nurse, was sharing about her co-coordinator role for a local hospital's Grace Closet, which supplied forgotten or needed items to patients. Most people, including Thea's husband, were too engrossed in Ellen's story of the patients Grace Closet had served the past week to notice Thea's faintly red cheeks and the way she kept her chin tucked as she skirted the front row and slipped in next to Todd, directly across the aisle from Reva. Had she been crying? If she hadn't been so cold to me every time I'd tried to talk to her, I would have been tempted to ask.

The tip of her perfect braid brushed the back of her chair. She immediately opened her Bible, presumably at the verse the discussion revolved around, and stared down at it.

"And we can always use donations of new underwear, bras, and socks," Ellen continued. "Toiletries are welcome too. There's a collection bin at the information desk at the main entrance."

"That's beautiful," Gio said, to murmured agreements. "Yes, please, if you all feel led to contribute, talk to Ellen more about it.

Thank you to everyone who shared those encouraging examples. You indeed glorify God when you put his Word into practice, even in the simplest ways. The world may not herald them, but heaven rejoices over them."

A soft chorus of amens rose.

"Let's move on to this week's verse." He pointed at the tidy blue letters on the whiteboard: Romans 16:16. "Todd, would you please read the first part of the verse for us?"

Funny he should ask the husband when the Bible Quizzing wife probably could have recited it from memory. I pulled my Bible onto my lap and flipped to the correct spot.

Todd read the short verse aloud with a little more theater than was warranted. "'Greet one another with a holy kiss.'" He guffawed and looked up at Gio. "You're not going to make us kiss people, are you?"

Giggles rippled through the room. A lame joke at best, but it did unlock a new fear within me. I drew the extroversion line well before kissing.

Gio grinned. "Some things belong to cultures that are not our own, and I'm perfectly fine with that."

"Me too," a man near the windows said, drawing more laughs.

"You will all be relieved to know," Gio said, "that Matthew Henry, in his commentary, explains the kiss was a cultural gesture in that Roman church of that particular time period. It was later replaced by the gesture we all know and probably take a little more easily to, the handshake."

My new fear shriveled, and as Gio explained that it wasn't the gesture that was the point of Paul's instruction but the intention behind it, the withered worry blew away like fine dust in a slight breeze.

"This wasn't just a way to say hello or a simple act of welcome," he said. "It was a show of unity and fellowship, a show of genuine care for the other believer. Let's unpack that for a minute. Why would greetings have been so important in the Roman church that Paul would call it out like this? What was happening at that time to the Roman Christians?"

"Persecution," a woman offered.

"Shunning," someone else said.

"Both often came from their own families, their own neighbors, didn't they?" Gio asked.

Heads nodded.

I leaned forward, burrowing deeper into the scene he described of weary, young Christians gathering together and finding reprieve from the harshness of their realities, from their uphill struggle to live set apart from the only life they knew—the long-ingrained patterns that seemed as much a part of them as the veins under their skin. I had never related so much to ancient populations before.

Gio rested his hands on the bottom corners of the lectern. "Think about how this command to greet other believers like members of the same holy family would have landed with an audience that knew the pain of being disowned by their earthly families. Imagine what those believers endured in those days and hours between church gatherings. What do you think they would have felt in those parts of their lives?"

"Rejected," a voice said, perfectly encapsulating how it felt. Nearly all heads in the room turned my way. Until then, I didn't realize the voice belonged to me.

Gio nodded. "That's a good word, Jess."

My cheeks filled with heat. I recoiled against the back of my chair as everyone refocused on Gio—everyone except Reva. Her gaze lingered on me a beat longer. I had showed another tell. I dipped my head, reading the words on the pages in my lap but not really seeing them.

Gio ended the segment with a single imploration: "This week, reflect on how you can be part of the reprieve your fellow believer finds."

The people in front of me bent over their notebooks, jotting down the insight. Where was that hunger when I sat alone before class? They didn't have to look that far to find someone shivering from the cold disinterest and sneers of those who were supposed to be friends. "Jesus stuff" very well may have been the real reason my own father refused to acknowledge any of the good about my new life.

For the rest of class, I followed along with the Scripture but didn't really latch on to anything except the steady tick of the minute hand.

At the end, Gio asked for prayer requests. Someone's cousin was sick. Someone sought a job. Someone's mother needed surgery. I knew none of the names mentioned or the names of the people who said them, until Reva spoke up.

"Some of you met my young friend from Lighthouse Ministries last week."

I sat up straight.

"She wasn't at our meeting this past Thursday. Word among the girls is that she is facing some significant family challenges at the moment and is quite vulnerable to veering off path again."

My brow furrowed. Was she really just going to air Austie's business like that for all the class? Was that the update she was supposed to have given me after class, privately, well out of earshot of those looking for another reason not to think much of Austie?

Thea lifted her head for the first time all hour, attention fixed on Reva. I gritted my teeth.

"She lives with her mom and has a history of running away," Reva continued. "I would greatly appreciate prayer that she would remain strong and stand on her faith—however new it may be—and not fall under the wrong influences."

Unreal. Austie had trusted Reva, admired her. That's how Reva repaid loyalty? By ripping open Austie's private struggles and using them as Sunday school fodder like grist in a small-town rumor mill? *I* had trusted Reva.

"Remind us of her name," a woman prompted. Because none of them had bothered to pay attention to it when they first had the chance.

"Austie Russell," Reva said.

I slapped my Bible closed, but the noise blended into the promises of the group to pray. Austie was not an issue to pray over from a distance. She wasn't in need of strangers knowing her struggles like she was a TV drama to watch. She was in need of someone willing to give her a holy greeting. Wasn't that what we had just talked about?

Gio asked the class to bow their heads. Before he could finish the amen, I was on my feet, fixed on the door.

When I was safely inside Hank, I took out my phone. The opening lines of a new text message rolled through my thumbs unhindered.

Hi, Austie. It's Jess Becker, from the Sunday school class.

16

THE LATE-AFTERNOON SUN invaded Hobby Hill Park like a bad dream. Condensation dripped off the sides of the two plastic cups in my hands faster than the sweat beading off my temples. A stroll through a park on Wednesday had been Austie's idea, despite my every effort to move us somewhere air-conditioned and preferably stationary. Odds were great I would have my frozen soda from the Fast Stop gas station sucked down long before our walk ended.

I opted to wear a pair of the trendy canvas shoes that were so popular with young people. I had bought them the day before at the resale shop by Cost Cutter, because when one walks with a young person, one should attempt to be less of a fashion flop. Online, people swore by their comfort. On my feet, the shoes grated and pinched, every step sending a reminder that older bodies were not meant to don youthful attire.

Hobby Hill was only a few miles from my house, a thirty-two-acre preserve situated in the basin of two woodsy hills, with a wetland area in the middle. Austie had suggested it, adding she didn't know a lot of parks "up north," which, as I had pieced together from contextual clues, meant "north of the Missouri River" in Kansas City vernacular. The comment indicated that

Austie did not live "up north" like me, one of many things I planned to ask her about.

I reached the sidewalk along the parking lot on the southern hill and turned toward the pavilion and playground. A handful of kids zipped about the modern apparatuses comprised of coated metal, vinyl, and thick climbing ropes, all of which apparently repelled the effects of the sun, unlike the slides and bars and merry-go-rounds of my childhood that roasted exposed skin on contact. The chaperones lazed at picnic tables under the large pavilion, occasionally looking up from their phones to ensure their respective kids were still accounted for. Right before I reached the pavilion, the sidewalk forked off to the right, passed the restrooms, and intersected with a wide, paved trail that made a half-mile loop around the wetland area. The eastern curve of the trail was at least under the broad canopy of oaks and maples.

I settled the frozen sodas and myself at a table near the middle of the pavilion, where the shrieks of play and stamps of little feet danced around me. The woman a table over eyed me. I made a show of moving the second frozen drink in front of the seat across from me, signaling I was to be joined soon. Then I took out my phone and pretended to be as busy and important as every adult under the shelter.

Five thirty arrived, our appointed meetup time. No Austie. Two of the adults rounded up their charges and left. Dark rings seeped outward from the cups into the table's wood slats. I took a swig of my drink and touched the cool plastic to the back of my neck. Even as I sat, my feet chafed in their canvas cells.

Ten minutes passed. I took a longer drink and opened our text conversation to ensure I had the appointed time correct. No sooner had I confirmed than the rattle of an exhaust system in desperate need of a tune-up drew my attention to the parking lot entrance. A rusted blue sedan darted through the lot. The driver's door was a different color than the rest of the car, and the hubcaps were missing. The driver made a U-turn at the far end of the lot, raced back, then squealed to a stop near the pavilion.

Austie emerged from the back passenger seat. She had her backpack slung over one shoulder and the same jeans and tank top combo that she had worn to church. I rose to my feet, ready to wave.

Before she could shut her door completely, the driver gunned the engine. Austie pitched forward with the momentum but caught herself. Somehow, she managed to shut the door and keep all her fingers free. The driver paused briefly at the stop sign guarding the exit before wheeling out onto the street and cutting off an oncoming car.

The woman a table over muttered and glared at Austie. I bit my tongue, grabbed the drinks, and strode toward the new arrival, inserting myself into the line of sight of the annoyed stranger. Austie and I met at the sidewalk, her with chin dipped and me a shield against the nosy onlooker.

"Everything okay?" I asked.

The circles under her eyes had darkened. "My mom's boyfriend is late for his appointment."

"Was he the one driving?"

She nodded and cupped her right arm, the one he had nearly ripped off her body.

"What kind of appointment?" I asked.

She side-eyed the entrance to the park as if ensuring he really had gone. "Parole officer."

Family challenges, Reva had said. It became clearer how tumultuous they may have been. Clearer still how vastly different Austie's experience was from mine. I swallowed, unsure what to say.

She caught sight of the drinks in my hands. "Thirsty?"

"One's for you." I held out the spare cup to her. The pale-brown shaved ice I had dispensed into the cups twenty minutes prior had mostly pooled into dark, watery syrup, which sloshed against the sides of the translucent cup.

Her brow tightened. "What is it?"

"Frozen soda. Well, was. Ever tried one?"

She shook her head and hooked her left thumb behind the strap of her backpack, an interesting accessory choice for a summer afternoon walk. It bulged with its contents, much thicker than it had been by her feet in the back row of the Sunday school classroom. "I don't really drink soda," she said.

"On a hot day like this, it's bliss." I pushed the cup closer to her.

For a moment, she only stared at it. Then, slowly, she reached out her right hand and took the sweaty drink. "Thanks," she said and lowered it to her side. A drop of condensation fell and streaked down the lower part of her jeans.

How she could wear denim in this heat was a mystery. Even my earlobes were sweating. I took a sip from my own cup, relishing the cool rush over my tongue and down my throat. I had downed more than a quarter of the soda already.

"So," I said. "Still want to walk?"

She shrugged. "Why we're here."

Not exactly the excitement I hoped for. "You're welcome to put your bag in my truck," I offered. "One less thing for you to carry."

"That's okay. I'm good."

"Are you sure?"

"Yeah."

"We can put it behind the seat where no one will see it."

"I said I was good." The bite in her reply put me back on my heels.

I could only blink in response.

She sighed, looked down at the ground. In a softer tone, she continued. "Got some stuff in here I don't want to lose, is all." Her eyes flicked to mine, then quickly moved away, a veiled apology left in between.

Reva's other statement echoed in my mind. "*History of run-*

ning away." A history of figuring out how to survive on her own—needing to figure it out. Whatever was in that bag, her self-preservation depended on it. A weight I had never carried, at least not in the same way. And I had shown up with a frozen soda and a naive hope it would bring a smile.

"Fair enough," I said. "Offer stands if you change your mind."

She looked off to the side and said "Thanks" so softly the squeal of a child on the playground nearly drowned it out. Two more drops eased off her ignored drink and splashed on the concrete.

The rapport we seemed to have back in the Allelon class had either withered or been a figment of my imagination the whole time. But she was there, and so was I, and that had to mean something.

I nodded toward the trail. "Ready when you are."

She picked at the strap with her thumbnail, words almost visible on her lips. She shoved her mouth to one side, then turned and slunk toward the trail.

Only minutes into my grand plan of being a holy reprieve and already both of us seemed to question the wisdom of our showing up.

17

BACK IN MY EARLY TWENTIES, before Mick and I got together, I went on a date with a man who had been after me for a couple of weeks, largely thanks to what he had heard about me from a friend. For all the effort he had put into wooing me into his passenger seat, he was a dud and a half on our date. He said maybe three sentences the entire night and made more eye contact with our waitress at Pizza Hut than with me.

The walk with Austie had similar vibes. We were doing the thing she wanted to do, in the park she wanted to do it in, yet she clung to the strap of her backpack with her left hand and demonstrated far more interest in watching her feet traverse the trail than in anything else. Pearls of water continued to slide off the Fast Stop cup in her other hand every few steps, the ice shavings inside nearly gone.

At least we took our time through the shaded eastern portion of the trail. I matched my strides to hers, falling in on her left, and held my cup in both hands, relishing the cool against my palms while it still lasted. All the while, I tried to think of something unawkward to say.

I took a quick sip to prepare myself. "You picked a nice park," I offered.

Deadpan tone, attention on her feet, she replied, "It's close to the PO's office."

"Oh." It made sense she would choose the time and place based on when she could get a lift. "How long do we have until your ride comes back?" I asked.

"Hour or so. Depends."

"On?"

She shrugged and kicked a pebble off the concrete into the grass. "On when he feels like coming back." Resentment seeped from the words.

I treaded carefully, not wanting to reveal how much I already knew about her home life despite her not telling me. "Do you live with your mom and her boyfriend?"

She nodded.

"But I take it not up north?"

"South KC. Off Holmes."

I made a note to look that up later. "I live a few miles from here. Near 88th and Alton, in the neighborhood behind the Cost Cutter on Barry. Do you know it?"

She shook her head and let go of her backpack strap long enough to wipe away the sparkles of sweat on her forehead. A cold drink would have helped with that.

We followed the bend of the trail. Up ahead, the concrete gave way to a wooden bridge hovering over what water had not been sucked up by the blistering atmosphere. The bridge extended for a good portion of the north side of the loop, most of it in full light. The walk was about to get even more unpleasant. If only the chill from Austie could have offset the heat tormenting my skin.

I grasped at another small-talk straw. "So where do you work?"

"Nowhere at the moment."

I grinned. "Holding out for a management position?" To a fellow member of my generation, that Chevy Chase movie reference would have elicited a core memory. But for whatever generation Austie was in, it garnered only a veiled scowl in my direction.

"Hard to work when you don't have a car," she said.

I dipped my chin in the blaze of her stare. "Right. Sorry. Bad joke." So much for keeping my inelegance in check. I aimed my gaze at the approaching marsh, hoping the sting in my chest didn't show up in my expression.

A soft groan at my side was quickly followed by "Jess, wait."

We both came to a stop.

"I'm . . ." She struggled to hold eye contact. "I'm sorry. I guess I'm in a mood." She let go of her strap and ran her palm over her hair. The lion head profile on the inside of her bicep greeted me, the broad snout pointed to the sky. The strength the tattoo symbolized seemed to evade the young woman who bore it. "It's been a hard week. I'm just tired. You know?"

I turned to face her. "Reva said you were having family challenges." The part about Austie being a prayer request seemed inappropriate to share.

She let her hand fall to her side. "I got to get out of that house. My mom's boyfriend is the biggest a–" She caught herself, eyes wide, and quickly recalibrated. "Jerk."

Her original word might have been a little more accurate. "He leaves that impression," I said. She hadn't yet mentioned his name, and that seemed intentional. "Do you have somewhere to go? With friends, maybe, or family? Or someone at Lighthouse?"

"Wouldn't be much better with any of them. Besides, takes money to start over."

"That it does," I said. Even that ninety-cent gas station drink in her hand meant ninety less cents to put toward a box of mac and cheese or a set of plastic tumblers from the thrift store.

"How'd you know about Lighthouse?" she asked.

How I answered that question could lead to revealing how much others had been talking about her. Others knowing details about your life without your consent was one of the worst violations. It could dismantle all illusions of protection–and belonging.

My reply was simple but honest. "Reva said that's where she met you."

Thankfully, it was enough. Austie nodded. "She's been about the only person who gets it."

I hid a wince, a very different take on our Sunday school coleader ringing in my memory. "We all need someone who understands."

She nodded again, then looked at the cup in her hand. "I'm sorry I'm not drinking this. It was nice of you to get it for me."

"It's okay. You don't have to drink it if you don't like it."

"No, it's not that I don't like it." She looked behind us as if ensuring we were alone, even though no one else was on the trail. Assured of our privacy, she pointed at her right lower jaw. "I got this tooth thing. Soda makes it hurt."

Ailments took money to fix too. In Woodfield, the most common dental procedure was tooth extraction. Get rid of the problem the cheapest way possible.

"Totally understand," I said. "I should have asked you if you wanted something. Go ahead and toss it. I won't be offended."

"But you got it for me."

"Only because I didn't know any better. Here." I tucked my own drink into the crook of my elbow, took her cup in both hands, popped off the lid, then deluged the grass nearby with the dark, sugary liquid. Only a few ice specks landed in the splash. They quickly melted. "Ants will get a treat today," I said.

The humor came first to Austie's eyes, then to her lips. It was the first time I had seen her smile. Up ahead was a trash can. I gestured toward it, and we started walking, our heads a little higher, a little lighter.

"Did you grow up in Kansas City?" she asked as we arrived at the trash can.

I slipped the empty cup inside with its lid and straw loosely attached. "No, actually. I moved here about two weeks ago from a small town in Kansas. I understand what you mean about needing money to make a change. Took me a year to save up." There were hints at my past in those words, but none of them revealed too much.

We headed on to the bridge. Green algae framed the stagnant water, filling in the gaps between reeds along the shoreline. The sound of our steps on the wood prompted a small box turtle to slide off a rock into the cloudy water. Ripples winged out from his pointy head.

"You like it here in KC?" Austie asked.

"I do. I like my job. I like my little house with a porch and bay window on the side, and my neighbors. My neighbor girl, Kyla, the one who got me to take her to Trinity? She's great. She's teaching me to play soccer."

"Can't picture you playing soccer, Jess."

"It's quite a sight, believe me."

The turtle sailed deeper into the pool, his head getting lost in the sunlight glinting off the water's surface.

"You like that church?" Austie asked.

Another tricky question. "It was nicer with you there," I said.

She humphed, then looked at me as if discerning if I was serious or not.

I was, and nodded to indicate so.

Pink tinted her cheeks. She looked down. "You were one of the decent people there."

"That's good company to be in, thank you. I assume Reva is part of the elite crowd too?"

"Yeah." Her shoes scuffed on the boards. They were the kind of sneakers a sensible person would wear on a walk. "Reva's my guardian in Christ. That's what they call it at Lighthouse. Has something to do with a Bible verse, but I couldn't tell you which one. Basically she helps me with my faith and checks up on me. Makes sure I 'stay straight on the narrow road,' as she calls it."

"Like a mentor? That's cool. I should get me one of those sometime." My shoes rubbed so hard into the balls of my feet, chucking them into the water didn't sound like a half-bad idea. "How long have you been a Christian?" I asked, shaking each of my feet as I swung them forward in an effort to loosen the pressure.

"Few months. What about you?"

"Almost two years. It's a big learning curve, isn't it?"

She nodded.

It wasn't just what you left behind; that part was hard enough. It was also what you stepped into—a whole new way of thinking and seeing and living. It wasn't a simple off switch and suddenly everything was rewritten and made sense. It could be overwhelming. Like going from a shaded part of the trail to the sudden pow of sunlight. I squinted against the brightness, kicking myself for not bringing my sunglasses.

"I have to admit," I said, "I get lost pretty easily in Sunday school. I accidentally spoke up in class this past Sunday. It was one of the most mortifying things I've done in a long time."

She chuckled. "What was the most mortifying ever?"

"That's too hard to narrow down." I smiled on the outside, but on the inside, the long list of contenders scrolled like the end credits of a movie. Many of them centered on Mick.

We talked more about our goals. I told her about my first "big girl" job and my hope to earn a paralegal certificate someday. She told me about earning her GED last year, about dreaming of going to college someday. For what, she hadn't decided, maybe health or fitness.

We rounded back to the shaded portion of the trail. I wiped my upper lip with my shirtsleeve and slurped the last of my drink. The chill had long faded, unable to stave the sweat on the back of my neck. I was closer than ever to chucking my shoes.

"Has it always just been you and your mom?" I asked.

"My dad left when I was a baby. She's had boyfriends and one fiancé. He was the one who gave me my first drink."

"How old were you?"

"Eleven."

My stomach sank. Eleven. What was it about that age that could change the course of a girl's life forever? Austie had had a parent who could have put a stop to all that came next. So had I. Neither of them did.

Round and round that half-dark, half-light narrow trail we went. Side by side. One of us hardly sweating and the other ready to jump in with the turtle. We talked about movies, television shows, favorite foods, and celebrity crushes. I didn't have to explain the appeal of Paul Rudd because some things translate seamlessly from one generation to the next.

What had started out as a rough go became an actual conversation.

About an hour into our walk, the rattling car returned. The honk of the horn flung across the open green space, alerting everyone to the driver's impatience. Fortunately, we were on the bend nearest the pavilion.

"Better go," Austie said. "Thanks for the walk, Jess."

"Thank *you*."

She waved and hustled toward the rusted car that would take her back, unwillingly, to a life she tried so hard to escape. What would she face when she got home? What would become of her dream of college?

"Austie," I called.

She came to a stop under the shelter and looked back.

It was my chance to impart one last bit of wisdom, if I had given her any up to that point. One last encouragement of some kind from a grown woman who could name the traps that lay all around her.

"Hope to see you Sunday." It was a spectacular anticlimax of a parting note.

All the same, Austie smiled. The driver honked again, shouting something indiscernible. Austie waved once more, then turned and headed for the car, clinging fast to her backpack.

18

MY ALARM INVADED that soft, fuzzy place between dreaming and waking. The genteel bird chirps to the backdrop of acoustic guitar emanating from my phone had seemed like such a great choice when I set it up while fully cognizant. To half-asleep me, the noise lashed against my will. Without moving my head cradled ever so comfortably by my pillow, I flung my left hand toward the nightstand and swatted at surfaces until my fingertips landed on the right spot. The invasive sound ceased, but the Thursday morning light took over. It spread unobstructed into my room, no curtains on the windows to block it out.

I blinked away the imaginative scene that had seconds before been as convincing as real life. Me on the trail with Austie, but I was on the ground, lying on my back, clutching my right foot, panicked over how swollen it had become—three times its normal size, a giant ogre foot that flamed red with grotesque blue veins straining against the skin.

The swollen sensation had not disappeared with the images.

I sat up, eyes scrunched against the loud brightness, and yanked the covers off my lower half. Both feet were indeed human size and color, but the right one felt different, dulled, like it had turned into a wad of cotton. I brought it closer. A thin, oval blister burdened the ball of my foot where the shoe had rubbed. The sole of my foot between my arch and toes was redder than usual. My heel needed a good douse of lotion. Other than that, nothing seemed out of place. I tried wiggling my toes. They responded to my brain's command, but if I closed my eyes, I wouldn't have been able to tell they were moving at all.

I reached down and poked at my big toe, then across the top of my foot and around the side. The pressure of my finger registered, but not the skin-to-skin touch. I frowned, dug my fingernail into the skin on the top of my foot. The impression went deep, but my nerve endings caught only the pressure. Deadened, numb, on all sides, toe to heel, top and bottom, up to the lower edge of my ankle.

"That's not normal."

I shoved Thea's words away. What did she know? She wasn't a doctor. She wasn't there on the trail when the shoes angrily grabbed at my feet.

"Has to be a pinched nerve," I proclaimed. To test my theory, I swung my feet onto the rag rug and stood. I bore my weight without a problem, could even take several trial steps, without pain or anything "not normal" aside from the blunted sensation.

"Yes, got to be a pinched nerve," I said. For that matter, the tingling in my hand was probably one too. It did stand to reason that pinched nerves could either overcharge or cut off nerve endings. And some people could be more prone to getting them, such as those who lifted heavy boxes at Red Rooster or made poor decisions in footwear. Even Dad had one at some point, from all the physical labor he did.

"Probably hereditary."

I nabbed my phone from the nightstand and searched online for how to treat a pinched nerve. In more severe, painful cases, seek medical help, Dr. Internet said. In mild cases, treat with ice, ibuprofen, massage, rest. All very common, very normal things.

I would do them, and immediately put those canvas shoes in a donation bin somewhere.

Resolved, I began my morning routine, which would include ibuprofen until further notice. Medicated, dressed, and brushed, I aimed my half-alive leg to the nook to check on the divas. Unlike me, they got brighter and better with time.

"Morning, Shania. Morning, Mariah." I dug into the soil of their plant pots in search of moisture. Each had plenty. "Surprised you're not thirstier in this heat," I said and brushed the soil crumbs off my finger.

Movement outside the bay window grabbed my attention. Across the lot, my neighbors loaded into their Toyota, Kyla ready with her school backpack and dressed in an adorable sporty outfit complete with her go-to white crew socks and Birkenstocks. She had worn a similar getup the night of the impromptu pizza and blackjack party. The nook still rang with her giggles. I smiled. Until the ghost of heartburn past floated up my esophagus. Extroverting always resulted in me developing physical ailments.

I proceeded to the kitchen, onward with the agenda for the day. Coffee, breakfast, check-in with Dad, work, a load of laundry, maybe a trip to the store for bedroom curtains—the heavy blackout kind. I set my coffee to brewing and placed the call to Dad. As the other end rang, I grabbed a bowl from the cabinet and laid it on the counter.

"Yes, I'm still alive," he said upon picking up.

"That's good news. What are you planning to do today with all that aliveness?"

"Clean up whatever mess these boys got me into now. They're still dumb as a box of rocks." He paused to clear his throat, choosing to do it directly into the receiver so that I had to move my phone away from my ear.

As I poured a bowl of cornflakes and retrieved my mug of coffee from the machine, he informed me of the latest evidences of their idiocy. The examples were more differences in opinion on how to manage inventory and what tools to use to pinpoint the root cause of a fuel line issue, but I didn't argue.

I resealed the cereal box and put it back in the cabinet. "Sounds like hard work keeping after them."

"They try me. How's city life?"

"Great. Job's going well. The neighbors are sweet, and I started going to a church up here."

"Mmm." That was his reply for both "good" and "not impressed." Both uses sounded identical.

I took a spoon from the drawer and stuck it in among the cornflakes. "Out of curiosity, Dad, do we have a family history of pinched nerves? You've had one, right?"

"Long time ago, in my hip. Why? You got one or something?"

"In my foot. Wore the wrong shoes on a long walk yesterday. I've had one in my hand before too, I think."

"Don't know about family history," he said. "Little ice'll help, though."

"Thanks. I'll try that."

In the background, a woman spoke, her words too muffled to make out. A click and rustle followed as Dad jostled his phone.

I leaned in, as if that would help my ears latch on better to whatever was happening. There must have been some kind of conversation because the next word that came through clear was hers: "Okay."

"Who's that?" I asked.

"No one. Just someone from town."

I frowned. "Are you at home or at the shop?"

More background conversation. "Listen, Jess, I gotta run. You need anything else?"

An answer to my question would have been great, but I let it go. "I'm good," I said. "Thanks for chatting, Dad."

Per usual, our phone conversation ended in less than five minutes. When I was home, we would eat breakfast together, talk about the town's goings-on and weather and livestock commodities report. Someday, I would bring us back to those conversations, bring us back together under one roof. My roof.

I set my phone on the counter and stepped over to the refrigerator for milk. The Daily Allelon list held me in place for a moment. My eyes landed on the verse at the top of the second column.

With patience, bearing with one another in love—Ephesians 4:2.

I sighed. Only by the grace of God would I find patience enough for Dad to have the epiphanies I longed for him to have.

Throughout the day, I steadily worked out my agenda, ticking boxes, being productive. I took more ibuprofen, draped a bag of frozen peas over my foot, tried elevation, and worked in a couple of massages during my lunch break of microwave pot pie and an episode of *Boy Meets World*. Nothing awakened my senses, though experience with my hand told me pinched nerves could be as stubborn as an old mechanic refusing to retire. Both needed time and reflection to relent.

Still, as my mouse pointer hovered over the log-out button at the end of the day, a glimmer of an idea lit in my mind: Check my health insurance coverage. The next day was September 1, the day coverage began. I could follow Ellen's advice, find a doctor, casually drop into the conversation the fact I get these pinched nerves.

But I shook my head, clicked the button, and shut my laptop. "Doctors don't tell you anything you don't already know," my dad would say. His medical advice had served me well for four decades. No sense switching it up at this point.

19

"THIS HAPPENS SOMETIMES, Jess. It's okay." My self pep talk got me to plant both feet on the rag rug next to my bed the next morning, but the stir of worry grew within me. A stir that carried the notes of Thea's warning. *Not normal.*

I slowly eased my weight onto both feet. Only my left one could tell me about the scruff of fibers against my sole. The right one was a hollow peg leg. The night's rest should have amplified the healing effects of the meds and treatment of the day before. Instead, it had allowed the numbness to seep up over my ankle, through my lower leg, to my knee. Every nerve ending had powered down, except those parts that registered the pressure of the floor.

"But I can still walk," I said over the worry. To prove it, I moved my right leg forward. My toes caught against the rug and dragged it with them, bunching it between my feet. I worked my toes loose and settled my right foot firmly on the floor beyond the rug. My left foot moved easily to catch up. On my second try, the tips of my first three toes skimmed along the hardwood before my foot flopped into place. But it was a step. A successful step. Nothing hurt, ached, or throbbed. No stabbing pains screamed up my leg. The internet claimed such things existed in "severe" cases of pinched nerves. I wasn't severe. Inconvenienced, maybe, but not severe, which meant I was still somewhere close to the neighborhood of normal.

At least I didn't have to leave the house. My boss at Red Rooster would have taken one look at my draggy foot and sent me home without pay. I didn't have the risk of Paul laying eyes on me walking, or anyone else at HML. No one needed to see me. No one needed to know. If I could get the numbness to retreat that day, no one would ever know.

I doubled my morning dose of ibuprofen. By the time I logged on, I had the painkiller coursing through me, my leg propped up on a dining chair, and three bags of frozen vegetables straddled over various spots on my dumb appendage. Sweet corn on my foot, peas on my ankle, green beans on my tibia. Five minutes into prioritizing my assignments for the day, a text message popped up on my phone next to my laptop. It was from Reva.

Have time to talk?

I chewed my lip. We had not interacted since our brief exchange by the doorway of the Allelon classroom. Did I want to talk to her? If I ignored her request and said that I didn't respond because I was working, it wouldn't be a total lie. It also would not be "greeting one another." I sighed and threw back my head. Of all the times for my brain to recall a Bible verse, it had to be that one.

"Fine," I muttered, then messaged her back.

I do.

Thirty seconds later, my phone rang. The woman was eager about something. I answered on speakerphone.

"Hi, Reva. Hope you don't mind that I'm working while we talk." A subtle laying of groundwork should I need an excuse to end the conversation quickly.

"Not at all, and I'll make it brief. I saw Austie last night at Lighthouse. She said you all met up."

I continued to click through my new tasks, determining which would be the easiest and fastest to complete. "We did. We had a good time."

"She said something similar. You apparently made an impression."

"A good one, hopefully."

"Sounds like it. She said she told you about her home situation." Reva paused. "She also said she told you about wanting to go to college."

I clicked open a task, judged it would take less than five minutes. "She did. Wants to study fitness, maybe, though she's undecided."

"Right." Reva's voice softened. "Jess, I think you should know how big of a deal that is."

"That she wants to go to college?"

"Yes, but also that she told you. It was the first time she told anyone else."

My hand came to a halt on my mouse. "Really?"

"Girls with her background often don't share such aspirations easily. She obviously sees you as a safe person."

A new dimension of Austie's upbringing painted across my mind. Instability was not fertile ground for dreams to grow in. Did Austie have anyone besides Reva pulling for her?

"There's something else you should know," Reva said. "It's about what happened after she left the park the other day." She was sparse in the details, taking a matter-of-fact route through the altercation at the house. No one was hurt, but the police were called to defuse things. "Her mom is pressuring Austie to leave. She believes Austie is the instigator."

I traced the edge of the folding table, caught between gratitude for knowing and guilt for holding something so private without Austie's consent. Her dark under-eye circles and stuffed backpack spoke to the unpredictability she endured. How much of what she carried, though, was because of hushed conversations like this one?

I squeezed my eyes shut as I spoke. "I don't know that I want to talk about Austie when she's not around."

Reva was silent. Maybe judging. Maybe processing. At last she replied, tone gentle. "That's a noble attitude, Jess. I respect it. But please understand, I'm telling you this so we can rally behind Austie, provide her support—to one-another her, not to tear her down. No sister in Christ should walk the narrow road alone."

"Still," I said. I dropped my hand to my lap.

Another moment of quiet passed.

"I have an idea," Reva said, tone unchanged. "What if we all have lunch at my house after church on Sunday? You, me, and Austie. We can talk more then. Together."

I wanted to say no. But Reva had taken my concern seriously, and that deserved something. I also could find out for certain how Austie felt about the prayer requests circulating about her. "Sounds like a good idea," I said.

"I'll arrange it."

Time ticked deeper into my workday. My laptop started to go to sleep. I jiggled my mouse to keep it alert.

"How are you doing?" Reva asked. "How is your week?"

I shifted my leg on the chair, my hip already shouting about the need to reposition. "I can't complain. It's Friday."

"One day closer to Sunday." The upturn of her voice at the end indicated her keenness.

"Yes, it is. Listen, I'm sorry to do this, Reva, but I should get back to work. My boss left me a long list of tasks for the day."

"Of course. Thanks for letting me interrupt. Hope you have a good day, Jess, and I'll see you Sunday."

"See you Sunday."

Once the call ended, I rolled my eyes and rubbed my face with both hands. Why did I agree to lunch?

Austie. Austie was why. Just like Kyla was why I would be back at Trinity on Sunday morning.

"This is what you get for being friendly," I groaned into my palms.

My hip protested louder. It was time to put the vegetables away anyway. I gathered the makeshift ice packs and gingerly pulled my leg to the floor. Faint pink stripes stretched across my skin, evidence of the long, slow, cold kiss from the bags I couldn't feel. As I walked to the kitchen, my left foot moved at an awkward cadence to match the drag-flop of my right. At the freezer, I ignored the Daily Allelon list and tossed the bags inside.

On the way back to my laptop, I stopped at the bathroom so I could grab the bottle of pain relief to keep with me. A stronger dose all day seemed to be in order.

I flipped on the light, stepped inside, reached for the cabinet—and sank with a heavy thud onto the hard tile floor.

20

STIFF. SHOCKED. Everything utterly still. Suspended in place, in time.

I gasped. The sharp, painful intake roused me.

Where am I?

The bathroom floor, on my right side. Right leg bent back underneath me. Based on how close my face was to the lower cabinet door, my head had sailed mere inches from the blunt edge of the counter. My veins burned with the intense rush within them.

I anchored my hands to the floor and pushed up onto my right hip. I patted every inch of my face and head, paranoid that I actually had whacked my skull against the counter. There were no gashes, no bumps, no tender spots. I lifted my right hand, the one that had absorbed the brunt of the fall, and held it in front of me. My fingers trembled as I turned my hand side to side, bent every joint. No injury there either. But could I stand?

I gripped the edge of the counter with both hands and hauled myself up to my knees. With my left foot into position first, then, cautiously, my right, I pushed halfway up to a stand. Somehow, the weaker leg held, but I didn't dare let go of my support. I lifted my eyes to the mirror above the sink. Terror looked back at me.

What if it happened again? What if I smacked my head the next time? What if I passed out and bled on the floor for hours, for days? No one would know. No one would be there. What if Kyla came knocking? Or Ron? Or worse, what if Paul called me, wondering why I wasn't logged in? He would be furious. He would fire me.

What would I do? What should I do?

I slid my left hand onto the countertop, rooted it there, then used my right to splash cold water onto my face. The jolt calmed the rage of adrenaline enough for my rational mind to churn. It churned around one word.

Doctor.

It was the first day my insurance was in effect. Could that have been a coincidence? Were Christians even allowed to believe in coincidences?

Another round of cold water. The splashes peeled down my cheeks, fell off my chin, but could not wash away the tremble in my core.

Doctor.

Doctor.

Doctor.

"Think, Jess." I bowed my head, letting water drip from my chin, nose, eyebrows.

The workday had barely begun. I was still in my thirty-day probationary period. But maybe Paul would let me go a few hours early. He had said it was possible to leave early on Fridays if all the work was done. It was Labor Day weekend to boot. If anything could put him in a more gracious mood, surely it was a Friday afternoon before a three-day weekend.

It was the only shot I had.

I pulled the hand towel from the rack over the counter and dried my face, neck, and hands. My message to him formulated. No details about why I wanted to leave at one o'clock, only a promise to get everything done. Keep it casual, breezy.

I kept one hand on a wall wherever possible as I returned to my computer.

Paul did say yes, adding for good measure, "Some of your list can wait until Tuesday. Enjoy your long weekend!" The permission, given so freely, solidified the situation was real. Really happening.

My hands shook as I tried to enter data, causing frequent retypes. My mind rattled with scenes of buckled legs and blood-matted hair. I worked through lunch, getting every task accomplished, even those Paul said could wait. Before powering down my computer a little before one, I looked up instructions for downloading my insurance company's app.

It was real. Really happening.

Stomach as tight as a knotted oak, I rose from my chair and collected what I might need. My purse, my keys, a snack bag of trail mix should the missed lunch catch up with me. Then, at the front door, I paused. On a hunch, I shuffled back to my nightstand and grabbed my phone charger. Just in case.

The afternoon sun reflected off Hank's windshield, giving him a bright crown that assured me of his trustworthiness. He would get me to where I needed to go, even if I had only one foot to command him. Dad had huffed at my preference for an automatic transmission in a quarter-ton pickup, but once again, Hank proved he was everything I needed.

I climbed into the driver's seat and situated my left foot on the pedals. It was odd and risky, but Hank and I could make it work. An urgent care clinic in my network sat across the street from Cost Cutter, mere minutes away.

Engine on. I backed onto the street, then pointed Hank in the direction of the clinic. But as I approached the entrance to the shopping center in which my destination resided, something compelled me to keep going. Keep driving. I proceeded to Barry Road, then turned right.

I drove west, toward the emergency room of Northland Memorial.

21

A FULL HOUR PASSED in that small room. I lay in the hard bed and questioned for the third time if I had made the right choice. I avoided looking at the IV catheter in my left hand. A foreign object protruding from my body aroused the haunting nausea. In the crook of my left elbow, the white medical tape holding a piece of gauze in place started to make my skin itch, but the lab person had instructed me to leave it on for at least an hour. She had drawn several vials of blood but couldn't tell me why. No one told me anything. They just came in with needles and tape and assurances that the doctor was on her way.

For all the bustle in the hallway outside my door, it seemed impossible the doctor hadn't come yet. I had no one to ask where she was or to provide a more precise ETA. I was surrounded by strangers with unreadable expressions and full agendas.

One of the nurses had given me a thermal blanket from the warmer to ward off the room's chill. My exam gown was hopeless to that end. The blanket had long lost its boost of warmth, but it was still my best defense. I pulled it up over my shoulders, snuggling underneath as much as I could. The same nurse had also left the television remote control on my tray table and informed me they had movie channels, a subtle way of telling me to settle in.

Finally, around half past two, my door opened. In strode a woman with a smooth complexion, a white coat, and the stereotypical stethoscope draped around her neck. She parked herself at the foot of the bed, partially blocking the still-blank TV secured to the wall.

"Hello. I'm Dr. Duke. Are you Jess?"

She didn't have my chart or a clipboard or tablet like the ER doctors carried around on TV shows. She didn't have anything to write on at all, like those restaurant servers who angled for a tip by overconfidently trying to remember every detail about every order. Servers like that couldn't be trusted.

"I am Jess Becker," I said, ensuring she was clear on exactly which patient she was in front of. I moved my right arm outside the blanket so the ID band the nurse had secured around my wrist was in full view.

Dr. Duke didn't look at it. Instead, she cozied her hands in the pockets of her coat. "Tell me what's going on."

I repeated all the same symptoms I had literally watched the nurse type into my chart on her little tablet. What happened to that tablet, and why didn't Dr. Duke have it, or apparently look at it?

The doctor listened and nodded along, expression flat. Not the stoic-yet-compassionate kind that Reva had, but the kind of stare that said I was a puzzle she was determined to solve. When I finished describing the numbness and the fall, she stepped to the head of the bed and pulled a handheld contraption from the wall. It had a pen light at the end, and she shone it directly into my eyeballs.

"Have you ever had numbness or weakness before, in your leg or elsewhere?" she asked.

I fought not to blink. "No."

"What about tingling or burning or any other abnormal sensations that didn't go away quickly?"

"Tingling in my left hand, a couple of times. That was a pinched nerve, though, I think."

She returned the device to the wall and unfurled her stethoscope. As she listened to my heart and lungs, she probed me for more answers. How long ago did I have the tingling? How far apart where the occurrences? Any recent pain or injury? Recent fevers? Drug use? Fatigue? Bowel issues? Dizziness or vision changes? With each answer I gave, it was harder and harder to track what scenarios might have been cycling through her mind.

Satisfied with how my internal organs sounded, she slung the stethoscope around her neck and rested her hands on her hips. "Lift your left arm for me and hold it for a few seconds."

I did so, turning my head far enough the opposite direction to not see that IV catheter.

"Now your right." Every few beats, she gave me a new instruction to follow. "Smile for me . . . Good. Now raise your eyebrows . . . Good. Stick out your tongue and move it back and forth."

I was a circus monkey, performing for the nods of approval from a stoic woman with "MD" behind her name.

"Let's give your legs a look." She held out her hand for the top of the blanket.

I gave it to her, and she peeled it back to the very end of the bed. Cold snaked across my skin. I folded my arms across my middle, staving off the goose bumps and the wash of vulnerability as best I could. Inherently trusting a stranger, even if they did wear a white coat, was not natural, and my body's warning system flared.

"Place your right heel against your left calf for me," she said.

An odd request, but I did as she requested, then vice versa at her prompt.

"Now straighten both legs."

As I complied, she stepped closer to the bed and cupped both hands around my left thigh. I flinched. Her hands were as icy as the room. Slowly she traced her fingers down my leg, light as feathers, tickling the nerve endings all the way. "Can you feel my touch? Any place you can't?"

"I can feel it."

She started on my right side, with the same light grip. "How about now?"

When her hands slipped below my knee, I shook my head.

She squeezed my calf. "That?"

"I can feel the pressure."

She asked dozens more questions, had me get up and walk across the room to evaluate my gait. It was a whole lot of input for her not to write anything down.

With her permission, I climbed back into bed and pulled the blanket up to my chest.

Dr. Duke folded her hands at her waist and leaned one hip against the footrail. "I'll take a look at your labs once those are available. We're running all the standard BMP and CBC tests, plus magnesium and thyroid counts."

She did not explain what any of that meant.

"I'd also like to get a CT scan of your brain to check for any time-sensitive things that could be causing these symptoms."

"Like what?" I asked.

"No sense in worrying too much about specifics at this point. The CT will help rule out some things and narrow down to others. We'll know more with those results, Tess."

I set my jaw. The wrong name was one thing, the minimizing and sidestepping was another. I may not have known what a CBC was, but I was smart enough to piece together that an ER doctor wanting a scan of my brain to look for "time-sensitive things" may—just may—be cause for alarm, and she wasn't being forthright with me.

If she detected any hint of my annoyance, it didn't stop her. "A radiology tech will be in soon to get you. I should have the results within an hour after your scan. I'll update you when I can. If the CT doesn't give a clear answer, we may have to run some more tests, but we'll just take it one thing at a time. Okay?" She tapped the footrail, clearly wanting to mask her pressing desire to leave as soon as possible.

"Are you confident this is not a pinched nerve?" I asked.

"We'll know more with the results," she repeated, then took a step toward the door.

"Okay," I stammered back.

She was gone seconds later, leaving the door ajar. Voices and beeps and clangs leaked into my room. The nausea roused. I swallowed.

Beside the bed, my purse rested in the visitor's chair. My phone stuck out from the front pocket. I could look up my symptoms, could weave together a story that Dr. Duke didn't want to tell me, could verify for myself if a severe case of a pinched nerve fit the profile. But a heaviness settled in my hands, my head, my whole body. The post-adrenaline crash.

I left my phone where it was and picked up the remote from the tray table. As luck would have it, *Clueless* was on. The movie was about halfway through, but I had it committed to memory.

I leaned back against the pillow. Soon I was absorbed back into simpler times when I watched movies on VHS with my parents, Mom on the couch with me and Dad in his recliner. We ate Twizzlers and drank diet soda. We laughed together, because those were the years when we laughed in the Becker house. I closed my eyes, sank deeper into that orange-and-white couch with the scratchy upholstery and homemade afghan draped over the back. Delighted in the carbonation fizzing over my tongue. Searched harder for that scent of Mom's floral perfume and the rumble of Dad's throaty chuckle.

Could either of my parents hear me searching for them?

I mouthed the dialogue along with the actors, anticipated my favorite one-liners, and waited for someone to walk through the door. Funny how "time-sensitive" could require such a long wait.

22

DR. DUKE SAID it all so fast, I could barely make out her words. I asked her to repeat everything, the whole spiel, and wished I was the one with something to write on.

"CT results showed nonspecific white matter changes," she said at a slower pace. "While that rules out some things, we still don't have an answer. I am going to admit you so we can continue to monitor your symptoms and get you in for an MRI. Unfortunately, we don't have a regular room available at this time. We'll keep you here until something opens up."

My head throbbed. Its ability to process dwindled. But it hitched on two things right away: white matter changes and admitted.

"I'm waiting on confirmation for the MRI from the on-call neurologist, but I have no doubt he will agree it's the right next step. The MRI is a much longer test and gives us clearer detail."

She said more and more, but what she didn't say was, "No, Jess, this isn't a pinched nerve. This is something else. Something serious."

Was it connected to my hand? What did she think was wrong? Was it a tumor? Was it cancer? How much did an MRI cost?

Would my insurance cover it? Would it cover the whole visit? My pulse raced.

"Tess?"

I snapped to attention. The doctor stared at me as if waiting for a reply. "Yes?" I asked, no energy to correct the repeated misnaming.

"I was asking if you're hungry," she said. "We don't want you to eat a lot, but we do have some saltines and other small things you could have."

My brow lowered. Hungry? That was what she thought I would be feeling? *Hungry?*

I shook my head.

She didn't ask me if I had questions, nor did she take my silence as anything other than a sign she could make her exit and dash on to the next patient. Based on the amount of yelling I'd heard when the latest patient across the hall arrived, she had her hands full.

"Hang tight," she said as she exited.

As if I could do anything else.

The door latched behind her. I was alone again. The room squeezed in on me. I breathed, prayed for help, then quickly found a new movie to have something other than the ringing silence as company.

Around half past six—five and a half hours since I'd arrived at the ER—a young man arrived with a wheelchair and the first smile directed my way all day.

"I'm Jimmy, one of your MRI techs," he said, sidling the wheelchair against the side of the bed. "Ready for your photo shoot?"

I hit the power button on the remote. "If I say no, what happens?"

He shrugged. "I help you escape out the back and plead ignorance."

"I like that plan better."

The jest, the gleam in his eye, the way he extended his hand to help me out of bed made him by far my favorite person at Northland Memorial. He couldn't have been much younger than Dr. Duke, but he was worlds more in tune with the abundance of nervous energy that poured off me like sweat. Unnamed strangers were about to look into the intricate recesses of my most complicated organ. They would see things no one else had ever seen and discover things about me, about my situation, that they had the power to keep from me.

But Jimmy didn't let me linger in that mindset. As he piloted me to the elevator and then into the maze of hallways and double doors, he asked me questions about my interests. Nothing invasive, all focused on the things that brought me joy, and that was clearly intentional. I told him about my little house, my divas in the dining room nook, my truck, my ability to quote *Clueless* extensively.

After many minutes, we arrived at the MRI imaging department. He scanned his badge and the automated door hummed open.

"So, Jess," he said, "I have some MRI questions for you now."

"Fire away."

He rolled me into an outer room, then came around the wheelchair to face me. "I like to start by asking everyone if they have ever had an MRI before. Have you?"

"I have not."

"Did the doctor tell you what to expect?"

The automated door clicked shut behind us. I wrapped my hands around the ends of the wheelchair armrests. "I'm gonna be honest, Jimmy. No one has exactly been forthcoming on anything."

He nodded. "I get it. The ER can be like that, people moving so fast. Let me give you the lowdown on what we're doing."

He explained how I would be flat on a table that would slide into a cylindrical machine. They would scan my brain and my spinal cord, which meant at one point during the test, I would be in the machine down to my waist. And the machine would be loud. Very loud.

"But we'll give you headphones to help block the noise," he assured me. "We can pump in some music if you want. I'll be able to speak to you through them. Are you claustrophobic?"

"I don't think so. Then again, I've never been stuffed into anything."

He chuckled. The sweetness of it took the edge off. He pointed at the next door. "High-powered magnets and wheelchairs don't mix, so I'm going to escort you into the MRI room and get you set up. If at any point you start to feel anxious, let me know. We can give you something for that."

Loud. Tight. Long. It probably was enough to make anyone freak out. "Good to know," I said.

After ensuring I had no piercings in or jewelry on, he told me it was time to move, held out his hands, and helped me to my feet. Into the room we went.

The large, round machine looked like it could swallow me alive. It emanated a sinister churning sound like a giant, human-zapping washing machine. Outside the opening was a table with curved edges to cradle me in place. Several sets of Velcro straps lined the sides. A small pillow and what looked like a miniature cage waited at the end nearest the opening.

I swallowed against the brute grip on my throat. "It looks like an electric chair."

"I promise it doesn't hurt." Jimmy held on to me as we shuffled forward. "I've had one several times. I can't tell people what it's like unless I've done it myself, right?"

If only all medical professionals took such an approach.

Opposite the big machine was a window to another room. Inside was a second tech who was engrossed with whatever was on one of the many monitors in front of him. The innards of my brain would soon be displayed there for him to scrutinize.

Jimmy brought me to the side of the body-length table. "The

trick is to lay perfectly still. The scan will take about ninety minutes, which I know is a really long time to be still. We will be as fast and thorough as we can. I'll check in with you through the headphones periodically, and I'll be able to hear you through the microphone in the room. In between check-ins, the mic is off, but you'll still be able to get our attention if you need to. See this ball-looking thing here?"

I followed his pointing finger to the rubber object with a cord streaming out the bottom.

"I'll give you that to hold," he said. "If you need us to stop for any reason, you just squeeze that and it alerts us."

I nodded.

He asked if I'd changed my mind about the sedative. I said no, but in the presence of that machine, the no was shaky at best.

"In that case, Jess . . ." He patted the table. "Ready?"

Getting strapped in didn't take long. Jimmy explained every step before he did it, telling me what to expect during the scan and allowing me time to understand and react.

"You're a saint for being so patient with me," I said.

"Not a saint, just someone who understands. I was once an orderly in a skilled nursing facility. Nothing teaches you the importance of going slow quite like that."

He ensured I had the ball secure in my palm, let me practice squeezing it, then held up the noise-canceling headphones. "Want us to switch on some Mozart?"

Hold music didn't seem to be an effective distraction against the reality of magnetic waves piercing my brain, but it was worth a try. "Sure," I said.

He fit the headphones over my ears, then secured the plastic cage over my head. He mouthed, *Okay?*, then motioned for me to blink once if yes.

I blinked once.

He signaled that he was going to the room behind the glass, and I blinked once again.

When he left, the ominous mouth of the machine loomed wide and shadowy over my head. My scalp prickled. Soon, the music began. Violins, then woodwinds and percussion. Last, a voice.

"Jess, it's Jimmy. We're going to get started. Remember, if you need to stop, squeeze."

I blinked once, out of new-formed habit.

The giant tubular machine kicked into higher gear. The table moved toward it, sliding me backward into the beast. Every muscle in my body stiffened. What if they found something? Would they find anything? What if they found nothing and all of it was a waste of time? What if the doctor had been completely wrong? What if she was right? How could it possibly be that I needed an MRI?

What in the world was happening? How did I make it all stop?

My head passed into the machine. I closed my eyes. Clicks. Knocks. Whirrs. Buzzes. Every noise more unsettling than the last. My breaths were no deeper than necessary. I held the ball loosely, praying I wouldn't twitch and squeeze it by accident. The roar around me was a harsh antithesis to the soaring melody trying so hard to instill peace. I fought every instinct to move, to cower. Only one other time in my life had I been helpless and trapped in a cacophony like that.

I had been twenty, maybe nineteen. In my first truck, a 1985 GMC tank. I was on my way from my place in town to my then-boyfriend's in the country, driving through a heavy downpour, wipers on full blast, Garth Brooks on the radio. I was miles outside town, on a shoulderless county road, open prairie on either side. I could barely see. Suddenly the rain stopped. An eerie calm. Then the bile-green tint every prairie dweller feared. A distant rumble, louder, louder, closer, closer. The entrance to a ranch was to my right, and potential shelter somewhere down that lane. I downshifted, aimed for the turn. My foot slipped off the clutch. The engine stalled.

Louder, closer.

Engine started again. Gas pressed to go forward, but the truck started to slide to the right. I turned the steering wheel into the slide to correct. On ice, the maneuver was wise. In that moment, useless.

Louder, louder. *Roar!*

The entire truck shook. My teeth rattled. The station signal jumbled. I couldn't hear my own scream. "God!" I pled. Over and over.

I clung to the steering wheel, hunched as low as I could. The truck flipped once. Twice. I was flung like a rag doll inside the grip of my seat belt.

And then, just like that, the noise was gone. Replaced by a violent pummel of rain and hail. When the storm finally subsided, I lifted my head high enough to get my bearings. A gray-blue eased through the quiet sky. Somehow, the truck had landed on all four tires, smack in the middle of the ranch's driveway, on top of the cattle guard. The windows had held, but not the outside mirrors. The driver's side one dangled from its last remaining bolt. The passenger side one was gone altogether. The end of the hood was crumpled.

I reengaged the engine and drove home. The nausea had stuck for hours.

Click, click, whirr. Roar. I was trapped in the deafening noise once more, but it wasn't passing over me. It hovered, pressing me against the table. That same plea rose in my soul. "God!" He had protected me once, saw me safely home. Would he set me down gently again and spread the blue over me like nothing had happened? The Bible told me he was able, but twice in a lifetime seemed a lot to ask.

23

THE LATEST NURSE stood at the foot of my bed collecting my responses, tapping and swirling her stylus on the tablet cradled in her left arm. New room, new floor, new medical team, same round of questions I had answered three times already. No one in the entire hospital system seemed to communicate with one another. No wonder Dad distrusted doctors so much.

My replies were brief, a syllable or two, all I could manage.

The room had a window that ran the full length of one wall, with a shelf underneath for flowers or visitors or personal effects. The blinds were drawn back halfway. Headlights slipped along the street on the edge of the hospital campus. Beyond it, twinkles of light spread out into the inky black, like stars that had fallen to earth and nestled among the trees. Every light that slipped or twinkled represented life being lived. People carried on. Friends got together. Parents tucked in their kids. Friday night movies played in family rooms. Comfortable couches embraced work-worn bodies.

Three stories above them, I lay half upright in a bed that was not my own, in a room that contained nothing of mine except the purse on my tray table and the white plastic hospital bag in the visitor's chair with my lone change of clothes inside. What if I put my outfit back on? What if I yanked out the IV, ripped off the ID and Fall Risk bands, and set out to find that back door Jimmy had mentioned? I'd scuttle down the corridor when no one was looking, bust through the double doors, clamber down the stairs, and escape among the fallen stars. Test results didn't exist if they didn't reach you.

"All right, Miss Becker, that's all I need for now."

I turned from the window.

The nurse clicked the stylus into its holder on the side of the tablet. "I'll come back periodically to do checks. Try to get some rest in the meantime. The doctor will be in as soon as he has the report from the radiologist."

"Soon" had wildly different meanings to patients than it did to hospital staff. The clock on the wall next to the television showed half past nine, more than eight hours since I'd arrived at Northland Memorial. Eight hours, two beds, two scans, two blood panels, two doctors, and who knew how many nurses. The wheels of my brain started to grind slower, harder, begging for a break.

The nurse tucked the tablet to her side. "Are you hungry?"

Why did everyone ask that? I sighed, shook my head, then resumed my watch over the steady, easy slip of headlights.

"Any questions for me before I go?"

I pointed at the window. "What street is that?"

"That's Barry."

The road that led to home.

I thanked her, sent her on her way. She left the lights dim and the door closed.

Stillness. The very thing my mind wanted but my body didn't know what to do with. Stillness came both before and after the worst of the storm. But which stage was I in?

My phone chimed. I wheeled the tray table closer and retrieved my phone from the outside pocket of my purse. A new text from Reva.

Confirmed for Sunday lunch. See you then.

It took a solid ten seconds for the connection to click into place. Our conversation earlier. About talking with Austie. Had our call really only been that morning? Had I really been innocently ticking through my daily routine less than thirteen hours before? Sitting at my laptop, a load of laundry ready for the washer, a cold diet soda in the fridge, a holiday weekend waiting to be spent as I saw fit. Then, like that, I was in a second hospital room, chained by "soon," haunted by silence. Not normal. Only God knew if any of it would relent in time for Sunday lunch.

I liked the message and lay my phone on my stomach. I closed my eyes, leaned back on the pillow. I tried to sleep, tried to turn off the lingering roar that had followed me up three stories. How was it not a dream, a bad, horrible dream?

My lips trembled. I opened my eyes and picked up my phone. A few quick taps and Dad's number was on the screen, ready.

"Please answer."

I placed the call, held the phone to my ear. Surely he was still awake, dozing in his recliner as he "watched" some ridiculous cop show and waited for the ten o'clock news to come on.

Ring. Ring.

I pulled the blanket up, wrung the hem in my fist.

Ring. Ring.

Breath came faster. Throat burned.

Ring. Ring.

Then his voice, the one I had known since birth, the one with which the tides of my emotions could rise and fall, saying he couldn't come to the phone.

I squeezed against the rush of tears. I hung up, tucked my phone to my chest, and curled onto my side.

I cried until I was too exhausted to do anything else but fall into the silence.

24

IN THE FOUR O'CLOCK HOUR, when night started to prepare for dawn, someone knocked on my door, pulling me from shallow rest. I lifted my head, rubbed my eyes as they adjusted to the low light. Headlights still eased by my window. A Hallmark movie played on the TV. And at last, there was a white coat in my room. He was tall, my age, with a silvery voice.

"Making sure you're awake," he said from the doorway.

"I am." I raised up to a seated position, blanket draped over my lap, and muted the television. The scene in some small-town hardware store flickered on unabated. I used the bed's control panel to turn on the light above me.

He stepped inside and shut the door behind him. "I'm Dr. Abrams. I know you've been waiting on me for a while now, haven't you?"

I waved my hand. "Flew by."

He grinned, activating the lines at the corners of his mouth. "Mind if I sit?"

"Please."

He came over to the visitor chair next to my bed, then gingerly moved the plastic bag of my clothes to the tray table next to my purse. "I know it's been a long wait tonight," he said as he sat, "so I'll get right to it."

It had arrived, at last. All that time, and suddenly, I wouldn't have minded a bit longer to prepare. I bit my lower lip, held my breath.

"The radiologist has provided a full report. Your scans show several lesions. They are located in areas that would affect both your foot and your hand. You said you were experiencing some tingling in your hand, correct?"

I shook my head, still two sentences behind him. "Lesions?"

"They are areas of abnormality in the tissue."

My brow lowered, the term as helpful as "nonspecific white matter changes."

Seeing my reaction, he explained. "They are signs of damage."

"D-damage?" I knew the word, and yet I couldn't grasp its meaning, or the implications. "Wha–but–how?"

"We don't know exactly how the lesions formed, but we do know that, based on your history, it wasn't trauma to the head. We also know that those lesions combined with the symptoms you've been having all point to one likely explanation." He paused. "Miss Becker, the location of the lesions and your symptoms are consistent with multiple sclerosis."

The words whipped against me.

"Are you familiar with MS?" he asked.

"I . . ." My tongue froze, as if the hidden, creeping lesions already sucked away my words. "Maybe. I think."

He said more things, so many things. "Neurological disease . . . chronic . . . more common in women . . . relapsing-remitting form . . . unpredictable . . . different for everyone . . . neurologist will confirm diagnosis . . . can manage symptoms . . . several medication options."

I clamped down on my lip, tried to keep the quiver under control. Tried to keep all the whips, the roar, the helpless rag doll at bay.

A hand touched my arm.

My gaze locked on Dr. Abrams's.

"This is a lot to take in, Miss Becker. You'll have other opportunities to hear this again and ask questions. Okay? Don't feel like you need to absorb it all right now."

My lungs cried for air. I inhaled, pulling hard against the clench, against the rise of tears.

"For now, here's what I want you to know most," he continued. "The on-call neurologist will be in to see you later today. He'll be able to better determine if this is truly MS. In the meantime, we are going to start you on an oral steroid called methylprednisolone. It will help with regaining sensation in your leg and foot. With relapsing-remitting MS, you will have flare-ups that can be treated with medication like this. In most cases, the symptoms remit most if not all of the way."

On the TV, the couple had crossed paths at a food table at a town event of some kind. They made eyes at each other, accidentally reached for the same coleslaw spoon at the same time. In the background, townspeople waved to one another, smiled in conversations no one else could hear.

I grimaced, found my voice. "It's . . . not curable, is it?"

He shook his head. "I'm afraid not."

The man on the TV slipped his hand into the woman's, lifting his chin in an epiphany that his future didn't make sense without her.

I gathered the edge of the flimsy blanket in my fists. "How bad can it get?"

"Like I said, we still need to confirm diagnosis, and no one can predict what a patient's MS experience will be."

"How bad?" I insisted.

He folded his hands in his lap. As if consulting the page of an invisible medical book, he spoke slowly. "Symptoms can reoccur in the same place or present in new areas of the body. They could be on the mild side, like what you've been having, or could worsen over time. Issues with balance, vision, cognitive abilities, incontinence, or bowels, as well as dizziness, heat sensitivity, and fatigue, are common. Symptoms can come on suddenly, and it's impossible to know when."

Whip, whip, whip of words. I leaned back against the bed and pulled the blanket up over my arms and chest, my fists still clinging to the edges. On the television, the woman smiled up at the man, her face aglow with the promise he had made to be hers forever.

Dr. Abrams unfolded his hands and rubbed them down his thighs. "With a disease like this, it can be hard to plan for the future. We've found that having a strong support system around you is key to living with MS. Do you have that?"

I turned to the window. Steady, sliding lights. "Of course."

"That's good. Please know that you are welcome to have guests. I expect you'll stay another night, depending on what tests the neuro might want to do. We'll take it a day at a time."

Another night meant canceling the lunch with Austie. I needed to tell Reva. But I didn't need to tell her why. I didn't have to tell anyone anything. I pulled the blanket to my chin.

"I encourage you to make note of any questions you have for the neurologist and be sure to bring those up when he comes." Chair legs scratched on the floor, drawing my attention back to the doctor. He stepped to the side of the chair, leaving it in place presumably for my visitors.

"Thank you," I mumbled.

"We'll get you started on the steroid." Before he took a step away, he paused and looked at me once more. "It often takes people with symptoms months to get in to see a neurologist, and sometimes years to get an MS diagnosis. In that sense, you are fortunate."

I forced my lips to curve upward. Doctors, even the kinder ones, had a knack for completely missing the emotional mark. I wasn't hungry, I wasn't a puzzle to solve, I wasn't unaffected by being called the wrong name. And it took a lot of audacity to tell someone to be thankful about anything associated with a disease that could take away everything at any moment.

25

MY CLOTHES HAD wrinkled after days of being folded in the hospital bag. I attempted to smooth the worst of the folds in my shorts as the nurse wheeled me toward the front entrance of the hospital just before noon on Tuesday. Outside the sliding glass doors, a free shuttle waited for me. I was going home, almost exactly four days since I had arrived. Almost exactly four days since natural light had caressed my skin.

The wheels bumped over the tracks of the doors. At the curb on the other end of the wide awning, the shuttle driver pushed off from the side of the open minivan and smiled. Beyond his vehicle, the horizon was clear and blue and taunting.

The nurse brought the wheelchair to a stop a few short steps away from the driver and handed him my plastic bag, now containing a thick stack of discharge papers and a large plastic mug with a flexible straw and the same blue Northland Memorial logo that adorned the bag. He stowed it in the back next to the seat I was to ride in.

Exchange complete, the nurse turned to me. "Ready, Miss Becker?"

Her name hadn't stuck with me. She had been my fifth nurse, maybe seventh, and had been the one to call the free shuttle service of a local nonprofit to take me home. They didn't trust me to drive myself. Hank, my trusty boy, would have gotten me there no problem. Instead, he was forced to wait in the parking lot outside the ER until I could figure out how to come back for him.

With the nurse's support, I hauled myself up. My right leg held, mostly resensitized thanks to the round of steroids and the help of a physical therapist. My purse flopped against my stomach as I shuffled, aided, into the van. I had to have looked as weak to passersby as my body acted.

After careful maneuvering, I secured myself into the seat and gave the driver the okay. He zipped the door shut. As he returned to his spot behind the wheel, the nurse waved from the curb, one hand on the wheelchair. I nodded in return, silently vowing to never see her again, so far as I could help it.

The engine started. Into the mild midday we went, first through the parking lot and then onto Barry Road headed east, following the same white line that had guided countless vehicles past my third-floor window. I hugged my purse to my stomach. All around, scenes of the everyday unfolded. A pickup's flashing turn signal, a mowing crew on an office building's lawn, a car pulling up to a pump at the gas station, a man reading a book at the bus stop, a discarded fast-food cup in the gutter. Glimpses at routine once so full of assurance that the thrum of possibility beat on were now assaulting reminders that the thrum was only for some people. How swiftly things fell apart.

My phone pinged. I reached into my purse and pulled it out. A return message from Paul.

HR confirmed you can take a paid sick day. Feel better soon.

The three-day weekend had not been enough to cover my stay at Northland Memorial. Though Paul showed nothing but understanding, I winced. Underneath that congenial reply had to be a disappointment he was too professional to let show. I had a strike against me, even if he wouldn't say it. From that point forward, I would have to be careful about how much I asked of him and of HML. A new hire who guzzled company money in time off and insurance was an employee on the watch list.

I slipped my phone back in my purse, but no sooner had it left my hand than another chime rang out. The new message came from Reva.

Following up on my text on Saturday. Think this
Sunday would work for lunch?

She had waited for days for me to respond to her offer to reschedule, waited for me to acknowledge she heard my concern about Austie's privacy and understood and wanted to accommodate. But it was impossible to know what the next Sunday, or any point in the future, held.

"We are ninety-five percent certain it's MS," the on-call neurologist had told me as he swabbed my lower back with an alcohol cleanser. "With a spinal tap, we can look for certain proteins that can help diagnose MS." And then he shoved a three-inch needle into my spinal column. The results would be in "soon." If he was right, then an unpredictable disease would loom over every minute of every hour for the rest of my life, holding the power to implode my world at its whim.

I hid my phone deep in my purse, leaned back against the headrest, and shut my eyes to everything. Purse held tight, feet planted to the floor, jostled by the bumps and sways of the minivan. If only the driver would keep going, back far enough to rewind time and undo all that had thrust itself in.

I shifted to my side, dipped my head, held back what welled.

Minutes passed. At last, the van slowed, then made a sharp turn before coming to a stop.

"We're here," the driver said.

The announcement lifted my head. Outside my window, my

house sat with its postage-stamp porch and mature trees in back. The well inside me grew. I released my seat belt and picked up my bag, determined to get inside before anything burst out.

"Let me help you with the door." The driver started to unbuckle.

"It's okay. Really. Thank you for the ride." I slid the door open and aimed both feet to the driveway. I kept a firm grip on the crash handle as I transferred my weight onto my legs. They held strong, the way they were supposed to. As I started to shut the door behind me, I suddenly paused. "I'm sorry, am I supposed to tip? I don't have much cash on me, but–"

The driver waved away the offer. "This is a free service. No tip."

"Are you sure?"

He smiled, shook his head. "No tip. Be well, ma'am."

Despite his reassurance, I closed the door with caution, waiting for him to show any indication I had misunderstood. The door latched closed, and the driver waved goodbye. The gears shifted into reverse, and I stepped away as the tires began to crank backward. For the first time in days, my feet were on my own driveway.

I turned toward my house. Crisp lines in the grass spoke to Ron's recent mowing. An envelope stuck out of the mailbox on the porch post like a white tongue. The serenity did little to quelch the shake in my bones. I pushed ahead for the mailbox.

"Jess."

I froze. The voice young and familiar. Sure enough, coming up the lot with a soccer ball pinned to her hip was Kyla.

"What's going on?" she asked. "Where's Hank?"

Before I could reply, she stepped onto the driveway, close enough to see the plastic bag I had neglected to hide and the wristbands fixed to my arm.

Her eyes widened. "Were you in the hospital?"

"I can explain," I said without any idea of what that explanation would be. I licked my lips as Kyla came over to me. "I . . . hurt my foot. Needed to get it checked out." Technically, it was all true.

"How'd you hurt it?"

"One of those crazy clumsy-people injuries. I'm fine now. Really."

She frowned. My skin burned under her scrutiny. She took in the wristbands, my feet, my face. "You look kinda rough."

Teenagers were nothing if not brutal. "Your concern is touching," I said. "How come you're home, by the way? Isn't this a school day?"

"They gave us a four-day weekend. I thought maybe you went out of town for the holiday or something. I came over Saturday to see you. Pop made hot dogs again. I was hoping you had pizza."

Standing in one place made the ache of exhaustion wail in my bones. I smoothed my hair, feeling the greasiness that had made Kyla comment on my appearance. "Sorry about that," I said.

"You missed your visitor too."

"Visitor?"

"She came by yesterday afternoon. Pop and I had just gotten home from the store, and she was knocking on your door. When she saw us, she took off."

"In a car?"

"Didn't have a car. Pop kept an extra eye out in case someone was casing the place. He said they may have been targeting your house since it looked like no one was home."

One more thing to worry about. All the more reason to figure out how to get Hank back home too. My boy was a protection in many ways.

"Thanks, Kyla. Tell your pop thanks too. I'm going to go shower."

She nodded. "Good idea."

I shot her a look, to which she grinned. Then she headed back to her solo practice. I moved on too—to the mailbox to grab the delivered contents, to the door where the key slid snugly into the lock, into the house that carried the scent my presence had created within it. That first inhale was deep and stilling. Then my gaze landed on the divas, lush and content in the touch of the golden rays.

The shake rattled up my body, ignited a fire in my chest. Even the divas' well-being was in jeopardy. My plans, my hopes, my job, my home, my savings to fund a retirement nest for Dad—cut off in their infancy, replaced with an immovable barrier I could not demolish. What lurked in my nervous system could return like a thief in the night and steal everything I had worked for and sacrificed to reach.

And what if I had brought it on myself? What if it was justice for all those years of destructive living and rebellious choices?

My throat clenched. I tossed my things on the table, kicked off my shoes in the middle of the hallway, and thrust open my bedroom door. The uncovered windows framed an open view of the sovereign heavens. So distant, so silent, so incongruently clear.

I fell face-first onto my bed. The burn ravaged up my chest and out through my eyes in streams.

"God," I said into my pillow, "please."

26

THE PHONE CALL from the neurologist arrived at the tail end of my shift on Thursday, at the moment I was about to log off and pile into bed to chase away the lingering grogginess from nearly a week of disrupted sleep. The results were "conclusive," he said. The presence of oligoclonal bands in my cerebrospinal fluid put me in the same class as most MS patients across the world. I was in a company of millions, yet the entire earth seemed to shrink around me to the size of a foxhole.

"We highly recommend getting in to see an MS specialist as soon as possible to establish care," the neurologist said. "They will be able to get you started on a treatment plan."

He told me about the MS clinic within the Northland Memorial system, which number to call, and to check with my insurance first.

"In the meantime," he said, "try to minimize stress as much as possible. We do see a correlation between stress and aggravated symptoms. Rest will be your best medicine for now."

I promised I would make the call, promised to take it easy.

Instead, I cleaned. No corner escaped my diligent hands, no cobweb my eye. For nearly two years, I had been the cleaning ministry at the Woodfield church. Tillie Watts had asked me to take over for her not long after I started attending. Her old, angry knuckles often refused to let her grip a dust rag, she said. The dozen or so other women in the congregation were in the same position or not far from it. It made sense she would ask me. Every Thursday night, I came directly from my shift at Red Rooster, where I had plenty of practice sanitizing toilets and mopping floors, and arrived right around the time Tillie and the three other choir members shuffled out the side door after practice. I started in the basement, sweeping, vacuuming, dusting, polishing, and worked up to the vestibule first and then to the sanctuary with its earthy scent of limestone walls and pine pews. The simple stained-glass windows diffused the late-evening light into multicolored smudges. The softened air held fast to the wisps of song and prayer that had been lifted by the choir members. Many of the hymns they sang were still outside my repertoire, but often a bar or two of a refrain hummed from my lips as the vacuum whirred by my feet.

In some ways, Thursday nights outshone Sunday mornings. It was me, my work, and the God who delighted in what he saw. Just me with a genuine desire to please, a heart filled with gratitude for where he had brought me, the promises he gave breath to, and the dreams of better things he had started to give life to.

That same sun now cut through the plain windows of my bedroom and warmed the hardwood floors I scrubbed with a mop. The rivers and knots of the grains surrendered their dirt bit by bit. It was the last room to receive attention, the last to be cleared of dust and germs. The dryer tumbled the final load, puffing out the powdery incense of the dryer sheet.

Did God see? Did he delight? Would he still allow any of those dreams to take their full shape? The questions of my heart lifted through the windowpanes, but they refracted somewhere in the atmosphere.

A knock on my front door drew me to a stop. I set the mop aside.

Ron waited on my porch, keys in hand and right on time. “Ready to go get your truck?”

He had promised he would help me retrieve Hank from the hospital parking lot, and that was the extent of our conversation about the holiday weekend. Nothing about why my truck was there or how I hurt my foot or by what kind of magic I was able to get around on a foot injured enough to warrant a hospital stay. He let my business be mine.

Hank sat in the second row from the ER entrance, his headlights pointed away from the red awning. When Ron dropped me off at Hank’s bumper, he waited until I was inside the cab before driving away. Hank still smelled faintly of oil and gravel roads, a familiar scent that stirred both relief and longing. He was a source of protection, but not the kind most necessary. His protection did not come with arms and a voice and a heart to break alongside mine. The only person on earth who could possibly stand guard in such a way was Dad.

There in the purview of the red doors that had transported me from Before to After, I pulled out my phone. My fingers shook as I placed a call to his cell. It wasn’t a pinched nerve, I needed to tell him. It wasn’t something a little ice could fix.

“Hello?” he answered louder than normal. Cheers and shouts filled the background.

“Catch you at a bad time?” I asked.

“At a scrimmage with the boosters. Team’s lookin’ real good. Best in years, I’d say.”

He had always been a big supporter of the Woodfield R-1 High School Boosters Club. Not for softball, though. Only football. He attended every home game and scrimmage in his Woodfield Lions shirt that was worn thin with age and not quite long enough anymore to cover his belly. The schedule was probably already on his fridge, home games underlined in red. His life, his routine, his world rolled onward unchanged. Meanwhile, I could no longer count on my appendages to function properly day after day or my optic nerve not to suddenly fizzle to black.

A sting bloomed in my chest. "Sounds like you'll have some exciting games to watch this season."

"Should. Got one or two boys might make All-Conference."

"That's great." I gritted my teeth, searched for the next words. "I called you Friday night."

"I saw."

"Were you asleep?"

"Guess I didn't hear the phone. Why were you calling so late anyway?"

The red-marked doors reflected in the rearview mirror. The memory of whirs and beeps and needles intensified the sting. "Wanted to talk," I said.

"What about?"

The crowd erupted into cheers. Dad joined them, screaming his approval directly into my eardrum.

I yanked the phone away and dipped my head. Was he even listening?

The crowd settled. Dad returned to me, voice back to normal volume. "You say something?"

I had plenty to say. A weighty load of things to say. But it would be wasted energy to try to unpack it in that call, not with his attention divided and the lack of privacy amid Woodfield's rabid fans. We needed time alone, together. An idea sparked.

"What're you doing for Thanksgiving?" I asked.

"Thanksgiving? Beats me. It's only September."

"Never too early to think about turkey."

He grunted. "Suppose not. Why you askin'?"

"I was thinking of coming home for a long weekend. My company is closed that Thursday and Friday. I could fix us a big meal, and we could watch football, catch up." Emphasis on the last part.

The shrug was evident in his reply. "If that's what you want."

"Perfect," I said. "It's a plan."

I had nearly three months to figure out what to say. Nearly three months to find an MS specialist and get more answers about what came next. Answers that could provide the clarity on whether any of my plans—especially the one involving Dad—had strength of their own.

27

"YOU'RE KIDDING ME." My writing hand slumped against the partially filled page of the notebook lying on the kitchen counter. "January 4 is the earliest available appointment?" It was only September 8, a nearly four-month gap.

The scheduler's apologetic tone underscored how often she heard that response. "It's a much longer wait than Dr. Levan would like too, but she has a full patient load. I will put you on the call-first list should she have any cancellations for a sooner appointment time."

Four months was an excessive amount of time to wait to be seen for a debilitating disease. But Dr. Levan at Fountain City Neurology was the only physician in Kansas City who specialized in MS and whom my insurance considered in-network. The next-best option was four hours away, in St. Louis. Even the people trained and paid to help me understand the future were unhurried to get me out of limbo.

"If that's the soonest, I'll take it," I said. Beside the notebook, my cheese sandwich waited on a paper towel, untouched. Only ten minutes remained on my Friday lunch break.

The scheduler gathered some more information, then confirmed the time, date, and clinic location. "You'll be getting a couple of text messages. One is an appointment confirmation and the other will have a link to our online patient portal. We ask that you fill out the online forms and questionnaires prior to your arrival."

I scribbled notes as fast as I could. What to bring with me, how soon to arrive at my scheduled time, what to expect.

"Between now and your appointment, Miss Becker, please make note of any symptoms, whether new or recurring. If you experience any sudden onset of severe symptoms, however, please go to the ER immediately. This could include vision loss, difficulty swallowing, severe pain, mobility issues that impact your safety, or any stroke-like symptoms."

My pen had lifted from the paper somewhere around "severe pain." The enormity of it all ballooned like a mushroom cloud, and I was the dark speck standing powerless at its base. The only answer, the only certainty at that point, was that the next storm was coming for me. When would it hit? No one knew. How bad would it be? Also unknown. But it would come, a determined thief poised to steal and maim.

By the end of the call, both sides of the notebook page flowed with notes. Things to remember, tasks to complete. The promised text messages arrived within minutes. I opened the calendar on my phone to January 4, 2024, and entered the next known mile marker on the road for which no map existed. January 4 was a Thursday, which meant I would need to take time off work. There were bound to be more days off, more hours here and there for appointments or symptom management. When? No one knew. How often? Also unknown. Whatever happened, I had to keep the missed work to a minimum, raise no red flags, sound no alarms. A sick employee was dead weight and the first to be pruned.

I sighed as I tore the paper from the notebook and folded it in half. I left my sandwich in the refrigerator for later, stuffed the notebook back in the kitchen drawer, and took the folded paper to the top drawer of my dresser, where I buried it with the discharge papers under my socks. Then I went back to work.

Later that day, Paul released me an hour early, citing a slow holiday week and my "impressive" ability to make up for the sick day. As long as I held that title in his mind, I might be able to weather the next storm, and the ones after that. Maybe.

"Have a good weekend," I wrote back.

He quickly replied, "You too."

It was only the third conversation I had had with anyone outside the health care industry in a week. I shut my laptop, rose from my chair, and shuffled about the house. No spot was left to clean in my home. No chores remained. Nothing to fill the raging quiet.

I rubbed my arms and traced into the living room. During my post-Mick days in Woodfield when I needed an escape, it usually involved a movie and food. I grabbed my purse and headed for the door. The library had the second season of *Boy Meets World*, Cost Cutter had Chinese food.

A defiant remnant of humidity clung to the September air, making the city long for fall all the more, and the colors that came with it. Hank waited in the driveway, the glint on his hood like a gleam in his eye at the thought of getting to take me somewhere. I was almost down the sidewalk when a figure on the street caught my attention. Someone walked toward me. Someone with shoulder-length dark hair and hands hooked around the straps of a backpack.

I halted. "Austie?"

She pulled her right hand off the strap long enough to wave, then put it back in place. She came to rest a few paces away from me, wearing the same tank top but different jeans. Both were wrinkled. The greasy roots of her hair made the strands hang limp against her scalp.

"I don't mean to freak you out by showing up like this. I just—I needed someone to talk to."

"Y-yeah, okay. You bet. But how'd you know where I live?" And why hadn't she called? Maybe that was a generational thing.

"You pretty much told me," she said.

"I did?"

She recounted the details I had thrown out on our walk without realizing they contained rather clear directions. Behind the Cost Cutter. 88th and Alton. Porch and bay window on the side.

My eyebrows shot up. "I guess I did tell you."

Austie was either clever for all the wrong reasons or desperate. Based on her appearance and the way her fists held fast to her bulging backpack, the latter seemed more likely.

The thump of a closing door traveled across the lot. Kyla came outside carrying her soccer supplies. Though she was clearly occupied with her own thoughts, Austie turned to the side as if trying to shield her face.

"So, can we talk?" Austie asked. Her eyes darted to my front door.

Something must have happened since the night the police visited her home. Something bigger than what I was qualified to talk her through. Still, she had come to me for help, for a "holy greeting." I couldn't turn her away.

I swept my arm toward my house. "Let's go in."

Out on the lot, Kyla set up her cones, her back to us, never looking our direction.

Once inside, I guided Austie toward the table. "How did you get here?"

"Bus. There's a stop by the library."

The library was a good half mile from my house, and the path included a decent hill.

As we neared the table, Austie paused at the divas. She lifted one of Shania's leaves with the tips of her fingers, her touch feather soft.

"Want something to drink?" I asked. "Cold diet soda?"

She looked at me with a cocked eyebrow, and in an instant the frozen soda discourse flooded back.

"Sorry," I said. "Your tooth. How about water? Or milk or coffee?"

"Water's great. Thank you." She slipped off her backpack and chose the chair closest to the door. "Hope I'm not interrupting anything. Looks like you were on your way out."

"Only to get some food." I pulled two plastic Red Rooster tumblers from the cabinet, added a few ice cubes to each, and filled them with water from the tap.

When I brought the cups to the table and handed her one, she chuckled and pointed at the logo. "Thought you were a Fast Stop fan."

I smiled and sat opposite her. "Definitely prefer it."

Both of us took a sip. The ice cubes clacked against the side of my cup, the only sound for several moments.

Austie lowered her water to the table, keeping both hands wrapped around the sides. Her backpack sat at her feet. "Feels kinda weird being in your house, not gonna lie."

Something we agreed on. Outside the window, Kyla dribbled a soccer ball through the series of cones she had arranged at equal distances.

Austie watched her, a certain wistfulness filling her expression. "I used to play soccer." The longer she watched, the more her lips contracted, like she was carried deeper into long-held memories of days she wanted back.

"So, what's happened?" I asked, pulling her into the present. "What did you want to talk about?"

Her eyes flitted to me, then down to her cup. She rubbed her thumb across the rooster silhouette. "Couldn't take it anymore. Either of them."

Each word sat heavy between us, packed with unshared pieces of the story.

"You left home?" I asked.

"Monday."

"Where've you been staying?"

"Wherever I can."

"Which is where?"

She glanced at me, her gaze weary.

I backed off. The less she relayed, the better. By the grace of God, I'd had somewhere to go when I reached the breaking point. It wasn't a place I wanted to go, but at least it was an open door. Sometimes life didn't offer open doors. With a history of running away, Austie probably knew that better than anyone.

Something Kyla said the morning I returned from the hospital surged forward. I tilted my head. "Did you by chance come by on Monday?"

Eyes down, thumb tracing across the rooster again, she nodded.

"You must have stayed close to here, then."

She didn't answer. The wrinkled clothes. The unwashed hair. Had she had any kind of roof over her head this week? A meal?

"Does your mom know where you are?"

She scowled. "I'm not talking to her!"

I held up my hands. "Fair enough."

My reply softened her expression. Her thumb resumed its steady movements.

"What about Reva?" I asked. "Have you called her?"

"She's had family in town this week."

"You didn't see her last night at Lighthouse?"

"Didn't go."

Considering Reva's insistence to get me to reply to her texts, it was likely she had been doing the same with Austie. "Think you should call her?" I asked.

She shrugged.

"Mind if I call, then?"

She took a sip, stalling, then shrugged again.

"That sounds like a yes to me." I rose from my chair, gaze

locked on Austie, waiting for any indication she preferred another option, but she didn't protest. Instead, she turned to the window and watched Kyla line up a shot, as if acquiescing to whatever waited on the other side of Reva's hello.

With that unspoken permission, I stepped into the living room with my phone. I would connect the two of them, let them figure it out. Reva would know what to do, and I could go back to my show and Chinese food and hunkering against my own unwieldy life.

Reva answered within two rings. "Jess, we finally connect."

"Sorry about the delay. It's been a week."

"That's okay. I'm ready to reschedule the lunch with Austie anytime you are. Does this Sunday work?"

"Actually, Austie is why I'm calling." Back at the table, my guest slouched in her seat until her head rested on the chairback. She settled her folded hands across her waist and closed her eyes. Despite her relaxed appearance, I spoke loud enough for her to hear that I wasn't revealing anything I shouldn't. "She's here right now, at my house," I said.

Reva's normally even tone carried notes of surprise. "She's at your house? Were you expecting her?"

"No."

A pause. "She left her mom's, didn't she?"

Austie deserved to tell her own story in her own time, and she deserved to tell it to someone who knew how to act on it. "You should talk to her," I said.

"Text me your address. I'm on my way."

My lips parted. I had meant on the phone—talk to her *on the phone*.

"Thank you for calling me, Jess. This is another indication that she views you as safe. I'll be there as soon as I can."

Being someone's safe person was never my aspiration. Being my own safe person was challenging enough. If either of them knew me, the real me, the *full* me, they'd agree. I tried again to head Reva off, to tell her I was simply going to hand the phone to Austie, but her next words set me on my heels.

"And, Jess, don't agree to anything before I have a chance to talk to her."

What in the world did that mean?

28

AS STRANGE AS it was having Austie in my house, it was doubly so when Reva arrived. Reva, with her pristine Acura and put-together outfit, strode through my door shortly after five. In her eyes was relief at the sight of Austie. In her hand, a Bible. I closed the door behind her and hung on to the knob, suddenly unsure how to act in my own home.

But Reva, as I had estimated, seemed to know exactly what to do.

"Is there a place Austie and I could talk privately?" she asked me.

"My office, down the hall there. Take an extra chair with you, though."

She headed in the indicated direction and nodded to Austie. At the command, Austie picked up her backpack and the chair she had been sitting on, then followed after.

I lingered at the front door, giving them a wide berth. Though my questions about what had happened had grown in number since the call with Reva, most of the answers were none of my business. Not at that moment, anyway, and potentially never.

When the duo reached the office entrance, Reva stood aside

and waited for Austie to go in first. Before she shut the door, she asked Austie, "Got your Bible with you? . . . Good."

For half an hour, they stayed holed up in the room. Voices rose, then fell. Chair legs scooted on the floor once. Footsteps several times. I allowed myself to go no deeper into the house than the table, and only to get a drink. The divas were due for one too. I took my cup over to them and dabbed water into their soil beds, enough to moisten but not soak. Out in the lot, Kyla packed soccer balls into the mesh bag. Dinnertime drew closer.

I took the cup to the kitchen and refilled it halfway. I guzzled it all standing by the sink. Eager to keep my hands occupied, I wiped down the counters even though they still sparkled, swept the floor that had attracted little if any dirt, refolded the blanket draped across the back of the futon. What must Reva have thought of my sparse home? Hers was full and decorated, with well-appointed furniture—or furniture, period—and memories framed on the wall. I didn't have curtains, or a real desk in my "office."

The evening seeped past six o'clock, closing time for the library. Though my stomach hadn't demanded much food all week, it decided at that moment it had no bigger priority than being stuffed with nourishment. The cheese sandwich from lunch called from its lonely place in the refrigerator, but I drank more water to satiate the pangs and sank onto the futon to wait it out. Surely the ladies wouldn't be much longer. When they left, I would still have time to get Chinese food, then maybe find a free movie on YouTube.

About fifteen minutes later, the office door creaked open. Footfalls filled the hallway.

I rose from the futon and met the guests in the dining room.

"Thank you, Jess, for letting us use your space," Reva said.

"Of course. Did you get things squared?"

Austie passed by me with the chair and set it back in its spot. Her backpack was already loaded on her shoulders. She stared at the table, her lips tight.

"We did," Reva said. "Another Lighthouse volunteer said Austie could stay with her for a few days, so I'll take her over there tonight."

"Glad you have a place to go." I smiled at Austie, but she didn't look up. She held on to the back of the chair, smoothing her thumbs across the wood. Her eyelids were redder than they had been when she stepped into the office.

Reva crossed her arms, tucking her Bible to her chest. Even she carried a heaviness in her posture. "It will give us some time to figure out next steps."

Austie tightened her grip on the chair. In her own way, she faced a road for which no map existed. And for her, the stakes were just as high.

My chest hitched. Words jolted loose from deep within me and blurted out before I could stop them. "Maybe you all could stay for supper."

Both women snapped their gazes to me.

No one was more surprised than me, though. The offer had been made; no taking it back. Supper and a show by myself had scampered out of reach. "I was getting ready to get some food. You could—you're welcome to join me. I can order pizza."

Austie looked at her mentor.

"That is a kind offer," Reva said.

"If you can stay," I added. "I think you may have family in town, Reva?"

"They left this afternoon, actually." She deferred to Austie. "I can stay if you want to. We're in no hurry."

Austie let go of the chair and hooked her thumbs around her backpack straps. Her voice was soft. "Pizza's good."

The lift in Austie's posture, the way Reva slid her Bible onto the table, all confirmed it was set. Ready or not, I was about to host my first meal.

"Great," I said. "Tell me what you like, and I'll pla—"

Knocks cut into my reply. We turned to the front door.

"You're popular tonight," Reva said.

"So it seems. Please, make yourselves at home. The futon is more comfortable than it looks, I promise."

As they made their way to the living room, I went to the door.

There was Kyla, with sad eyes and slumped shoulders. "It's hot dog night," she said.

The creaks of the futon frame told me the ladies had found a comfortable place to wait. I lowered my voice. "Sorry to hear that. I have company tonight, though."

Kyla peeked between me and the doorjamb. Her face lit up, and she waved.

"Hi there," Reva said from across the room. "I've seen you at Trinity, haven't I?"

Kyla nodded. "I go to the youth class with Wren."

Of course Reva would recognize her. Reva took her greeter job seriously. She took every ministry she had seriously. She rose from the futon and came over to join us.

I stood aside for the two to better see each other. "Reva, this is my neighbor, Kyla Torres. She's the one who coerced me into taking her to church."

"Thank God you did, Kyla. Job well done." She nodded toward the younger woman still sitting across the room. "This is Austie Russell, a friend of ours from church."

Kyla's bright smile and innocent wave drummed up a similar response in Austie, though it was not as enthusiastic.

"You all having a party or something?" Kyla asked.

"Not a party, really," I said. "They're visiting."

"Although, did I hear something about hot dogs?" Reva asked. "Sounds like you're the one having the party."

Kyla scrunched her face. "Umm, no. My pop makes them literally all the time. I'm so done with them."

A twinkle shone in Reva's eyes. "I can understand." Then she looked at me, tilting her head slightly. The look said everything. It wasn't her house, wasn't her place to invite Kyla in. Only mine.

Taking the hint, I cleared my throat. "Reva, Austie, would you all mind if Kyla joined us for pizza?"

Kyla rocked on her feet and folded her hands under her chin.

Reva winked at her. "I don't think we can say no at this point."

From her spot on the cushion, Austie nodded, her lips tipping up.

I turned to Kyla. "Looks like you're in, kid."

In she was, squeezing past Reva and me before I could finish telling her there was soda in the fridge. Austie watched her cross the room with a palpable curiosity. Her backpack lay on the cushion next to her, untouched.

"Can we play blackjack again, Jess?" Kyla called over her shoulder.

Reva swung her gaze to me. My cheeks warmed. The iconic casino game probably wasn't a thing a Sunday school leader condoned. But only bemusement coated Reva's tone. "Sounds like you two have had some memorable hot dog nights."

I cringed and shut the door.

When it came time to order the pizza, we decided on two kinds—one for the older, more acidic stomachs and one for those whose bodies could process calories as if they didn't exist. Reva insisted on paying.

As we waited for the food to arrive, Reva helped me prepare drinks, plates, and other essentials. Kyla found the card deck in the drawer, and Austie started to teach her the far more appropriate game of Crazy Eights. Austie's hint of a smile soon grew into quick, soft chuckles.

Reva noticed too, and grinned. A real, actual grin. She came up to me at the silverware drawer and leaned close. "You probably don't realize this, Jess, but you're living out this week's Allelon verse."

I paused with forks in hand. "I am? What's the verse?"

"First Peter 4:9. 'Show hospitality to one another without

grumbling.'" She touched my arm. "Blessings come with obedience."

I pulled on a smile, kept my tone neutral. "They do." Was what she claimed true for everyone? Including those whose old mistakes seemed to far outweigh any amount of present obedience?

At the table, Kyla slapped down her last card. "Bam!"

Austie playfully threw up her hands.

There was something cozy about the scene unfolding in my home, something that brought light and closeness. It wasn't just our elbows rubbing together; it was our lives.

And that was terrifying. What if they discovered the real me? The *full* me?

More than once as we ate our supper, my mind drifted back to the folded notebook paper in my top drawer and the eerily quiet sky.

29

THE PIZZA BOXES sat half empty on the counter. Drinks were almost gone, napkins wadded onto empty plates. Kyla noshed on the crust of her final slice and huddled with Austie over her phone. A tutorial for some kind of fancy soccer spin move played for the second time.

Austie pointed at the screen. "Watch. See how he's leading with his dominant foot when he jumps but lands with his back foot controlling the ball?"

Kyla paused in her chewing and leaned closer.

To my right, in the chair nearest the bay window, Reva marveled at the interaction, her hands tented over her plate. She glanced at me, and I urged myself to smile because it was a sweet thing happening right in front of us. But my social battery was almost as drained as my cup. My brain ground like a braking freight train. A belly full of dairy and carbs didn't help.

"You could one hundred percent do this," Austie told the young soccer player. "You'll be breaking someone's ankles for sure."

Kyla giggled and popped the last bite of crust into her mouth.

The "Maradona spin" was a new term to me, and the way the man in the video described it, I would break my own ankles if

I attempted it. A wave of sleepiness passed over me. I massaged the bridge of my nose, battling it down.

Reva noticed. She turned to her charge. "Austie, I know we said we were in no hurry, but it is getting late. We probably should head out soon."

"No!" Kyla said, pausing the video. "Can she please stay a little bit longer and help me practice this?"

"Ten minutes," Austie broke in. "Ten minutes, and I'll have her slaying."

Her confidence was admirable.

Reva nodded toward me. "Why don't you ask your hostess?"

Both girls looked at me, a silent plea in their tweaked eyebrows and bated breath. Ten minutes more meant that much to Kyla. To Austie. Ten minutes more meant Austie could relish the company of someone who wanted what little she had to offer because, to that someone, it was gold. I could give them ten more minutes.

"Honestly," I said, "I wouldn't mind seeing Kyla do this Madonna or whatever it's called."

"Maradona," they both said at once, then looked back at Reva for confirmation.

"All right," she said. "I'll help Jess clean up. You two go practice."

Kyla sprang for the door, phone in hand. Austie thanked us both, then hustled after her. On their way out, Kyla asked her companion, "Want to come over every week?"

A simple, poignant question.

In the wake of their departure, Reva's gaze hooked to mine. "You have been a gem tonight," she said. "You truly have. I hope we're not overstaying our welcome."

"Not at all," I said at the same moment a sudden yawn flung my mouth wide. I covered it with my hand and apologized.

"Kind of looks like we zapped you," Reva said.

"No, really, I'm glad you all stayed. I've been sitting in this chair too long, is all." I rose and stretched to the ceiling, feeling the release from my fingertips down to my glutes.

Reva did the same, and when she dropped her hands to her sides, she asked, "Do you happen to have any Tums?"

"That's a great idea," I said. "And yes, I do. In every room in the house. Let me grab us some."

"Every room, really?" Reva asked as I headed to the kitchen.

"It's my dad's hack. He never wanted to be without." A medicine cabinet was something else he'd need for his retirement nest. I opened the first cabinet door on the left and grabbed a bottle of the fruit-flavored tablets. On the shelf above sat the plastic mug from Northland Memorial, stuffed in among my collection of water bottles and travel mugs.

"By the way, Jess, I'm glad you're feeling better."

Cold shot through me. I swatted the door closed, afraid she could see the mug, but Reva wasn't magically standing behind me, nor was she facing my direction at all. Instead, she stood with her hands on her hips, observing the action outside.

"What'd you say?" I asked, playing partially deaf.

"I said I'm glad you're feeling better," she repeated over her shoulder. "I missed you Sunday."

"Right. Sorry about that. I did want to get together for lunch." I brought the tablets over to her.

She held out her hand and requested two. "I know you did, but in the end, the Lord brought us together in a much timelier way tonight."

Timelier wasn't necessarily the word I would have chosen. Hopefully none of what had happened that evening would become part of an updated prayer request on Sunday morning. The risk was less if Austie was present.

I shook two tablets out for her and poured four into my palm, a good, strong, preemptive strike against heartburn. "Think Austie will still be at church this week?" I asked.

"Probably. Especially now that she's met Kyla." She munched

and pointed to the action outside the window. "They've really hit it off, haven't they?"

Down in the lot, Austie demonstrated a move that involved a pivot of her entire body while in the air. Kyla took the ball and did her best to imitate her tutor, but her back foot came down too early. She set up the ball to try again as Austie gave her more pointers.

"It's wonderful to see," I said, then cupped the tablets into my mouth. They broke apart between my teeth, chalky at first, then pulverizing to a fruity goop that eased down my throat and quieted the vague niggling already forming at the base of my esophagus. Kyla's effect on Austie had been similar, instant and calming.

Reva turned to the table. "Shall we get started too?"

Together we worked in a systematic fashion to gather alike things for easier transport to the kitchen. Plates stacked, forks bunched, cups congregated together. I picked up the deck of cards Kyla had left in a clumsy pile next to its box. Each card I tapped into alignment was like filing a laugh or a smile from the pre-supper game. First Austie helped her learn Crazy Eights, then a famous spin move with the potential to set Kyla apart from the others at tryouts. In one short evening, she had invested lifetime memories in Kyla. Had we done the same for Austie?

I opened the box and aimed the straightened cards inside. "What do you think the next steps will be for Austie?"

Reva put the bundle of forks on top of the plates. "That's to be determined. Her goal is a place of her own and a steady job, but there are lots of steps in between then and now."

Uncertainty was something Austie and I had in common. Hers, though, wasn't a "what if"; it was a pressing "what now?" At least I had a roof and a job and, should those be taken away, a parent who hadn't kicked me out before. Austie had a backpack.

I traced the edge of the box lid. "Does Austie know this woman from Lighthouse? The one she's going to stay with?"

"She knows who she is. I'm unclear how much interaction they've had." Reva lifted the stack of dirty dishware and headed for the sink. She crossed through the spot where the three of us had met after their long meeting in my office, the spot where Austie's rubbed-red eyes revisited mine.

A vulnerable young woman with nowhere else to go had come to me for help, pieced together clues to figure out how to get to me, trusted that I would be "safe." Had I helped her the way she needed? Or had I just passed her off?

In the kitchen, Reva turned on the water and began rinsing off the forks for the dishwasher. I headed for the junk drawer, carrying the deck of cards, an everyday object that had brought out an entire side of Austie probably few people had ever seen. How often would she get to display that side again? Would she ever? Would she arrive at the stranger's house and wonder if she was truly welcome or just the object of a favor? And after the few days were over, then what? If Reva, the keeper of answers, didn't know, then no one did.

A different kind of ache formed.

I pulled open the drawer. The contents shifted with the movement. I paused to push items back where they belonged.

"By the way," Reva said, "I love it that you have the Daily Allelon on your fridge. What are the stars for?"

"I keep track of the verses we do each week." A tight space formed for the deck, and I wriggled it in.

"Is that right?" she asked over the splash of water on a plate. "In that case, maybe you'd like a preview of this coming week's verse. It's also from 1 Peter. It instructs us to use the gifts we have received to serve one another."

I froze. Gifts like a deck of cards. A table full of food. An open door. A house big enough for two. Given to be shared.

All other things fell away—my drained battery, the folded notebook paper. What were my troubles compared to hers anyway? I shut the drawer and turned to Reva. "What if Austie stayed here?"

For several beats, the only sound was the dance of water on ceramic. The only movement was Reva twisting to face me. Then she reached over the sink and shut off the water. "Jess," she said, her hands dripping into the basin.

"I have the space," I said. "She could stay for a bit as she gets on her feet. I was planning to fix up the basement anyway."

She grabbed a towel and wiped her hands. "You understand Austie comes with a different set of circumstances? It's not simply giving her a place to stay. It's sharing the responsibility for her discipleship."

I frowned. "What's that mean?"

"It means you'd be helping her learn to live biblically and to function in a new way." She laid the towel aside and leaned against the edge of the sink. "You probably have a daily routine, right? You get up at a certain time, eat at certain times, arrange your waking hours around your job. Weeks and months have certain rhythms too. Maybe you do laundry at certain intervals or your grocery shopping on certain days."

I nodded.

"That's new to Austie. Your home would be more structured than what she's known up to this point. It's a learning curve you and I don't see."

The details I had amassed about Austie's life fit together in a clearer picture. The gravity of it pulled at my shoulders, squeezed away all space for altruism.

Reva came over to me and rested her hand on my arm. "I'm not saying it's a bad idea, Jess. I'm saying if you make this offer to Austie, you should make it with ground rules. For instance, she would need to contribute to household expenses, which means she would need to find and hold a job. She would be responsible for certain chores. She would need to respect and protect your sleep schedule as well as your privacy, seeking your approval before having guests over. You'd be modeling structure for her. Your entire life would be a model to her. Like sharing a yoke."

My entire life, including the what-ifs and doctor appointments, the limbs that could turn useless and eyes that could go blind at any moment. Things I couldn't keep hidden like a plastic hospital mug behind a cabinet door. Did I really want that?

"Of course, I'm part of this package too," Reva said, her hand lingering. "I'll be here to help when you need me."

She didn't say "if," but "when." I bit my lip.

The front door swung open. "Jess! Jess!" Kyla called from the threshold. "Come watch! I can do it!"

Slam. So thrilled with her new skill, she hadn't waited for a response.

Reva settled her attention on me again, her tone as soft as her touch. "What do you think? Do you want to take the next few days to pray about this?"

Kyla had never been so excited. Austie had never been more relaxed or trusting. I couldn't do much of anything about my what-ifs, but I could do that one thing for Austie's what-now. And maybe that was the kind of obedience that God saw the most—and blessed accordingly. If I could keep the focus on her, keep pouring myself out for her, instead of fretting over my own worries, then maybe those worries would stay where I hid them, only coming out when and to whom I wanted.

Only one way to find out.

"No," I said. "Let's talk to Austie tonight."

PART 2

TOGETHER

30

OF ALL THE UNIQUE TRADITIONS the Allelon class had, none was quirkier than the annual Costume Kickball Game against the youth. It was an event so anticipated, the entire church turned out on the Sunday before Halloween to watch the spectacle take place on the grass field behind the church. The older adults class set up a drink and snack buffet. The senior pastor and worship pastor were to serve as umpires because they apparently were gluttons for punishment. Rumor had it the young adults won almost every year.

Kyla and I stepped through the back doors of the youth wing a half hour before the four o'clock first pitch, as the chill of the fall afternoon started to fold around the city. She carried her costume, and I shouldered my camping chair. Spectators in sweaters or light jackets filed in around us and tramped across the open grass with lawn chairs or picnic blankets. The folding tables for the buffet were set up halfway between the building and the field. Several older women finished stocking the tables with individually packaged snacks, homemade cookies, and bottled drinks.

The field itself was freshly mowed, with the basepaths cut an inch shorter than the rest of the infield and cleared of stray leaves from the trees in the neighborhood along the back edge of the church grounds. The third-base line ran parallel to the church, with the rear tip of home plate pointing to the western horizon. Someone had laid down portable bases at each corner and a pitching rubber in the middle. Many of the players had already arrived, laughing at each other's ridiculous garb as they huddled around their team "benches," which were simply rows of folding chairs.

"This is something," I said to Kyla.

She grinned.

Merging into the flow of traffic, we continued to the field, our shoes occasionally crunching on dried, pale leaves. My feet moved easily, no hint of tingles or numbness. For almost two months, all parts and pieces of my body had behaved, arousing no suspicion in anyone. My worries had indeed stayed where I hid them, and the paper evidence remained buried under my socks.

About twenty yards behind home plate—a vantage point offering an equal view of the entire field—I came to a stop and swung my toted camping chair to the ground.

Kyla stood beside me. "Think Austie will get here in time?"

"Of course. She promised she would be here to play, and her shift ended just a minute ago. I'm positive she's on her way." Austie's new job as a stocker at Cost Cutter put her at the store at least twenty-five hours a week, eating away at her availability for hanging out. Kyla had been counting down the days to Costume Kickball, especially after they had found "the most perfect" costumes together at the thrift store.

"Want me to help you get dressed?" I nodded toward the bundle in her grip.

She glanced back at the church, as if debating whether to hold out for Austie, but nodded.

Soon we had the polyester-blend getup slipped into place over her sweatpants and long-sleeve T-shirt. The top protruded over her head like an odd elf hat. I secured the Velcro strips in the back and patted her shoulder to signal all done.

She turned around and held out her arms. "How do I look?"

"Exactly like a hot dog."

She smiled, her cheeks pushing against the edges of the face hole. Once more, she looked at the church. The only people streaming from the door were the other spectators or players.

"Austie will be here," I assured her. "Still plenty of time. She took her costume with her to work, so she'll be ready as soon as her coworker drops her off."

Kyla nodded, but worry shadowed her expression.

Someone called her name. Wren waved to her from the youth bench along the first-base side, using her entire arm and whipping the fringes of her cowgirl shirt side to side in the process.

"See ya, Jess." Kyla broke away toward her friend. Her costume would restrict her from a full run, but she didn't seem to have any regrets about her choice.

"What a perfect costume for her."

I turned toward the voice. Reva approached from the young adults' side of the field.

"You should see Austie's," I said.

"What is it, pizza?"

"Yep. Pepperoni."

A twinkle charged up in her eyes. It had become my mission the last couple of months to bring it out at least once during pizza and game nights. The Austie-Kyla duo often brought it out first.

"Any idea when Austie might get here?" she asked. "Gio's finishing the lineup now and was wanting to confirm she was still coming."

"As far as I know, she'll be here any minute. Kyla's super eager for her to arrive too."

"I wish she didn't have to work on Sundays."

"Me too." Many of Austie's shifts had less-than-desirable hours. The new person didn't get much choice, though. My Red Rooster manager had always scheduled me for the graveyard shift when I first started.

Reva checked her watch. "I can ask Gio to list her as a designated hitter if need be. We have more than enough players to cover. How is Austie doing with her work schedule, by the way? Is she getting there on time?"

"She is. I drive her if the weather's bad, but most days she walks. And she's keeping up with her chores and thinking more seriously about enrolling in the community college next fall."

"She's talked to me about that as well." Reva settled her hands on her hips and surveyed the field. Two more young adults arrived at the team bench. They checked in with Gio, who was both dressed as a stereotypical coach, complete with a wad of gum in his cheek, and ready to serve as coach. He marked their names on his clipboard.

When Reva spoke again, her tone was more cautious. "Austie has been doing well, Jess, and that's a credit to the stability she has. She's been speaking up more at Lighthouse meetings too. We have to stay ready for backsliding, though."

The House Rules, which Reva had helped draw up and then stuck to the freezer door next to the Daily Allelon, had prohibitions against the things that particularly threatened to throw Austie against the rocks, but as we had reviewed them together around my table, Austie showed nothing but zeal to put temptations and old ways behind her. A similar zeal had filled me when I started accompanying Tillie Watts to church. Austie's two-month track record was as solid of a start as mine had been.

"I think she'll keep surprising us," I said. "She knows how much there is to lose."

Reva shifted her gaze to me, resting it there for a moment. Gio's call broke her attention and zapped away anything that might have been playing on her tongue. He gestured for her to come back, and she waved in acknowledgment.

"Duty calls," she said to me. "Talk to you after."

"Want me to steal the signs of the other team? I'm pretty good at it."

"Maybe not at a church game." She winked and headed back to the team.

Around me, families had started to settle in with snacks and drinks from the buffet. The start of the game ticked ever closer. I pulled my camping chair from its tote and set it up on the most level spot of ground I could find. No sooner had I sat than Ellen strolled up with one of her sons and Thea at her side.

"Ready for your first-ever Costume Kickball?" Ellen asked.

"I am. I've never seen anything like it."

Thea stepped closer, her signature criminal-investigator stare taking me in. "Why are you not playing?"

I smiled up at her. "Kyla requested Austie play instead. I see your husbands are playing, though. Think they'll keep the young adults' record alive?"

"Hopefully." Ellen giggled. Her little boy grabbed her hand and urged her toward the buffet. Despite his insistence, she stayed put. "By the way, did I hear that Austie is staying with you?"

"She is, for now." Through May was what we had written into the House Rules, but with Thea hovering over me, that seemed one detail too much to share.

The boy's yank grew more urgent. Ellen allowed herself to move a step in his desired direction. "That's nice of you to open your home to her. Hope all is going well."

"It is. Very well." My gaze drifted to Thea on the last bit. The slight upturn of her lips was somewhere between smile and purse.

Soon the demands of Ellen's son became too great for her to ignore, and she excused herself. Thea followed a beat slower than was comfortable. I slipped on my sunglasses and rolled my eyes safely behind the tinted lenses. Sunday school classes and small towns were not all that dissimilar.

The kids' team had quieted as the youth minister began announcing the roster. His voice carried over the distance. Kyla was to play second base and kick fourth in the lineup. Upon hearing her assignment, she looked at the back of the church, then at me. I mimed that there was still plenty of time. She tugged at the face hole and rejoined the huddle. My assurance hadn't eased her mind, or mine.

When the first pitch was ten minutes out, I sent Austie a text.

Everything okay?

A read receipt came through. But no answer.

When the game started, she had yet to show up or respond.

31

AT HER FIRST PLATE APPEARANCE, Kyla had an opportunity to be a hero, a changemaker for the beleaguered youth team chasing their first-ever Costume Kickball Champion title. Bottom of the first inning, two runners on, one out. I set my phone to record every moment.

She strode to the plate, taking inventory of the situation like a master strategist and clutching her hot dog costume to her belly.

"Let's go, Kyla!" I cheered.

She readied behind the plate, a lean brownish blob with black sweats and white sneakers sticking out the bottom. She faced off against Ellen's husband, who was dressed as a red-shirt-wearing spokesman from a certain insurance company. He started his windup. Kyla crouched. The first pitch rolled toward home. Kyla moved forward to meet it at the plate. She swung her mighty right foot back, and *whack!* The ball roped through the infield and into the gap in center right. Perfect placement. Both outfielders slanted back at full speed.

One runner scored. Then the next. Todd in right field caught up to the ball and hurled it to the second baseman. But Kyla had legged out a double and earned two RBIs in the process.

She had put the young adults on notice, and her teammates

danced and whooped as if victory had already been secured. The crowd shared their exuberance, but no one more than me. The video on my phone would be a shaky, nauseating mess, but I intended to show it to everyone—Ron, Kyla, my next cashier at Cost Cutter, even Paul.

If only Austie had been there to see it.

I stopped the recording and wondered in a hushed tone, "Where are you?" More than twenty minutes had passed since the game started. The read receipt was the only proof of life.

When the side was retired and the teams exchanged places on the field, I got up with my phone and headed to the more private spot between the buffet tables and the back door. My path threaded through the other spectators and their admiring comments about Kyla's kick. "This just got exciting," someone said. The one person Kyla would have wanted making such assessments had not been there to see it.

As I passed by the buffet, I tapped Austie's name on my screen and lifted my phone to my ear. One ring. The second inning started with a pop fly. Two rings. I stuffed my free hand into the front pocket of my jacket. Three rings.

"I'm here, Jess!"

I swung around to the doors.

There was Austie. She trundled out into the grass with two people about her age and her pizza costume flung over one shoulder. The woman beside her was shorter, fuller, with jet-black hair and a lip ring. The guy behind them was tall and gangly with a beard that tried really hard. Austie's movements were looser than normal. Her feet plodded along like she wasn't trying to control them, and she held on to the arm of Lip Ring, who giggled at nothing in particular. The fluidity was a telltale sign of what had delayed her—and a direct violation of House Rule number 5.

"Oh no," I mumbled and ended the call. Before I could get more than three steps toward them, Austie stumbled. Though she managed to stay upright, her costume fell to the ground. She and her female companion plunged into a fit of laughter. By the grace of God, no one was at the buffet tables, and the nearest spectators didn't seem to notice.

I hustled over to them and snagged the costume from the ground. Sure enough, Austie bore that familiar fermenty musk. "You've been drinking?"

She landed her watery gaze on me. "Had a beer."

"And some other stuff," her companion mumbled, setting off a second round of snickers. The young man behind them cracked a smile.

I kept my volume low, hoping they would too. "Are you serious, Austie? You drank before you came to a church event?"

She steadied herself. "No."

"What do you mean, no?"

"I meant I'm not coming to a church event. I'm coming to give you my costume and ask you to take my spot."

Her short friend struggled to keep a straight face.

My hand fisted around the costume. "You promised Kyla you'd play."

"That was before Demi invited me to go to the haunted houses."

Demi smiled at me. "Hi."

"She works at Cost Cutter too," Austie added.

The source of her backslide came from the same place that was helping her advance. The irony was bitter.

Behind me, the crowd cheered. Gio's voice rose above the others, commanding his base runner to go.

I spoke a little louder to be heard. "Kyla has been watching for you. She's been asking when you'd get here."

"So tell her I couldn't stay."

"Austie."

"Look, she'll understand. She sees me almost every day. This is literally the only night we can all go to the haunted houses."

The costume sagged from my hand. Reva would have had the

right words, the right look, the right presence to put this nonsense to a stop.

"She'll understand," Austie repeated.

The gang stared at me, as if in challenge.

"At least–" I cleared my throat. "At least promise you won't drink any more tonight."

Demi scoffed. A scowl descended on her face.

Austie's tone matched her peer's energy. "Even if I do, I'm obviously not the one driving. I don't have a car."

"Max is the DD," Demi said.

I zeroed in on Austie, said as firmly as I could, "I really think you should stay. Come sit with me."

She took a step forward, brow drawn tight. Her glare burned my skin. "Who are you, my mother?"

I struggled for the words. "No, but–"

"Exactly," Demi said and pulled Austie back toward the doors. Max scurried in front of them. Soon they were gone.

I gritted my teeth. I wasn't her mother, but I cared about her far more than that Lip Ring and Scraggly Beard ever would. Hadn't I proven that to her? Why hadn't I thought of something better to say? Something to make her understand? More importantly, what was I going to tell Kyla?

I whipped around, ready to march back to my seat.

At the buffet, watching, was Thea.

32

ANIMATED CHEERS ERUPTED from the crowd. But Thea was locked on me. Her eyes traveled from the back door of the church, to the costume limp in my grip, to my hot face. If God had made me a quicker thinker, I would have done more than stand there like a dunce, would have said something to cover up the events, explain them away. All I could do, though, was clamp my lips shut.

She arched an eyebrow, slid her gaze away, and grabbed two snack bags of cheese crackers before prancing back to the sideline.

"Great," I muttered. The buffet was far enough from our hushed voices to have spared us some privacy, but the scowl of Nose Ring, the sneer in Austie's expression, and the way they flung themselves away from me would have been revelation enough.

The eavesdropper folded into the rows of spectators on the young adults' side, directly behind where Reva stood next to Gio observing play. Going to Reva and conferring with her in private about what had happened didn't seem feasible at that point. That left only one course of action: Return to my seat and wait out the game. I folded Austie's pizza costume as compactly as possible, stuffed the oblong puff under my arm, then grabbed a bag of chips and a bottle of water, as if they were the real reason I had gotten up. Back at my chair, I shoved the costume under my thigh as I sat.

Reva caught my eye, pointed at her watch. Unable to give any other answer, I shook my head. Clearly understanding my meaning, she twisted her lips to the side and resumed her duties.

Two kickers later, the youth secured the third out, protecting their lead and prompting the sides to exchange places once more. On her way to the bench, Kyla waved at me and mouthed the question that had been plaguing her. *Where is she?*

All I could do was shake my head again.

She slowed her steps, studying me as if hoping I would give anything else. When I didn't, her expression fell. At her next plate appearance, she dribbled one to the shortstop for an easy out.

Aside from that blip of underperformance, she played the rest of the game with gusto, knocking in two more runs, and I documented every moment I could. In the top of the final inning, as the sun inched toward the horizon and the bright reds and yellows of the leaves behind the field muted, the youth snagged the last out of the game and secured their historic win. Bragging rights came with a large washbasin of candy and snack cakes, which the Acardis hauled out to the pitcher's mound for the pilfering pleasure of the victors.

But one conqueror in particular showed little interest in the spoils. Kyla stepped away from the group and jogged toward me. Reva noticed and tracked the girl from her spot on the edge of the chaotic treasure hunt.

"What happened to Austie?" she asked. Sweat beaded on her forehead and seeped into the upper edge of the face hole.

I stood and gestured for her to turn around so I could open the Velcro closure. "She had something come up," I said over the rip. "She asked me to fill in for her on the young adults' team, but you all were doing so well, I didn't want to come in hot and burn it all down."

Together, we peeled the costume from the bottom up. Kyla asked from the bowels of the polyester blend, "She was here?"

"For a minute."

The sweep of the material over her hair jostled several strands loose from her ponytail. They stuck out like down. She turned to me. "Why didn't she stay?"

No easy answer existed. I did the best I could without stabbing at her disappointment too much. "She said she couldn't, but I did get your kicks on video for her. She'll watch them later. I predict she'll have some notes."

Despite my quips, Kyla didn't grin or nod or smirk. She gathered her costume to her side, her folding job worse than mine, and homed in on the scrunched pizza costume on the seat of my chair. "She promised she would play."

"Kyla! Come on!" Wren called from the infield. A line of parents had already formed with phone cameras at the ready.

"Picture time," I said.

She glanced over her shoulder. "Suppose I should go."

"Let me hold your hot dog." I took the sweaty wad from her and sent her off with a command to smile like it was pizza night.

She looked at me sideways, then started back to her team.

Pizza was probably the wrong thing to mention. Part of me wanted to capture that lonely walk on video for Austie too. Kyla had not understood Austie's choice. Frankly, it wasn't understandable.

I unfurled both costumes, then rolled them together for easier transport. As I loaded my chair back into its carrier, Reva approached me.

"Heard Austie was here?" she asked.

Easy to guess where she had heard that. At the young adults' bench, Thea was still in conversation with Gio, accompanied by her husband.

I pulled the carrier's drawstring tight, then picked up the co-mingled costumes and tucked them under my arm. "Yes, with two kids I've never seen or heard of before. You were right about the backsliding. She reeked of alcohol and attitude, snapped at me about not being her mother when I tried to talk her out of going with them."

Reva looked out at the infield. The youth minister herded the kids into a loose arrangement for pictures. Kyla was in the middle of the second row with an arm around Wren.

"I don't think Kyla saw her," I said. "Not based on the conversation I just had with her."

"Do you know where Austie is now?"

"Something about 'the haunted houses,' whatever that means. I didn't get a chance to ask."

"They're in the West Bottoms," she said. "They're a Halloween tradition in KC. Gio and I will go find her and bring her to your house. We can have a chat with her there."

I nodded, adjusting the bundle under my arm. "Didn't think the backsliding would come so out of the blue like this."

Reva kept her gaze on the band of smiling young faces. "The narrow road is prowled by thieves."

Spoken like someone who bore witness to it many times.

"Okay, now silly faces!" someone called to the kids. Tongues stuck out, eyes crossed, rabbit ears popped up behind heads. The lighthearted moment was captured in a dozen phones.

"What should I tell Kyla?" I asked.

Reva smoothed her shirtfront. "Tell her whatever she asks for." She started back to Gio, promising to text me when they were on their way to my house.

Tell Kyla what she asked for. But how far did that go with a fourteen-year-old?

When we were loaded into Hank, Kyla set her bag of treats in her lap and her elbow on the windowsill. She rode with her chin in her elevated hand, as solemn as if they had lost the game. We followed Barry Road homeward, skating by shopping centers, gas stations, dozens of restaurants, and eventually the hospital. I kept my attention on the dotted lane marker outside my window as the doomy building slid into the dusk behind us.

"You did great today," I said. "Your pop would be proud."

She nodded, her mouth rubbing against her curled fingers.

"Maybe next year you should ask him to come watch."

Her brow pinched. At first she turned farther away. Then, suddenly, she dropped her hand and looked at me. "Is something up with Austie?"

I took my time answering, checking my mirrors and repositioning my hands on the steering wheel. "What makes you ask that?"

"What happened when she came to the church?"

That part, at least, had a simple enough answer. "Like I said, she had something come up and she asked me to take her place on the team."

Kyla stared at me. "That's it?"

"Pretty much."

Her stare lingered. When I didn't say any more, she leaned her head back against the seat and aimed her gaze at the passing sights.

Technically I had followed Reva's advice, but something like lead weighed in the air between us.

We arrived in my driveway soon after. Unlike the church property, the lot was littered with leaves. A breeze stirred up a bunch by the soccer goal and pitched them against the net.

I unclicked my seat belt. "Want me to come show your pop the videos?"

She kept her face pointed away from me. "Wren told me, you know."

"Told you what?"

She brought her eyes to meet mine. "That Austie showed up wasted."

My breath caught.

"Wren heard her parents talking about it. Some lady said she saw it."

Thea. For someone who clearly prized innocence in her own life, she didn't seem to bat an eye at the risk of shattering an entire youth group's. I grabbed the ball of costumes and slapped them into my lap. Small towns and Sunday school classes really were one and the same.

"Is it true?" she asked.

I patted the bundle, drumming up the words to say. "Wouldn't call it wasted, but she had been drinking."

Quiet settled over the cab. Kyla's eyes narrowed. The anger coursing through me seemed to echo in her.

"I'm really sorry, kid. I know how disappointing it is. I wanted her to make a different choice too."

The dimming light lengthened the shadows on her skin. She shook her head and threw back her seat belt. "Bro, why did you lie to me?"

"I–"

She thrust herself into the evening and slammed the door behind her. The entire truck shook.

"Kyla?"

It was too late. She tore across the driveway and into the lot separating our homes. I should have listened to Reva's pure advice. Thea's words were not the threat to Kyla. Mine were. And I had no idea what to do with that. I had no idea what to do with anything that had happened this evening.

In the tree line at the back of the lot, a leaf broke loose. It brawled with the wind, tussling and tumbling, until it landed dizzy and spent on the fading grass.

33

LIAR. THAT'S WHAT I had become in Kyla's estimation. It didn't matter that my intention was to protect her, not to mention Austie. Didn't matter that I tried to do right by both of them. She disappeared into her house well before my feet touched the driveway. She hadn't even stayed to reclaim her sweaty hot dog wardrobe.

The balled costumes unraveled in my lax grip and sagged at my side as I trudged up to the porch. Inside the house, the aroma of meaty pizza hung in the air. Austie must have come home at some point and heated up a slice from the leftovers of the previous night's gathering. Had she swiped some for her uncouth companions as well? Salt in the wound.

I draped Kyla's costume over the back of the armchair by the door, where it would await her return—if she ever wanted to come back to the home of a promise breaker and a liar. My mood darkened along with the windows. For a night of historic victory, not one of us walked away from the field in celebration. Even my footsteps sighed.

Down the hallway, Austie's bedroom door stood open. I entered her private space for the first time since swapping out my workstation for her twin bed on loan from the Acardi basement. Her backpack was tucked in the gap between the bed frame and the plastic three-drawer tower that served as both nightstand and dresser. Even in abundance, she kept things minimal. The basement space, which I had offered to her first, was "too big" for her. So my workstation now resided under the windows in my bedroom, and we slept one wall away.

I smoothed her costume over her teal comforter, which coordinated with the teal-and-white chevron curtains on the window. They were the only curtains in the entire house, a fact she barbed me about on repeat. She barbed me about a lot of things. My lack of hair control, my inability to quietly digest raw vegetables, and my vast repository of facts about television shows "no one cares about." In return, I never missed an opportunity to challenge her to wear intact jeans and find a modern song that was not simply an unimaginative recycle of my generation's jams. I had always pictured sisters bantering in such a way.

Wrinkles cut stark lines across the face of her costume, creating shadowy valleys in the brown-red pepperoni. A grass blade stuck to the edge of the crust. The sting of her insult still pricked. I never set out to be her mother, only the holy reprieve. For nearly two months, that reprieve had been propped up and guarded on all sides by the ten House Rules. She had given nothing but allegiance to them, particularly the fifth one, the heart of the list: "Refrain from all forms of insobriety."

Reva had said she would be there to help when—not if—we needed her. When had come.

A few minutes after eight, Reva's text message arrived.

Headed to your place with Austie. She is ok.
Will talk when we get there.

I paced the living room, little else to hold my attention other than the ticking clock and the multiplying questions.

Almost an hour later, the beams of Reva's headlights illuminated the picture window. I waited by the coffee table. Minutes passed. Figures skimmed by the window. The door hinges whined. I folded my arms across my middle.

Then we were face-to-face again. Austie's eyes hitched to mine. Her face just as pinched as before, jaw just as set. Words stopped well before my tongue. I twisted my lips to the side. She swept her gaze away, as if unwilling to entertain my presence, but her attention landed on the costume strung over the armchair. She quickly looked at her shoes.

Reva came in behind her, Bible in hand, and shut the door with a quiet click. "Sorry it's a little later than I hoped, Jess."

For her, my voice returned. "Not a problem. I can stay out here if you all need to talk." I pointed toward Austie's room.

But Reva shook her head. "This is a three-person conversation. We're all part of this."

Austie stole a glance at her. The suggestion didn't seem that great to me either, but Reva had yet to prove unwise.

"Let's sit at the table." She held out her hand to Austie in the general direction of our destination.

Austie jiggled her leg, as if testing her feet's readiness to run, but under the fixed watch of her guardian, she had no realistic alternative. She stalked toward her chair. In her wake, Reva nodded for me to follow. I fell in behind my roommate and caught a whiff of the new odor she bore, a sharp, skunky stench that was a signature of a very specific type of smoke. I recoiled, both from the rankness and from the fact she had made a bad situation that much worse.

Each of us took up our normal place, me facing the door, Austie opposite me, and Reva in the chair closest to the windows. Many a meal had been shared in those exact positions, including less than twenty-four hours prior. But the phantoms of our laughter had numbed to silence, and the memories of our shared smiles were sheathed with tension.

Reva lay her Bible on the table in front of her.

Seeing it, Austie slunk low, her neck practically on the chair back, and crossed her arms. "Let's get this over with," she muttered.

"Get what over with?" Grace exuded from Reva's tone and the gentle way she stacked her palms on the leather cover.

"Whatever lecture you're about to dish out."

"This isn't a lecture, Austie. This is a reset. Emotions are high right now, but the best way forward is to refocus on why we are together."

If Reva's pulse thumped in the back of her throat too, it didn't show. Austie, meanwhile, rolled her head toward the kitchen and aimed her gaze at whatever it was that interested her over there. Despite her scent, the whites of her eyes were clear, and her movements seemed crisper than they had been at the church. Had she stopped drinking when I asked her to? Only been in the car with someone getting high? Reva wouldn't have insisted on talking if she thought Austie wasn't in a frame of mind to listen.

I folded my hands in my lap and tented my thumbs toward the ceiling, clamping the pads together.

"Do either of you know what the theme verse is for Allelon?" Reva asked.

The sign outside the classroom conjured in my mind. With Austie staunch in her silence, I answered, "Something in Romans."

"That's right, Jess. It's Romans 12:10. A verse that has not one but two 'one anothers.'" Reva slid her Bible across the table to her right. "Austie, please read it for us."

Austie's jaw joint bulged.

Reva scooted the book closer to her. "I have it marked for you."

Resistance lasted several long, angry beats. At last, in one furious swoop, Austie grabbed the Bible and threw back the cover.

I started to say something, to remind her of sacredness, but Reva caught my eye and subtly brushed her fingers in the air, calling me off. It was an assurance that God protected his own

Word. A fuming young woman wouldn't stop him. If anything, he would stop her.

Austie flipped to a page marked by a green sticky note and scanned the text. Still slumped at an angle that had to have put undue strain on her neck, she read in a tight, quick manner, "'Love one another with brotherly affection. Outdo one another in showing honor.'" She shoved the open book onto the table and recrossed her arms.

Unruffled, Reva gathered the Bible. Her fingertips anchored to the verses on the page, her expression still in her signature stoicism. She let the quiet sit with us for a moment, let it speak what she didn't have to.

Austie's eyes swiveled to Reva, caught her stare, and retreated. She shifted in her chair, changing to a slightly more upright position.

"Love, affection, and honor are what hold us together," Reva said. "And that not of ourselves, but of the One who designed us for community. When we chose Jesus, we chose his people too, every flawed, beat-up one of them."

I moved one thumbnail down into the soft flesh of the opposite pad. Was that true? Because how much choosing had I really done in my Christian life to that point? Besides the defiant young woman across the table, everyone had elbowed their own way into my life—showing up at my truck window, at my front door on a Sunday morning, at a church entrance with a lanyard. I dug into my thumb pad.

"We also recognize that we sit at this table at different points in our Christian maturity," Reva said. "We remember that God is working in each of us in different ways at different times, as our faith is ready to receive it, and we are responsible for guarding each other's well-being, even if that means we must drag a sister away from things that will harm her."

Austie shot her another brief sideways look. Part of me wanted to reach over and yank her fully upright by her shirt collar.

But Reva, full of a stalwartness I had not yet begun to dream of possessing, lightly tapped the pages. "Perhaps the most important thing we remember is that the way we one-another is meant to be a dazzling display of Christ's love to the world around us, especially to those whose lives rub against our own." She paused. "Especially those who may look up to us and who may be setting their compass by our example."

Austie's jaw slowly loosened from its clench. Behind her on the armchair, the hot dog costume lay in wait. Her cheek hollowed inward as she bit the inside. She wasn't the only one guilty of neglecting the example she set for our young neighbor. My nail dug deeper.

"Do we all agree with these reminders?" Reva asked.

Reminders or first time ever hearing them. I nodded.

Our leader focused on Austie. "What about you? Do you agree?"

After a brief stillness, Austie moved again, scooting farther back in her chair. She shielded her mouth with the side of her left fist, then nodded.

"In that case, I have some more questions for you, Austie," Reva said. "Do you choose to continue to be part of this community in the way Romans 12:10 instructs?"

A wrinkle bunched on the bridge of her nose. Her fist curled tighter. She nodded.

"Do you want to continue to be part of this household and be guided by the House Rules as you pursue good?"

Her gaze drifted to the table and the place where her plate would rest, one small reach away from Kyla's. The place where she had read aloud to me from her phone the Metropolitan Community College application process. She nodded.

"Do you trust us, your sisters, to help you keep your eyes forward, forgetting what is in the past and striving toward what is ahead?"

Behind her fist, on the side that Reva could not see but was the perfect angle for me, her chin trembled. Her head bobbed in ardent response.

Reva turned to me. "Jess, your turn."

I drew in a breath.

"Do you wish for Austie to remain part of this household, guided by the House Rules?"

For the first time since we sat, Austie looked at me. Those piercing blue eyes that had not long ago blazed animosity now held swells of tears. The plea in them panged through my chest. "Yes," I said in ardent response.

With that agreement came the start of the reconciliation process. An ask for forgiveness, a pardon given, a commitment to speak to Kyla the next day. Eyes wiped.

But as we rose from our chairs, filled and reset, a new question began to disquiet the deep recesses of my mind. If one-anothering required Austie to allow us into the best and the worst, the raw and the real, what did that mean for what I kept hidden in the sock drawer?

34

"AUSTIE," I CALLED as I poured another bag of miniature candy bars into the large orange bowl on the table. "Kyla's headed over."

Outside the bay window, Kyla made her way across the lot in her reclaimed costume. The western sky teemed with vibrant predusk tones, a perfect backdrop for a night of trick-or-treating.

"One sec," Austie replied from behind her closed bedroom door.

The last of the bars tumbled from the bag and skittered down the peak in the middle of the bowl. Two bags' worth of chocolatey glory was a good starting place. It was impossible to gauge how many kids would stop by my little house that night, but those who did come would not walk away empty-handed. I leveled the mound of bars with my still-symptom-free left hand and dug out my favorite, a sticky nougat layered with oozy caramel. The first bite lodged on my molars fast enough to make a dentist squirm.

The bedroom door creaked open. Austie stepped into the hallway, covered from neck to knees in a giant polyester pizza slice. The crust portion slanted over her shoulders and protruded far enough to the sides that the ends angled over her biceps. She held out her arms and spun like a runway model as she moved toward the table.

"Kyla's going to love it," I said, offering her candy.

"Hope so. This thing itches like crazy." She grinned and swiped a plain chocolate bar.

Handing out candy while dressed up had been Kyla's requested penance for Austie. Her request for me had been a bag of Takis and a dirty soda. Teenagers could be much easier to mollify than adults.

"Thanks for getting all this candy on your discount, by the way," I said.

"No problem, but . . ." She nodded to the five other value-size bags lying on the table. "Think you're being a little extra?"

"Unashamedly."

She smiled as exuberant knocks thumped against the door. She pulled away to answer them.

"Speaking of discount," I said to her golden-crust back, "let's chat about me purchasing one of those turkey meals the deli is selling for Thanksgiving."

She waved over her shoulder. "Bet."

"Bet," I repeated in a whisper, following her with the bowl. My mental dictionary of generational slang grew by the day.

Kyla's face lit up when Austie opened the door. The two launched into giggles and selfies, pausing only when I directed their attention to the first of the trick-or-treaters coming around the curve of our street. They grabbed the bowl from my arms and reported to their posts on the porch. By the looks of it, Austie was on track to more than make up for missing the kickball game, and by the immaculate state of the bathroom, which was Austie's offered penance to me, she was back on track to thrive under the House Rules, at least as long as she minimized her time around Nose Ring and Scraggly Beard.

The girls waited at the porch railing with the bowl, chatting about whatever young people chat about while dressed up as culinary delights.

Free from the bonds of extroverting with young strangers and their parents, I pulled a cold soda from the fridge and lazed on the futon with my phone. There was one other person whose well-being I needed to ensure.

I placed the call. The rings on the other end of the phone line gave way to Dad's voice and the grate of chair hinges.

"Hey, Jess."

"Happy Halloween. Expecting any trick-or-treaters this year?"

"Don't know. Gonna be at the shop for a while. Got a few jobs that need done yet." Though he spoke of being stuck at work, his tone contained no hint of disappointment. Avoidance of people ran in the bloodline.

"I may have a bit of candy left after tonight," I said. "If I do, I'll bring it at Thanksgiving. Put any more thought to what you might want to eat, by the way?"

"Got some of those chicken strips you left in the freezer."

"Very funny. For real, though, I can bring the food. Grocery store up here sells entire meals–turkey, potatoes, dressing, even pie. All we have to do is warm it up."

"Whatever you want is fine."

The first batch of kids arrived on the porch. I craned my neck toward the picture window. A little girl in a purple princess dress looked up in wonder at the giant-sized pizza.

I grinned. "Would it be a problem if I brought a friend? Haven't talked to her about it yet, but she might not have anywhere else to go."

"The gal that's livin' with you now?"

"Yes. Austie. I haven't asked her what her plans are, but I wanted to check with you first."

"Suppose that'd be fine. Got a bed in your old room now."

"Really? Thought you were going to turn that into a storage room or something."

"The bed's for when you come home."

A sudden wave of somberness rolled through me, dimming the joy. What if his innocent comment proved to be a prophecy?

What if I did have to "come home" for good and not just for a visit? The image was crisp and harsh: Me trapped in that bed, Dad click-stepping into the room with soup, back hunched, forced into a servanthood neither of us wanted. The image scudded away as fast as it had invaded, but it left behind a jagged trail.

I tucked my hair behind my ear and fought off the lingering shiver. "That's thoughtful of you." Somehow I had to find a way—and the courage—to tell him about my diagnosis. Despite my hope my symptoms would remain at bay as long as I willed them to, the reality was I lived in a wobbly peace. I could end up dependent upon him. That part would be the hardest to say aloud to the only family I had.

"'Course, if your friend comes too, you might have to sleep on the couch."

I nodded along. At least for now, that was the only concern he had. That and the idiot boys. "Shouldn't be a problem," I said. Though if Austie did come along, it would also be harder to find enough privacy to talk to him. Maybe I needed to hope she found plans of her own.

Out on the porch, the girls waved goodbye to their first customers, as equally unaware of my hidden worries.

"Since we're talking about Thanksgiving," Dad said, "guess I should tell you I got an invitation to a dinner that night."

Thankful for the diversion, I relaxed my grip on the phone and followed him down the new trail of conversation. "Really? From who?"

"Someone in town."

"One of the boys?"

He huffed, then elongated a profane word. "Hardly."

The "hardly" would have done the job fine, or even just the huff. "Who is it, then?" I asked.

"Someone from the boosters."

There was only one reason for him to be so annoyingly coy. "Are you saying this is a female someone?"

A pause. "Yes."

My eyebrows shot up. "Kevin Becker has a lady friend?"

"You don't have to say it like that."

"I think I do. This is a big deal. You haven't dated in . . . you've never dated."

"It's not dating. We get together from time to time."

"That's called dating, Dad. Granted, it has been a minute for me, but that's how I remember it going."

He grunted. "Whatever it's called, she invited me to her family's Thanksgiving dinner."

I sprang from the futon. "Hold up. She invited you to hang with the family? How serious is this 'getting together' you've got going on?"

"I'm old and I live alone, Jess. It's not that far of a stretch for her to invite me."

I passed around the coffee table and paced in the open space. "Who is this generous woman?"

"I'd rather you wait till Thanksgiving."

"Why?"

"Don't want you to have any preconceived notions."

"Why would I do that?"

He sighed. "Can you just wait?"

We both had things requiring courage to share. I couldn't begrudge him the request, or the fact he was a step ahead of me in the truth telling. "Yes, Dad. I can wait."

As the next wave of trick-or-treaters marched up my front lawn, I assured him I would place the order for our meal, let him know if Austie could come, and not bring up his mystery woman again. We ended right as the next distribution of candy bars began. More chuckles and coos over the "cute" costumes wafted from the porch.

The girls were happy. Dad was happy-ish. We had found a comfortable cadence. But into the tranquil harvest colors unrolling across the sky seeped notes of gray.

35

THE END OF DAYLIGHT SAVINGS the following weekend had shortened the days to the length of a gnat's life. At four o'clock on Wednesday, the sun sent clear signals it was preparing to call it a night within the hour, slowly fuzzing the light in my bedroom.

I paused in my work to click on the desk lamp. The bulb kicked on at the same moment another *whack!* drummed through the windowpanes. The truncated daylight also meant that Kyla wasted no time practicing after arriving home from school.

I refocused on the spreadsheet stretched across my laptop screen and Julio Varga's latest round of medical bills on my monitor. Mediation was the following Monday, and Paul had sent the assignment as a high priority. My eyes followed each digit of every itemized fee on Mr. Varga's hospital invoice as my fingers typed them verbatim into the spreadsheet, accompanied by the CPT code. One wrong number or excluded charge could cost Mr. Varga even more than he had already surrendered. The hospital bill was lengthy—and costly. He had needed an MRI too. Upper extremity joint without contrast, code 73221. His insurance had covered a portion of it. A shockingly small portion.

Cold tangled in my gut as I entered the total he had been charged for a single three-day stay. Four numbers before the period. Two months after my own ER stay, I had yet to receive statements from either the hospital or the insurance company. A small mercy in one respect, but an imminent sucker punch in another. What would I do when my own bills arrived? How would I absorb the cost? Would I have to ask Dad for help with that too? Telling him about my diagnosis was overwhelming enough.

Whack!

I jumped. The startle caused an errant strike of a key, which added an extra digit to Mr. Varga's cost column. I quickly deleted it and pulled myself back into focus mode. For the rest of the time it took to enter his statements, I avoided any more wayward keystrokes, despite the noises outside.

By twenty minutes to five, the descending sun had trumpeted pinks and purples across the atmosphere, and the whacks in the lot had ended. I switched to the billing system to record my time for the Varga case, the final task of my shift aside from a last check of messages. The delicious reward of a chilled diet soda waited—a normal, everyday element that served as a reminder that some things, at least, stayed comfortably predictable.

A new text message popped onto my phone, which lay next to my mouse pad.

Austie

Come outside

My fingers paused over the numeric pad of my keyboard. Outside? Why was she outside? The message above it, which had arrived around the eleven o'clock end of her shift, said she and Reva were going on some errands. That had been unusual enough.

With the efficiency that kept me in the good esteem of Paul, I hammered out my start and stop times along with a description of the tasks completed and submitted my log. The rest could wait until after I had investigated whatever was going on outside.

By the time I got to the porch, everyone else had congregated around a gleaming Beetle coupe parked behind Hank. I slowed to a stop on the top step. Reva stood in the yard on the passenger side, arms akimbo. Kyla leaned over the fender, smoothing the bright cherry hood with one hand while bracing a soccer ball to her hip with the other. Austie waved to me from the crook of the open driver's door, key chain looped around her finger.

She held up her arms in a V. "What do you think, Jess?"

"It's so cute!" Kyla answered for me, still petting the hood. "It looks like something you'd drive, Austie."

It did. But a *car*? How could she have afforded it?

I traced down the front walk. Hank had twice the length and girth of the coupe. He would have taken it out completely had they met on the highway.

"Is it yours?" I asked.

"Got her today!" She jiggled the flip-key remote, which hung from its key chain alongside a metal charm of a red Beetle.

"Still waiting on the title," Reva added. "But for all intents and purposes, it's hers."

How was that possible?

"Want to get in?" Austie asked me.

"Me too!" Kyla tossed the soccer ball into the grass and scampered past me for the passenger door.

"All right," I said.

Austie held out the key as I approached. "In case you want to check things out." Her eyes were ablaze with bliss. Her smile brought out my own, though it didn't squelch my curiosity of how any of it came to be.

I took the key from her and folded myself into the driver's seat. The inside was minuscule but immaculate. Whoever had owned the car before had taken great pains to clean it, from the stereo knobs to the brushed chrome fixtures to the crevices of the rubber floor mats. The cabin was awash with the scent of Armor All. I slid the key into the ignition and engaged the battery. The dash lit up. No warning notifications showed. Someone had even filled up the gas tank.

Kyla used both hands to explore, turning down the visor, opening the glove compartment, moving her automated seat in all directions. Suddenly she paused. "A CD player? How old is this car?"

Austie leaned in next to me. "Almost ten years. Only has eighty-five thousand miles, though."

The odometer confirmed the claim.

Reva squatted next to Kyla. "Gio had his mechanic look it over. He said it is a solid car, well maintained."

"Looks like it," I said. Very little wear marred the buttons and knobs. No sun fading on the dashboard or cracks in the windshield. I shook my head. "When Austie said you two were spending the afternoon together, this is not at all what I thought you were doing."

"It was somewhat unexpected," Reva said. "Our friends called me this morning, offering to sell it."

"Austie, can I turn on the radio?" Kyla asked, finger already jetting toward the power button.

"Do it! You should hear the sound system!" She leaned so far into the cabin to help Kyla that I had to ask for breathing space.

"Why don't you two explore together?" I said and started to extract myself, a process that required much more of my knee stability than getting out of Hank ever did. I managed to lift out of the coupe not long after Kyla figured out how to flip through the preprogrammed stations. Nearly all of them were Christian. Austie plopped into the seat with youthful ease and began teaching her how to adjust the bass and treble.

Reva met me in front of the car. We stood side by side, elbows nearly touching. "I think they both like the car," she said.

"No question."

She glanced at me. "You're wondering how this came together, aren't you?"

"Took the words out of my mouth." Or my head, per her usual.

Austie found an early-2000s hits station and cranked up the volume. A vaguely familiar pop-punk song blasted through the open doors.

"Our friends bought a different car yesterday," Reva said over the music. "They were willing to sell this one for a fraction of what it's worth. We set up a small private loan with the help of a banker from church. She'll pay a little bit each month for six months."

"What about sales tax?" I asked. "Property tax? Insurance?"

"Taken care of. The sellers are helping her with property taxes this first year."

The cumulative total had to equate to thousands of dollars, more than Mr. Varga's medically necessary MRI. Possibly more than an ER visit. Someone had helped shoulder an enormous cost on Austie's behalf.

"That is incredibly generous," I said. "Almost unrealistically so."

"Not so unrealistic," Reva replied. "The sellers have plenty, and they don't mind parting with the extra if it helps someone else. If memory serves, you gave me a similar rationale about two months ago when it came to your house."

Fair, but the house thing was different. Wasn't it?

Kyla led Austie in a dance that shook the entire car. Amid the thickening blur of daylight, they created a joyous and bright moment. Behind the wheel of her own car, Austie had a freedom previously out of reach. Freedom led to opportunity, like being able to travel for a better job or having transportation to community college. It was a giant step forward for her, and at that, I had to smile.

"Maybe Austie will be driving you all to church now," Reva said. "She mentioned that her schedule changes in a couple of weeks, and she won't be working on Sunday mornings."

My lips contracted. Sundays meant Allelon, and Thea, and the reputation she had ensured Austie was saddled with among that crowd. I shoved my hands into my pockets. "Maybe. If she wants to go back, that is."

Reva glanced at me. "Why wouldn't she want to go back?"

Laughter exploded from the cabin. The girls fell into each other in their merriment. To us, Austie was more than her mistake. But to the people at Trinity? Who knew what she was?

"People know, Reva. About what happened at the game. That's how Kyla found out. Wren told her what she heard from her parents, who heard it from Thea." All arrows pointed toward that one name.

A wind cut over us, rattling loose leaves across the grass. I huddled against it.

Beside me, Reva clasped her hands at her waist. With the same easy grace she had used to ask Austie to read from Romans, she replied, "As far as I know, Thea told only me. If someone overheard and failed to have the same discretion, that's not on her."

But how could they have overheard if she wasn't talking loudly enough, on purpose? I shook my head. "The fact remains, people know. Austie's been labeled. We both understand that labels are heavy things to lift."

She nodded. "It is true that once someone sees you a certain way, they can have a vice grip on that view."

Kyla changed the station to a new song, a high-tempo "bop" from youth group she had introduced us to over pizza one night. She and Austie sang loudly the bold, assured lyrics about standing in faith and doing whatever it took, exactly the hopeful path Austie strived to stay on. For an entire refrain of the song, Reva and I stood as stone-still antonyms to the rejoicing in front of us.

At last, Reva spoke, attention fixed on the girls. "I think it's important to tell you that the friends who sold this car are in Allelon. That's why they were aware of her need."

My breath paused. The prayer request Reva had shared with the class rolled through my memory, all of Austie's vulnerabilities she had listed in front of people who didn't even know the young woman's name. One of them had been the generous source? I turned to Reva. "Who?"

Kyla stuck her head out the open passenger door. "Austie's going to take us for a ride! Let's go!"

Reva met my gaze, ignoring the strands of hair the chilled breeze flicked across her cheek. "Doesn't matter who. What matters is we trust that some people do understand how labels kill grace."

The same breeze aggravated the cold lodging deeper in my gut.

She nodded toward the car. "Let's go for a ride."

It wasn't until we were almost out of my neighborhood that her statement's full meaning took shape: I was equally guilty of labels.

36

AS KYLA AND I CLIMBED into Hank for the drive to church the following Sunday while Austie was at work, I made an unspoken commitment to put aside all uncharitable assessments of the people at Trinity, starting with Thea. Maybe I had read her wrong the whole time. Maybe everyone knowing Austie's carelessness at the game really wasn't Thea's fault, and maybe her intention in telling Reva had been rooted in genuine concern. It was possible, regardless of what my instincts claimed.

The whole drive, I held fast to my self-imposed rule: No to assumptions, yes to grace.

On our walk up to the church doors, I filled myself with as much graciousness as I could muster. I would grace like no one had ever graced.

Then I stepped through the Allelon doorway and into the hot center of Thea's stare. Her eyes traveled the length of me, stuck firm to mine for a moment, then ripped away. Her skirt puffed as she spun around and engaged with someone apparently more to her liking.

I gritted my teeth. Whose labels were killing grace, exactly?

Reva, deep in a conversation with another woman in the center aisle, hadn't witnessed the interaction. If she had, would she have said something? Would she have agreed I was right to have concerns about Thea? I crossed to the other side of the room, grabbed a donut from the box, and stowed myself in the back row next to the windows. No one spoke to me, which was just as well, and class began only one minute late.

I stared out the windows at Hank in his parking spot for most of the first part, thought about the nap I would take that afternoon, the groceries I needed to buy, Mr. Varga's mediation the next day and whether he would find long-awaited relief.

My attention meandered back to the lesson right around the time Gio began to expound on the verse for the coming week, Galatians 6:2: "Bear one another's burdens."

Bearing, not taking, he explained. "Think of a yoke. A more experienced, stronger ox is yoked shoulder to shoulder with a less experienced ox as a way to train it. The stronger ox does not take the full burden. Instead, it shoulders part of the load, allowing the other one to learn to bear up and to stay on the path the farmer has carved out for them. The stronger one lends strength and guidance the weaker one does not yet possess."

Like a model. The way I was to Austie. The way Austie was to Kyla. The way Reva was to all three of us. In our own ways, we had rallied around Austie, shoulder to shoulder. Not taking the full burden but carrying it with her, training her to bear up and walk the intended path.

"Here's the trick of it, though," Gio continued. "We are often tempted to think of ourselves as the stronger ox."

I lifted my head, sure he could read my thoughts the way his wife could. But he wasn't looking at me.

"How willing are we," he said, "to admit we are the weaker ox? How ready are we to humble ourselves at the shoulder of someone stronger and allow them to lead us? And I mean outside the context of them teaching us Scripture, although that is certainly in view. I mean in our trials, in those moments when we would rather insist we can do it ourselves. That is the part we don't like to admit we neglect."

He described me. He described the mindset that Beckers were taught from a young age to espouse. I had to overcome that thinking if I was going to ask Dad for his help and get him to admit he needed mine too. The images returned of him with soup in hand and me sequestered to a bed. But instead of being set in my Woodfield bedroom, what if they were in my new one, inside the little house on the narrow street, the tops of the trees swaying outside the window? It made sense. My doctors would be in Kansas City. My pharmacy. My insurance. My job. A yoke would be exponentially heavier for us both in a health care desert like our hometown. His move to the city was all the more imperative. How could I convince him to let go of his own preconceived notions?

An idea struck. There was something I could do.

I counted the minutes until the end of class.

As soon as I delivered Kyla safely home after Sunday school, I gathered supplies and headed to the basement. Pencil in my back pocket, measuring tape clipped to my waistband, roll of masking tape around my wrist, spiral-bound notebook in one hand, and my phone for research in the other. In the art of persuasive arguments, visual aids were often powerful tools. For the matter at hand, those aids amounted to floor plans. If he could *see* the vision of his new living space, then maybe he would understand.

I started with cabinets.

Online retailers provided several options for freestanding bases, the dimensions of which I averaged out on a sheet of notebook paper, then taped off along the west wall. Dad could have an efficient kitchenette with two bases, a mini fridge, and a microwave on top. Next came a spot along the east wall for a twin-size bed. I also taped off places for a nightstand, a desk, and a TV stand in the corner under the window.

Of course, he would refuse to move anywhere without his recliner. That raggedy, stained thing had been a fixture in his house since my high school days. I staked out a spot in the direct line of sight of the proposed TV stand. It was the perfect perch, where he could see both the outdoors and the football game on TV. I lowered to my knees and yanked off a piece of tape I estimated to be roughly the width of his chair.

What would it be like to come down the stairs to him kicked back with a game on? His favorite brand of microwave bean burrito cooling on a paper plate on the armrest, the sunrays glinting off the frame of his glasses and soaking into his flannel shirt. The toe of one sock hanging like a deflated balloon, pulled loose when he pried off his shoes, which lay cockeyed next to his chair. The woodsy musk of his aftershave mingling with the pungency of his burrito. His occasional snore overlapping the commentators' chatter.

I smoothed the tape to the floor, running my fingertips over and over the textured surface to lock it into place. Was it feasible to see such a scene? Was it possible to find him resting in a home I created for us? A mutual safety net I had woven? *Me.*

Footsteps plodded overhead. I snapped to attention and blinked away the blurriness clouding my vision. The clock on my phone showed ten past noon. Austie was home.

She came to the basement door, which I had left ajar. "Jess?"

"Down here."

She clomped down the steps. Her white Cost Cutter polo hung free from the waistband of her black pants. "What are you doing?" she asked.

"Some daydreaming. I'm marking out some floor plans for what I hope will be a living space for my dad someday. If I can convince him, that is."

"Nice." She stopped on the last step.

I pushed myself up from the floor, making it to my feet with only mild windedness, and slung the roll of tape on my wrist. "Heard any more about your work schedule for Thanksgiving week? My dad said you are more than welcome to join us."

"That's what I was coming to tell you. The store's open Thanksgiving morning, and they have me scheduled for both that and the day after."

Being the new person meant working holidays too.

"That stinks," I said, settling my hands on my hips. "And Reva's going to Chicago to her daughter's. Hopefully you don't get too lonely."

She shrugged. "Got Kyla. We'll do stuff. Which reminds me, how soon are you planning to get started on all this down here?"

"It's a long ways off yet. Why?"

"Would it be okay if Kyla and I used the basement during the winter? She asked me to make her a conditioning program, and this would be a great spot for workouts."

"As long as you don't make me join, have at it."

She laughed and tapped the heel of her shoe against the riser. A dreamy look swept over her face. "Been thinking more about going for that degree in fitness at MCC. Helping Kyla might give me a taste, you know?"

I nodded. "It's a fabulous idea." If only Thea could hear it too.

Tap, tap. "Yeah." She let her gaze drift to the floor. "She said if I am going to be her coach, though, I can't drink anymore. Coaches don't drink."

"Clever girl."

Austie glanced at me. "It's also because her dad struggles. That's why her pop doesn't let him come around."

Until that revelation, Kyla's full family life had never been a discussion point. It explained a lot, particularly her esteem for honesty.

"What did you tell her?" I asked.

"That I wouldn't." She straightened, looked into my eyes. "And I'm going to keep that promise."

A smile came to my lips. "I have no doubt you will." Labels were heavy things to lift, but not impossible.

"Gonna go change my clothes." She waved and started to turn upstairs.

"If you haven't eaten yet," I said, bringing her to a stop, "I was thinking of going to price out some cabinets and stuff. Want to go? We could get some lunch."

"Thanks, but I'm meeting up with Demi and Max. They wanted to see the car."

I bit my lip, brought my hands off my waist, and fiddled with the tape roll. I had never tried to give her advice before, but in that moment, it seemed necessary. "Not trying to interfere, Austie, but considering what you just told me, I feel like I should say one thing. Some of my biggest mistakes were not actions but people."

No pinch came to her brow. No tightening of the mouth. Only a nod. "I got you. See you later, Jess." She bounded up the stairs.

The slap of her footfalls camouflaged my soft words into the empty room. "I really hope you do."

Labels may kill grace, but fools drown discernment.

37

I MOVED THE COOLER to my hip before attempting the porch steps. Behind me, Kyla wheeled my suitcase across the wood planks while Austie balanced both boxed pies in one hand and clutched the brown paper bag in the other.

"Tell your pop thank you again for letting me borrow his cooler," I said over my shoulder.

"He doesn't mind," Kyla said. "I can't even remember the last time we used it."

Sidewalk firmly under my feet, I swung the cooler back in front of me and proceeded through the nippy late afternoon toward Hank. Paul had let me off an hour early that Wednesday for the Thanksgiving break, so I made it a priority to get on the road while at least a sliver of day remained. Sunset was less than twenty minutes away as we traversed the front walk.

"What do you have in there, anyway?" Kyla asked.

"The usual Thanksgiving suspects. Sliced turkey, gravy, potatoes, green beans, rolls." All thanks to the deli staff of Cost Cutter. Austie's employee discount had proven quite useful yet again. I set the cooler next to Hank and popped open the passenger door. With only a little wriggling, I slid the cooler onto the floorboard and turned to take the suitcase from Kyla.

Her fingers brushed my hand as we exchanged the top handle. They were icicles, as surely as her bare legs were. At least she wore a hoodie with her shorts and sandals.

"I wish Pop would get a traditional Thanksgiving meal sometime," she said as I rotated the suitcase to lay horizontally. "We're having barbecue. Seymour always brings us some of his smoked brisket for lunch. He's, like, super into barbecuing. Pop says he won a bunch of competitions."

"No kidding?" I set the suitcase on top of the cooler, ensuring the end would not go past the edge of the seat, then I faced Austie. "Sounds like you'll be noshing on the handiwork of a pitmaster."

She grinned and held out the pies. "Can't wait."

The Cost Cutter meal included two whole pies, one pumpkin and one pecan, and that seemed like a spoil of riches for a small gathering of Beckers. I nestled the pecan, Dad's preference, into the passenger seat, then held out the pumpkin to Kyla. "Sounds like you need a little Thanksgiving in your Thanksgiving. Take this to your pop as a thank-you."

When she hesitated, I added, "You all might need it since there'll be three of you this year."

She looked at Austie. "You like pumpkin pie?"

"Love it."

At last convinced, Kyla cradled the pie in her arms like a treasure.

Austie chuckled. "Thanks for thinking of me, Jess."

"Bet," I said with a wink, then took the last item from her. The bag crinkled around the bottle hidden inside. My dad's favorite brand of whiskey, a gift for him to pair with the pecan pie and perhaps shake loose some of those preconceived notions. I tucked the gift into the gap between the cooler and the door frame. The cover provided by the bag had been for Kyla's sake, though she may have known all about veiled bottles.

Before leaving the cabin, I unzipped the front pocket of my suitcase and slid my hand inside. My fingertips brushed against the floor plans drawn on notebook paper. They contained careful notes, estimated dimensions, and plenty to discuss. They were, in the end, the only preparations for my impending conversation with Dad that hadn't fallen flat. I still had nothing coherent and convincing to say about why it was so important for him to move in with me. No persuasive argument to lead with. For a week and a half, I had contemplated, practiced in the mirror, tried to glean a few pointers from an online article titled "How to Talk to Your Loved Ones About Your MS Diagnosis," but most of the advice was far too in-the-feelings to work on Dad or sound natural coming from me. The best I could do was formulate an opener: *Dad, there's something I need to talk to you about, and I ask you to hear me out.*

I zipped the pocket closed and shut the door. The chill of the afternoon seeped through my sweater and prickled my skin. I slipped my hands into the pockets of my jeans for whatever radiant warmth they could offer. "Guess that's everything. You two will keep a close eye on the house? You won't let anyone burn it down?"

"Your house will be fine." Austie tilted her chin up in confidence. "Your plants, your soda, your movie collection, everything."

"Especially the movie collection," I said, pointing at her. "And you're more than welcome to keep using the basement for workouts. But hopefully you give your player at least Thanksgiving evening off."

"Have to," Austie said. "They're going to her great-aunt's for dinner. But that just means double the high knees on Friday."

Kyla rolled her eyes.

"Glad I won't be here to see that." I retrieved my hands from their warming spot and rubbed them together. "All right, gotta get on the road. Have a happy Thanksgiving, and I'll see you Saturday."

After bumping fists with each of them, I climbed into the

cozy embrace of Hank and turned the ignition. Fifteen minutes to sunset. I eased out of the driveway, past Austie's car parked sideways at the top of the lot, and onto the street. In the yard, the girls stood side by side, their dark hair giving them a visible common bond to complement the unseen one.

I waved one last time, shifted into drive, then followed the pavement out of our neighborhood for my first trip back to Woodfield. We were all, in some way, creating a new Thanksgiving tradition.

When I reached the first red stoplight, I pulled out my phone and called Dad. It rang through to voicemail.

"It's me," I said after the beep. "Letting you know I'm headed out. Don't wait for me for supper. I'll pick up something on the way."

The call ended. The stoplight turned green. The wheels churned forward.

Soon, it was only me and Hank, on a road toward an unknown outcome, susceptible to the whims of circumstances. A familiar scenario.

The Allelon verse of the week had to do with living in harmony with one another, an instruction found in the book of Romans. Harmony was the opposite of discord, Gio had said. It involved wanting the best for one another, even if it meant personal sacrifice. It involved letting go of a critical spirit in favor of a gentle and quiet one. It involved seeking to understand rather than making snap judgments and not putting people at a distance with a long list of "you should" imperatives. I couldn't expect Dad to understand all that or to act according to a command he was not under.

But I prayed he would anyway.

38

NIGHTFALL HAD SHROUDED Woodfield by the time I wheeled across Wood River on the edge of town, but I didn't need the help of the sun to know where the stream curved around a jut of land and how the gentle ripples glided by the willow rooted on that miniature peninsula. Many nights were spent there alone with my fishing pole, and more than a few nights with a cold can and the heat of company. No sun was needed to trace my way back to the steeple under which Jesus had broken the lull of that old life. Woodfield possessed some of the biggest moments of my time on earth, yet it seemed smaller, sparser, hollower than when I left.

Hank eased under the streetlights on the main strip. He at least fit right back in with the farm trucks and late-model sedans. Even in the busy evening hour, the activity on the strip was a fraction of that of Barry Road on any given midday. Vehicles huddled around three spots: the steakhouse that Gio vowed to bring Reva to, Shuckers bar, and the Red Rooster gas station. So much statement in that one fact.

I pulled into Red Rooster and parked in front of the store alongside several other vehicles. Hank's front end drank in the bleached light from the store's fluorescent bulbs. More than likely, Dad had only milk and beer to drink. Diet soda was a necessity, as was supper.

I stepped out. Wind blustered against my cheeks, carrying with it a strange aroma of gasoline and wet soil. Ahead of me, a man pushed through the main door, setting off the high-pitched chime that once haunted my sleep—a reminder of another long shift hefting boxes, selling lottery tickets to people with unreasonably high hopes, and cleaning up after teenagers who dared each other to smear chocolate bars on the restroom walls. That life was over too, but not by much.

The woman behind the counter gave a half-hearted hello when I entered, her home-dyed hair pulled back into a thin ponytail. She, too, probably heard the door chime in her sleep. I smiled at her, then wove through the aisles to the cooler where the multipacks were housed. The whiff of pizza and fried food sent a grumble through my stomach.

I pulled a six-pack of soda from the cooler and let the glass door slap shut. My reflection stared back at me. It was the same Jess—same hair, same face, same name—but different. I stood inside Red Rooster not as someone on payroll but as only a shopper. Someone who made far more than what she used to make and had an actual house and the start of a retirement savings. Anyone in town who saw the Jess of the reflection would see someone who had found a path to goals outside of Woodfield's confines. What they wouldn't see was how precarious it all was, teetering on a frail fulcrum. They wouldn't see those bright possibilities ahead of me laden with hints of gray.

I tore my gaze away and headed to the food warmer for a carton of chicken strips.

My stomach refused to stay quiet the whole time I paid for my purchases. As soon as the cashier mumbled, "Have a good one," I set the carton on top of the soda, popped open the lid, and pulled out a strip. The box was warmer than the food, but I ate all the same and carried my purchases toward the exit. I pushed open the door with my hip and folded back into the night. Three steps and one more large bite in, a woman called from behind me.

"Jess?"

Striding toward the doors was Jill Norman, the woman whose post had been my last vicarious update from Mick.

I shoved the food into my cheek and dropped the half-eaten strip in the carton. "Hey, Jill."

"Thought that was you." Her tight figure resembled the one she had commanded in high school. The strands of gorgeous hair framing her face bobbed with her movements as she walked over to me. "How you been?"

Chewing as quickly as possible, I nodded and gave a thumbs-up.

"Sorry to have caught you in the middle of eating. Didn't want to slip by you and not say hi. I heard you're in Kansas City now. You moved in July or something?"

I swallowed. "August." Right around the time of the party at Shuckers, with Mick and his new woman wearing the shiny ring that had never been meant for me. I told her about my new, steady job and cozy house in a great neighborhood—facts I didn't mind being repeated.

"Sounds like you're doing well," she said.

I shut the carton against the chill and discreetly wiped my fingers on my jeans. "How about you?"

"Same old, same old. Came by here to pick up some drinks for tomorrow. Are you visiting your dad for Thanksgiving?"

"Headed there now. Needed some food first. I doubt he has much more than Vienna sausages in his house at this point."

She laughed. "Sounds like my dad too. Though I assume your dad's special someone keeps him well stocked."

Of course Dad had given the town of less than one square mile some excitement to twitter about, though it remained to be seen how much of it was accurate. There had been a number of rumors about why Mick and I broke up, none of them wholly true and most of them not in my favor.

"By the way . . ." She glanced to the side as if checking for any other ears in range. "Is it weird for you? That they're together, I mean?"

I shrugged. "He's never dated before, so it's weird in that way, I guess. But he's a grown man. He can date if he wants."

"Right, but I mean, it's gotta be weird. Isn't it?"

Whatever it was she dug for or why, experience said not to get tangled in the web, and the cold that leaked through my sweater said to get back to warmth. "It's fine." I nodded toward my truck. "Better get on with it. He's expecting me."

"Totally, yeah. Good to see you, Jess."

"You too, Jill."

We waved and went our separate ways, probably for another year or more. The door chime stung the air as I rounded Hank to the driver's side.

Dad probably didn't have a clue regarding the chatter circulating about him and his lady friend. The boys in the shop wouldn't have dared ask him if they had heard something.

Another certainty stood out from that interaction with Jill: It wasn't Dad who had sparked the wildfire of wagging tongues. In his rule book, family stuff was meant for the family alone, and sometimes not even that widespread. In the first weeks after Mom died, he refused to accept any meal brought to our doorstep and changed the subject if anyone brought her up, including me.

If it wasn't him who stoked the embers, that left only one viable culprit. Someone whose identity he had yet to reveal. A female someone in whom he may have confided everything, even things about his daughter.

The contents of the conversation I needed to have with him were not the kind of thing I wanted whispered about over back fences and among the barstools. Which cast a large question mark over the entire plan.

39

RAVENOUS HUNGER and nervous energy proved a potent combination when it came to finishing off my supper on the go. All three chicken strips had disappeared down my gullet by the time I pulled into Dad's driveway. Hank's headlights brushed over the pristine red paint and polished chrome accents of Dad's Sierra truck. I parked beside it. His house may not have been the cleanest, but his GMC got the royal treatment. The tired porch light tried its best to illuminate the front walk, and the glow of the living room lamps wrapped around the partially open curtains.

More than three months had passed since I had set foot inside the house that protected all my earliest memories. Three months and one season change. The humid summer had faded to early fall sunsets, yet the house itself remained as it always had been. Inside waited the human whose smile meant the most to me.

I turned off the engine.

Transferring everything from Hank to the house would require more than one trip, but I consolidated where I could anyway. The bagged bottle of whiskey and the empty chicken strip carton fit inside the cooler. The six-pack of soda balanced easily on the cooler lid. That left only the pie and my suitcase to come back for.

I hoisted the first load and headed up to the front door. The closer I got, the more the sirens and tire screeches of Dad's favorite detective show bled through the wood. I knocked with my foot.

The television noises muted. A moment later, the light of the living room splashed across my face. Dad grinned from the doorway, the plume of hair sticking out from the back of his head as usual. "Hey, Jess."

My heart leapt. "Hey, Dad. Happy Thanksgiving."

"Need some help?" That meant he had missed me.

"Nope, got it." I had missed him too.

He shuffled to the side and let me pass. His cane was propped against the arm of his recliner. On the end table next to his chair sat an open can of beer and a half-eaten burrito. The TV flashed silent images of *Blue Bloods*. All the things that hopefully would play out in a comfortable house on a narrow street two hours away.

An unfamiliar smell wafted over me. I paused by the couch, sniffing. "What's that scent?"

"Made myself some food."

"It's not the burrito I smell. It's fruity, kind of."

"Must be that, then." He pointed at an air freshener plugged into an outlet by the door. "Island Breeze or something."

The boys at the shop would have had plenty to say about that decision. At least Island Breeze was far better than the trace odor of engine the house typically bore.

"Got any more in your truck?" He craned his neck to peer outside.

"I do, but I can get it."

"Might as well make myself useful." Leaving the door open, he hobbled out into the night.

"Take your cane at least!" I called after him.

His reply was too garbled to understand.

"Stubborn as ever," I mumbled, then hauled my load into the kitchen, but my heart lifted a little more. He truly had missed me.

My back cried in joy when I set the cooler down on the floor next to the refrigerator. A magnet from his insurance agent held up the high school football schedule. All the home games were highlighted in yellow, documentation of where he had been every Friday night from September to mid-November, including the night I was in the ER. I picked up the pack of soda and pulled open the door.

As it turned out, Dad did have a stock, and it was well beyond the bachelor fare. Milk, eggs, juice, grapes, strawberries. Just like Jill had suggested I would find. In fact, all around the kitchen, more clues of a woman's influence showed. The end of the counter by the entrance was no longer cluttered by mail. The sink sparkled in the absence of dirty dishes. His work boots rested on a new rubber shoe mat by the garage door.

"Interesting." Had it really gotten to the point that he was changing his home for her?

Dad lumbered inside. His uneven steps mixed with the light rumble of suitcase wheels, followed by the thump of the front door closing. I returned to the cooler to unload our holiday meal dishes and placed them amid the foodstuffs he clearly had not purchased for himself.

"Got cold out there," he said as he came into the kitchen with the boxed dessert (and his cane, a delayed obedience to my imploration).

"It's chilly," I agreed.

"Pie looks good, Jess. Been a while since I had pecan." He slid the box onto the counter where the mail used to pile up and stood admiring it.

"You can have some if you want," I said and grabbed the bagged bottle from the cooler. "Here's a little something to go with it."

He took the bag, leaned his cane against the lower cabinet, and extracted the whiskey. A low, slow whistle rang from his lips. "The good stuff."

"Up to you when you want to crack that open." I continued transferring items onto the refrigerator shelves. "Noticed you have a few more things in here. Didn't think you liked strawberries."

"Like to keep them on hand."

"Can only guess for who."

He smirked and set the bottle on the counter.

The tray of potatoes and container of gravy were the last to go in. I set them on top of the turkey and green beans, then shut the door. "What time is your lady friend going to be here for lunch tomorrow?"

"You really don't have to call her that."

I picked up the package of rolls and tossed them on the nearby counter. "You could tell me her name, then I won't have to."

He started to fold the paper bag. The crinkle stood as his answer.

"What time?" I asked.

His fingers worked the bag into a small, sloppy triangle. Dark oil stains still rimmed his fingernails. "Early."

The coy game again. I crossed my arms. "Meaning?"

He set off his lower jaw from his upper, the way he did when he had something uncomfortable to say.

"What?" I asked. "What's going on?"

His knuckles whitened as he squeezed the folds of the brown paper. "She'll be here around midnight, when she gets done with her shift in Emporia."

"Midnight?" Even as the word came out, all the clues collected together in one clear image. The air freshener. The shoe tray. The clean kitchen. The foods he despised sitting in his fridge. My stomach dropped. "Are you—does she live here?"

A direct question with only two possible direct answers. He committed only to a single, shallow nod.

I dropped my hands to my sides. "Dad."

He tossed the bag on the counter. The paper expanded with its freedom. "This is why I didn't want to tell you anything before. I knew you'd be all judgy. She and I both knew you would be."

I scrubbed my face. So much rode on this weekend, and the reunion threatened to veer off the rails after ten minutes. If we had any shot of making it through and getting to the real reason why I ensured we were together for the holiday, discord could not prevail. I had to model letting go of a critical spirit and seeking to understand. Harmony was the path to the future we both needed.

Cleansing my lungs with a deep breath, I slid my hands into my pockets. "My aim is not to judge but to understand. Surely you get that this comes as a surprise to me. Three weeks ago you weren't convinced you were dating, and now she's living here. It all seems so fast."

"Ain't got much time to be slow."

Desperation was never a good decision-making tactic. Those years spent on Mick were a living testament to that truth.

"It's my job to look out for you," I said. "That's all I'm trying to do."

"Don't need lookin' after. I'm fine as I am."

Said the man who had zero idea of what was being shared about his private business all around town—likely fueled by the woman who deemed me "judgy." A woman who must have been young enough to still be working late into the night in a city thirty minutes away.

"Will you at least tell me who she is?"

He flung his hands in the air. "Back to this again."

"You do realize I can just go to Red Rooster and find out in two seconds?"

"Ain't no one there who—"

"They know, Dad. Trust me on that. I ran into Jill Norman tonight, and even she knows. So just tell me. Who is she?"

His brow narrowed, a visible part of his mental calculations.

As if determining I was correct, he snatched the mangled bag and squeezed it back into its compressed shape. "Bonnie Gregory."

I sank against the edge of the counter. Jill had looked at me like I was clueless because I was. She had insisted it was weird because it was.

"You're dating Mick's aunt?"

No, he was *living with* Mick's aunt. She and I had been to several of those family Thanksgiving dinners together, her always with a deep-cut neckline, loud voice, and wild tales, often at others' expense. That was the woman he had allowed into his life—and back into mine by extension. He had made us both the subject of sentences that started with "Did you hear?"

I clutched my arms to my stomach. "Why, Dad?"

"See? I knew you'd get bent out of shape."

"I'm not bent out of shape. I'm asking why."

"Why not? I can date who I want. Is it because you never got over Mick?"

I righted. "What?"

"That's what Bonnie thinks."

My fists balled. That woman knew nothing of me anymore. She had barely known me back then, not the real me, only the me I was compelled to convey.

I seized the empty chicken strip carton from the cooler and crushed it in my hand. "You don't have to worry about that." I marched to the trash can near the garage door and hurled the wadded carton inside.

"Don't know why you're so upset about this," he said to my back. "I never cared for that Mick but didn't say anything."

The sting pierced my heart. If only he had said something. If only he had cared enough to save me from myself. My relationship with Mick had been rooted in the convenience of proximity and a fear of what might happen if my standards were higher. The price paid for convenience was so much higher than Dad realized—yet another reason why I needed to get him out of here, away from this town, even if the plan only became more complicated.

I rubbed at the burn in my eyes. If a gentle and quiet spirit spoke louder than argument, like Gio had said on Sunday, then I could only hope mine shouted loud enough.

I dropped my hand and faced him. "I don't want to fight. We haven't seen each other for months, and I want nothing more than to enjoy the time we have together."

He worked the bag and kept his eyes averted. Maybe his silence was an unspoken agreement to at least think about it.

I headed for the living room. "Gonna go unpack."

The closer I came to him, the farther away he turned his head.

My face burned as I crossed the living room. All the memories that had been built in our home together became like friction dragging against the unfolding present.

40

EVERY JOINT, MUSCLE, tendon, and inch of marrow complained as I pushed off the thin pillow the next morning. After the tense evening with Dad, sleep had been sporadic. The rock-hard bed Bonnie had brought from her house, complete with a gaudy bedspread that reeked of cheap dryer sheets, didn't help. Nor did her arrival at quarter after midnight, right as I had begun to sink into dreams. She and Dad had stayed up and talked in the living room, where he had waited for her in his recliner. When they finally went to his room, I covered my head with the sheet, queasiness tumbling in my stomach.

As the morning sun plied through the spaces between the mini-blind slats, I massaged the pulsating ache in my temples and eased into a seated position. In the hall, Dad's door opened. Two sets of footsteps padded on the carpet. Bonnie said something about breakfast as they passed by my room. Dad grunted.

Heaven only knew what he had shared with her about our conversation in the kitchen. Considering the way things ended, he gave her something to add to her list of reasons to label me judgy. Facing her would require all the painkiller I could responsibly ingest.

I swung my legs to the floor and eased up with a heightened body awareness that had become my norm. After confirming all limbs were functioning and sensitized, I stretched my arms high above my head. Pops and creaks brought a smidgeon of relief to some of the stiffer joints.

Dad kept a robust supply of medication in the bathroom across the hall. I tiptoed to the door and cracked it open as quietly as possible. In the kitchen, a drawer opened, silverware clanked. Bonnie's voice carried unhindered through the house.

"You should have seen him," she said. "You would have had a fit. All that sobbing and talking about how the court would rule against him and take away his kids. He was a mess. Manager had to send him home early."

I dodged into the bathroom. Whoever the poor soul was she blabbed about, he didn't deserve to be analyzed by people who didn't have skin in his game. Why would Dad want to be involved with anyone who made sport of other people's pain? Deep down, he had to desire some version of "live in harmony" too, and that, by necessity, could not include her. Somehow, I needed to get time alone with him, to convince him to listen, to tell him all the things my daughter's heart wished to say.

After a dose of Aleve, I readied myself for the day, donning my best pair of jeans and a cotton shirt with orange flowers and a neckline appropriate for women over forty. I styled my hair and took extra care with my makeup. Satisfied with what showed in the mirror, I steeled myself and headed for the kitchen.

Dad saw me first, looking up from his place at the table. In front of him sat a bowl of oatmeal with sliced strawberries strewn on top. He hated oatmeal. He hated strawberries. Across the table, Bonnie perched in the chair I used to occupy, and before me, Mom. She was unaware of my entrance and had paused her chatter long enough to slip a dainty spoonful into her mouth.

"Morning," he said.

Her eyes zipped to me.

I froze in place.

"Jess! There you are!" She sprang from her seat. Her gold bracelets jangled as she came at me full bore.

Before I could stop it, her hug was upon me. Her ample chest smashed against me as her hair-sprayed strands bristled across my cheek. We had never hugged each other. Ever.

"Bonnie," I said. "Long time."

She pulled back and cupped my shoulders. Her smile and gaiety screamed performative. "You look good. How have you been?"

A sour taste crept into my mouth. "Fine. How are you?"

"Can't complain. It's Thanksgiving!"

I nodded. "Happy Thanksgiving." Her fake nails dug into my skin. I took a half step back, prompting her to release me from her grip.

Her ruby-red lips stayed high and wide. "I suppose Kevin told you about us."

Kevin? Like he was just some guy we both knew and not my father? "He did," I said.

They were easily ten years apart. In so many ways, they didn't belong together. Why couldn't he see it?

She wrinkled her nose in faux camaraderie. "Kinda ironic us being together, huh?"

Dad's gaze moved between us.

"Unexpected," I said.

She laughed. "For us too. I don't think either of us were looking to find love at this age."

Dad quickly focused on his bowl and swirled his spoon around the contents.

Not that I had vast experience from which to draw, but it sure seemed that love didn't compromise values. Lust did, but not love.

Bonnie's neckline plunged in a deep V, exposing the web of veins under the thinning porcelain skin of her chest. Her hair, perpetually dyed to a youthful brown, flowed in carefully curated waves over her shoulders. Everything about her was as curated as the gossip she loved to spout.

I forced a polite smile, then stepped over to the refrigerator.

"Got breakfast laid out on the table," she said. "Good bowl of oatmeal is the best way to start the day."

My sodas were perfectly chilled after a long night on the shelf. I grabbed one. "Not too hungry yet, but thank you."

"If you change your mind, help yourself to anything we have."

I should be saying those words to her. I should be the hostess, not the other way around. I leaned against the counter and cracked open the soda. It was bound to be a long day. A long weekend.

"By the way, Jess," Bonnie said as she returned to the table, "I was looking at the dishes you brought and thought maybe we needed a bit more balance. Maybe another vegetable or some fruit. If you want, I could roast some carrots."

Though it was a bit of a slight toward my gift, her suggestion inspired an idea. An excuse to get Dad alone.

I pushed off the counter. "That's a good idea. I can run up to Emporia real quick to get another side, maybe a salad mix. Dad, would you want to come with me?"

He looked up with a frown. "You can't go on your own?"

"I wouldn't mind the company. Maybe there's something else you need from the store."

He shook his head. "I'm set."

Bonnie reached across the table and swatted his hand playfully. "Honey, she's wanting your company. You should go."

The fact she was on my side mostly outweighed the fact she had called him by a pet name in front of me.

Dad shifted in his chair.

"Go," Bonnie said. "And you never know, maybe she'll stop and get you the sausage biscuit I know you'd rather be eating." She giggled and winked at me like she knew oh so much about him.

Whether it was the promise of a fat-laden breakfast or the persuasion of the woman occupying his table, Dad relented. A trip to Emporia meant we would be alone for at least an hour. I would use every minute of it.

God, give me the words.

41

DAD WASN'T MUCH BETTER than Kyla when it came to dressing appropriately for the cold weather. Despite the windchill being deep in the thirties, he wore only a Snap-on jacket over his flannel long-sleeve shirt. He did, however, wear jeans to cover his legs. Using his cane for leverage, he pushed himself up into the passenger seat of Hank. I waited until all of him was safely inside, then shut the door.

Bonnie waved from the front step. "Have fun!"

Fun was not the right word. Reva would have come up with the right one. She would have had the entire conversation with Dad mapped out, with Scripture references to boot. Not me. My legs quivered as I crossed in front of Hank to the driver's side door. I bit my lip and got in.

"Truck still looks nice," Dad said as he attempted to match his seat belt's latch plate to one of the buckles at his hip. After watching several of his failed tries, I reached over and raised the correct buckle high enough for his hands to find it.

"I take care of the things I love," I said.

His eyes grazed mine over the click of the buckle. Then he turned to Bonnie.

She waved again, more exuberant than before.

"Don't feel right leaving her alone," he said.

"You're leaving me alone all evening to go to her family's dinner."

"Come with us, then. Everyone knows you anyway."

"Which is exactly why I won't be going." I started the engine and shifted into reverse.

Dad shook his head at my reply, wedged his cane between his knees, then lifted a hand with fingers more bent than ever to wave at Bonnie.

We wheeled backward into the street. The church steeple held its skinny cross above the treetops, like a farewell salute of its own.

"Emporia, here we come." I edged us forward, slowly at first, then gaining speed.

Two turns later, we were on the main strip. At that early hour on a holiday, few others were out. The gas station had a single car parked in its lot, which likely belonged to the cashier. The steakhouse was closed. Shuckers was shuttered, at least until after the family dinner ended. By that point on a holiday, everyone needed to tie one on, or so Mick's marketing philosophy went. The actions of his customers always proved him right. Bonnie would no doubt stop in too, "to say hey," but really to look for a fresh harvest of what kept her going. How could Dad be so oblivious about her? More importantly, why was she really with him?

We traced down the thoroughfare. Up ahead was the river and the bridge that would transport us out of the town. I could gun it, drive and drive until we were at my house. How easy it would be to just take him and root him where he was much more likely to thrive, away from people he shouldn't trust. I could thrust him into a new life before he was thrust into a broken one.

Closer, closer the bridge came. The water slipped underneath in steady, determined movement away from Woodfield, as if even it understood the perils of sticking around too long. How could I let him stay? I couldn't.

The entrance to the riverside park opened on the other side of the road. I jerked the steering wheel hard to the left. Hank banked across the opposing lane and into the park.

Dad threw his arms out to brace himself. "What are you doing?"

We rumbled over the pocked gravel lot, kicking up dust behind us. When we reached the far edge that ran parallel to the shoreline, I hit the brakes.

"What in the world, Jessica?"

I ripped the keys from the ignition and turned to him. "We need to talk."

He groaned a curse and slapped his hands in a pile on top of his cane. "If this is about Bonnie—"

"Do I not have the right to ask questions? As your daughter, do I not have a right to understand? Because ultimately this isn't about her. It's about you. It's about us."

He sighed and stared out his window toward the bridge that we should have been crossing.

"Why did you have Bonnie move in?"

"I already told you."

"You gave a reason for why you started dating her, not for why she's living with you."

"What difference does it make?"

"Why, Dad?"

He started to look back at me but settled on the windshield and fiddled with his cane handle. "She doesn't have any kids. I don't have any at home. It made sense."

It didn't. It was a flimsy excuse, and I pressed into it. "Are you going to get married?"

"What? No."

"Are you even in love with her?"

He shot me a look. In my childhood, a response like that would have tied my lips tight and sent me scuttling for cover. But I wasn't a kid anymore. I held my chin level, waiting.

He heaved a sigh and turned back to the passenger window. A car passed over the bridge. The sun glinted off its roof. He watched it until it glided around a curve and out of sight.

Reva had been so calm, so patient with Austie. I channeled her unflappable nature as best I could. "The biggest lesson I learned in my years with Mick is that you have to make sure the person you choose to hitch your wagon to is someone you trust with every little thing in that wagon. Your money, your possessions, your well-being. Your privacy."

He flicked his eyes my direction, then pulled them back to his window.

"You have to trust them so deeply that if something happens to you, you wouldn't dare think of anyone else to have at your side. Is she that someone for you? Do you see her driving you around when you can't anymore? Wiping your mouth when you can no longer chew? Bathing you?"

He slung a swear word and pierced me with a glare. "Why you gotta be so over the top?"

But he needed to hear it, to think about it. "I would be that person for you. I would do all those things. I would wash your clothes and keep track of your medicines and bring you soup. Because—" My chest hitched at the touch of the rare words on my tongue. "Because *I* love you. I want to take care of you, for the rest of your life."

He clawed the air between us and looked away. "Jess, stop."

Ignoring his request, I leaned toward him, pulse quickening. "I would stay with you in the ugly. Because in the end, we are all either of us has. You and me."

He shook his head, refusing every plea.

When I'd sat in the ER bed hundreds of miles away, I had called him and prayed for him to answer. He hadn't. In that moment, I sat an arm's length away and prayed for him to answer. Would he? "Please, Dad. We need each other."

He scrunched his face and threw back, "Don't need nobody."

The barb of it ripped open the fragile storehouse of tears. I squeezed my eyes shut, but it did no good. Streams cut sharp courses down my cheeks. I let them. He would see me cry, and I would let him. My voice cracked. "But *I* need *you*, Dad."

His attention swerved to me. Heat rose in my wet face as he took me in with those narrowed gray eyes behind the cloudy lenses. "What are you talking about?"

My chin trembled with the gravity of the moment I had tried so hard to imagine but could never make crystallize. The moment that would change his view of me forever. Us, forever.

Every muscle fought against the release of the truth. "I have MS."

His brow dove deeper. "You what?"

I had said it. He had heard. No taking it back. I was exposed. A fresh wave of tears swelled. Shadows and light muddled together in a chaotic jumble. I wiped and wiped, smearing off all my carefully applied makeup in the process, until my hands were soaked and streaked black and brown. My breath came in irregular gasps.

"Since when, Jess?"

I dried my hands on the inside of my shirtwaist, where stains wouldn't matter, and sucked at air until I could speak and my vision was clearer. "Found out about two months ago. Had symptoms for a while."

"Before you moved?"

I nodded, dragging my entire palm over my cheek.

"And you still moved?"

"Didn't know I had MS. I thought it was a pinched nerve."

"Maybe it is."

I rubbed my palm with the hidden part of my shirt. "It's not, Dad. They've run the tests."

He fell silent and looked out at the river. Did he think of Mom? All her appointments and prescriptions? Did he think of the precariousness of life with a chronic illness? Did he at last understand why I wanted him close?

"I'm doing well now," I said. "But I will need support. There will likely be days I can't drive or walk." Or worse, but that was for another time.

He stared at the flowing water. When he spoke, his voice, for the first time, had softened. "You know your room's always open."

I winced. "No, Dad. I can't leave KC. Not now."

He faced me. "Why not? Thought your job was a from-home thing."

"It is. But my doctor would be there."

"Can't find one in Emporia?"

The small city was big enough to have more than one endocrinologist for Mom, but not the kind of help my disease demanded.

"It's not that simple," I said. "Not with MS."

His expression hardened. "So what, then? You want me to move up there with you, is that it?"

The fire that had warmed my cheeks reignited in the center of my chest. It whipped at the strength in my voice. "I really do think you'd like it."

He huffed. "You might know my whiskey, Jess, but you definitely don't know my likes. If you want help, my help is here. You can't expect others to uproot everything because you want them to."

"But—"

He whacked his cane against the mat. "I'm not moving! That's final!"

My mouth tried desperately to form words. His only offer to help, his only show of compassion, was on his terms. He would watch out for me, but only if it didn't cost him too much. Had that been why he took me in after the breakup? Because it didn't cost him anything?

"Look at it this way," he added. "If you moved back to your room, you'd have Bonnie to help too."

The fire erupted, sending flames up and out through my words. "I am not having her anywhere near me!"

In the face of my rage, his reply was cool, his shrug chilling. "Sounds like you're the one too stubborn to change, then."

He didn't care. His only child was suffering under a load too heavy, and he refused the yoke. Instead, he heaped more burden on, requiring enormous sacrifice for the privilege of his help. The blaze within me numbed everything. I could focus only on the bowtie emblem in the middle of the steering wheel.

"Sorry," he said without an ounce of remorse in his tone. "That's how it is."

I hunched against the hardness of his words. That's how it was.

"I think it's best if I leave this afternoon," I said.

"Do what you want," he bit out.

42

AS SOON AS WE WALKED back into the house, Dad went straight for the whiskey and then his recliner. He stayed there the rest of the morning, nursing a two-finger depth and muttering at the parade on TV to end already. I stayed in the kitchen, mixing the salad and babysitting the prepared food as it warmed in the oven.

To her credit, Bonnie said nothing about the change of mood or my ruined makeup, perceptive enough to not pick at the wound. At one point she did come into the kitchen where I huddled at the table with my phone and my second soda of the day and asked if there was anything she could do to help. Assuming she meant with lunch, I told her I had it handled and sent her back to the living room to field Dad's complaints about not knowing who in the world the B-list celebrities hamming it up for the cameras were.

I only went near the living room when I had to, whether to grab silverware to set the table or to check on the food in the oven. One of those times, a hushed conversation underlaid the excitement of the announcers. Bonnie spoke first, her voice too soft for her words to be clear. But Dad's response rang vibrant: "No!"

After a lunch that lasted long enough for Bonnie to recount her favorite parts of the parade and her one experience being on a float, Dad retired again to his recliner for his annual marathon of football games, which I had promised to watch with him. It was supposed to have been the highlight of my stay with him. In reality, he refused to look at me. His cane smacked against the floor like a string of exclamations.

I quickly stacked plates and took them to the sink. Active hands led to a stilled tongue.

"Let me help you clean up," Bonnie said as she brought over the silverware and glasses.

"You don't have to." I flipped on the hot water and doused the basin with dish soap. A foam soon formed on the surface of the water.

"Are you sure? Because I don't mind missing football. It's all he ever watches."

The TV kicked on, pulling the NFL theme song into the house. He was probably pushed back in his chair, feet up, hands folded across his belly, which I had filled by my own money and time. In that supine position, he would doze off and on until it was time for pie.

"It's okay, Bonnie. I got it. But maybe you could see if he wants more whiskey now or with his dessert."

For a moment, she lingered at my side, watching me dip the cups into the water. Maybe she felt the loneliness of that statement too. The pie and whiskey I had picked especially for him, to treat him, to please him, and he ate and drank and watched as if I wasn't there.

She nodded. "Good idea."

When she left the room, the air rushed from my lungs. With it came a press of tears. I bowed my head, kinking the hose of their flow. More crying would do no good. If it didn't affect him the first time, it never would.

I took my time washing what few dishes we had dirtied. The hot water turned my hands pink. As I set the last plate to dry in the rack, my phone chimed in the back pocket of my jeans.

It was a picture from Austie to Reva and me. In it, she sat with Kyla and Ron at their meal of smoked brisket and sides of coleslaw and cheesy corn. Austie's smile was the widest of them all. Accompanying the picture was a simple message.

Happy Thanksgiving!

A moment later, another picture came through, from Reva. She was crouched in an apron with her arms around two of her grandchildren. Each child wore a chef's hat. One held up a wooden spoon smeared with mashed potatoes. In the background, her daughter smiled at the memory being captured in her kitchen.

Reva's caption was more verbose.

Praise God for the many blessings we have!
Happy Thanksgiving, sisters!

It was my turn to add to the chat. But what did I have to take a picture of? Dad asleep in his recliner and Bonnie looking bored on the couch next to him? A stack of clean dishes? No photos had been captured of our meal, or of any of the memories made. And that was for the best. I sent a GIF of a turkey eating pie, wished them all a happy holiday, then took a wet paper towel to the table.

A half hour later, we ate pie in front of the TV. The only talking came from the people on the screen. Afterward, in the middle of me washing the plates and forks, Bonnie came into the kitchen. She wore heels, a cloud of perfume, and her coat.

"Hey, Jess, wanted to let you know that my sister asked me to come over and help her get things ready."

"Oh, okay." I rinsed the forks and slipped them into the rack with the others from lunch.

Bonnie looked over her shoulder at the living room doorway before adding, "Kevin's going with me."

I paused. "You mean right now?"

"Yeah, sorry. She's freaking out about having it all done in time for the family. Gotta go save her. It's what sisters do, right?" She smiled and glanced back at the doorway.

It was not even two o'clock. The TV was off. Dad's cane clicked against the living room floor. He was up and moving and headed even farther away from me.

I dried my hands and followed Bonnie to the next room. Dad was at the door, slipping his arms into his Snap-on jacket. While Bonnie strode toward him, I stopped near the coffee table.

"We should be back around ten or so," she said as she reached Dad and fixed his jacket collar.

"Probably won't see you again, then," I replied.

She frowned. "What do you mean?"

"She's going back to KC." Dad's words were about me but not directed toward me.

"Are you really?" Bonnie asked.

I nodded.

"Oh." Her face fell. She looked between us, the question right there under the surface. But she pushed it aside, at least in front of me. What she would ask or say when they were alone—or with her family—was another matter. "Thank you again for lunch, Jess. It was delicious."

"You're welcome."

Dad studied his hand that gripped his cane.

"Glad everything's going so well for you in Kansas City," Bonnie added. "Please don't be a stranger."

"Good to see you again, Bonnie."

Both of our gazes moved to Dad. When he didn't notice, she tapped his arm. His attention went to her first, then, as a flicker, to me.

"Drive safe," he said, then reached for the door.

Only Bonnie waved to me as they exited.

I rooted myself in place, my arms wrapped around my middle, until his engine grumbled down the street. Outside the window, the church steeple kept its eye on me. All my life it had had its eye on me, though as a mere background image most of that time. The stormy night I sat under it with all my earthly wealth and cried in my poverty, Tillie Watts had found me, brought me to shelter, sang over me with her choirmates. Theirs were songs about streaming grace and goodness that fettered hearts to heaven. Was it possible that I'd welcomed brokenness back then because I was naive enough to believe that all my problems would be solved if I just let go?

What would I do if—when—MS attacked again? What if I was the one who became bedridden? What if I was the one who could no longer chew? Had I ever really believed that Dad would be the one to stay in the ugly with me?

My bottom lip shivered. My legs weakened. I rushed to Dad's recliner and curled up on the sunken cushion. I planted my cheek against the worn upholstery embedded with his scent. There, in the embrace of his proxy, under the view of the steeple, I let every trapped word, every rejected floor plan, every design for the future, fall with the tears.

By the time the last one crashed, afternoon had softened to early evening.

43

THE ONLY THING I WANTED was my bed. My own bed with my own pillow that cushioned in all the right ways. The two-hour drive to Kansas City took an eternity. The city's pristine overpasses and wide lanes and towering high-rises were no longer the emblems of possibility; they were markers of how far away I was from the only family I had.

What would I do now?

I pulled into my driveway shortly before seven o'clock, almost exactly twenty-four hours after I had reversed out of it with a goodbye wave to Austie and Kyla. The front window glowed with light from the living room like a beacon directing me to the only solace I had remaining. My sweet bungalow, a holy reprieve in its own right.

Park. Engine off. I gathered the keys in my palm and exhaled slowly. The silence of the cab and the cold, still night enveloped me. But it could not drown out the snap of Dad's voice or the smack of his cane against the floor mat. I shook my head, shook off the haunts, and stepped out into the dark.

Despite the lights on in the house, Austie's car was missing from its normal place in the grass at the top edge of the lot. I checked my phone. No read receipt from the text I had sent her before leaving Woodfield to let her know to expect me. Maybe she had gone somewhere. Maybe with the Torreses to their extended family. Across the lot, our neighbors' vehicle was gone as well.

Maybe her not being there was a good thing. It gave me time to figure out how to face her questions about the turn of events and gather strength to cling to "everything's fine" appearances.

I went around to Hank's passenger side. The cooler was easier to tote now that it was empty. Every morsel it had transported to Woodfield had stayed in Woodfield, along with the floor plans, which I had left shredded and stuffed among the food scraps in the kitchen trash can.

Lightened cooler in one hand and the handle of my rolling suitcase in the other, I trudged up the front walk.

Bed. Pillow. Peace. All I wanted.

The suitcase wheels bumped against the steps as I ascended onto the porch. The light from the living room flooded over the boards, making my shoes almost luminescent under its touch. I took a step one split second before my gaze drifted to the glass—and locked onto the scene inside.

The blood froze in my veins.

Beer cans. Scattered on the coffee table. Discarded on the floor. Lined up on the kitchen pass-through window. Some lying on their sides, bent into Vs. A few inverted with brownish streaks fanning out from the rim.

The cooler dropped from my grip, clattering against the wood at the top of the steps. I rushed across the porch, pulling my suitcase behind me. The front door was unlatched. The strike rested against the end of the plate. A mere touch and the door gave way, opening to more irrefutable evidence that people had violated my home in untold ways and then fled. On the table, in corners, across the floor were more cans, bottles, crushed cigarette butts. One clear bottle lay on its side with its contents puddled on my hardwood. Mariah had been knocked over, dislodged from both her ceramic decorative pot and her drain pot, her roots dangling in open air. A crack snaked down the side of her ceramic pot. And that stench. The unmistakable, skunky stench.

I flung my suitcase and purse aside and flew toward Mariah. Her ceramic pot held as I set it upright. I tucked her into the plastic drain pot and slipped it inside the decorative one. With both hands, I scooped as much soil back in with her as I could and set her on the floor next to Shania's stand.

"I'm so sorry," I whispered and wiped a splatter from her leaf. The liquid carried the distinct sweet-spicy cologne of rum. She was covered in it. Which meant it had probably seeped into her soil.

I thrust myself up to standing, fists balled. Who had Austie let into my home? Why? Why would she do it?

A fried chicken box from Cost Cutter lay in the kitchen doorway. I kicked it aside as I passed. The refrigerator stood open. All my soda had been taken, likely mixed with the rum and vodka.

The bathroom was worse. Toilet lid up. Rug soaked. Sink spout trickling water. Medicine cabinet open and in disarray.

I slammed the faucet lever into the off position. "Why, Austie!"

Her door was closed, but her bedroom was the least of my concerns. Because my bedroom door gaped open, the opposite of how I had left it. My breath stuck in my lungs, fingernails dug into my palms. I stepped inside. The corner of my sock drawer angled open, wide enough for someone to reach in their hand. Had they been looking for money? Jewelry? They wouldn't have found either. I slammed the drawer shut and turned to my workstation. By the sheer grace of God, whoever had been in my intimate space hadn't bothered my laptop, either too drunk or too stupid.

I marched to her door, pounded three times. No answer. I threw open the door. It thudded against the stop and reverberated back, hitting my shoulder.

Empty room. Bed undisturbed. Closet closed and plastic set of drawers unbothered. Apparently her belongings were too precious to touch.

Why would she let those people into my house? Why would she ruin the trust I had in her? The trust Kyla had in her. I flopped against the threshold and buried my face in my hands. The same question kept howling over and over: Why? On its tail rode the second resounding question: Where was she? If there was even a small chance Austie would answer my call, I needed to place it.

I tore back to the front door, where my purse and suitcase waited. After locking the dead bolt tight, I fished my phone from my purse. As I located Austie in my contacts, I slung my purse strap over my shoulder and gathered my suitcase to my side for the trek to my room. The other end started to ring. A second later, an acoustic guitar melody floated from somewhere deeper in the house. I dashed toward it, across the living room, around the chicken box, down the hall, to my door. The melody glided from my top drawer.

I hung up, left my suitcase and purse in the hallway, then plunged my hand into the pile of socks and underthings. My fingers found Austie's phone, shoved deep among the cotton intimates.

A new kind of cold pulsed through me. Was she still in the house? I dropped both our phones onto my dresser and raced for the only other place in the house yet to be searched: the basement. From bedroom to basement door was normally a good ten steps. I reached it in about three and grabbed the knob.

It wouldn't budge. Since when did it lock? I jiggled it madly, as if that would somehow help. Then my knuckle brushed against a depressed button. I popped it, turned the knob, yanked open the door.

There was Austie. Sprawled sideways on the illuminated landing, head against the wall, pool of blood under her cheek. Motionless.

44

"AUSTIE!" I SCRAMBLED DOWN to the landing. My pulse hammered in my ears, nearly as loud as the thump of my feet. I eased over her body to the lower set of stairs and sank onto the first step. She lay on her right side, her face pointed to the basement, to me. Deep red streamed from her busted nose and fattened upper lip.

"Austie? Can you hear me?"

A soft moan. She was at least breathing. Her legs were elevated against the upper stairs. Her arms stuck out in front of her on the landing. My shins bumped against her fingers as I reached out and slid my hand under her cheek. Gently, I tilted her face up, bringing the injuries more fully into the light overhead. Her eyebrows puckered at the movement, then slackened. The skin over her nose had turned unnatural colors. Blood rivered down her cheek. An angry goose egg protruded from her right temple.

I needed to get her to a doctor. Fast.

"Austie, we gotta go. Hear me? We gotta go."

Northland Memorial was only minutes away. I would get her there. But somehow, I had to move her to Hank.

"Think, Jess."

The hallway light above threw its glow down to me. Taking

her up would mean reversing her body direction, then lugging her up the flight of steps, through the house, across the porch, down the front walk. I could hurt her even worse. And what if someone saw?

I turned to the basement. The outside door!

I thundered down the steps. At the bottom, I flipped on the light, then dashed across the outlines of masking tape to unlock the dead bolt. I flung open the door, creating a clear path out, then sped up the stairs.

"Be right back," I promised as I hurdled over her and onward to the main level. Pausing only long enough to grab my purse and our phones, I flew toward the front door, upsetting a beer can on the way. It ricocheted off the wall with a tinny clank. I locked the door behind me, tore across the porch and straight to Hank. Moments later, he idled mere steps from the basement entrance, and I was back at the helpless young woman.

"Here we go, Austie. I got you. I got you."

I rolled her onto her back, giving me more space to plant my feet on the landing. Crouching at her side, I slipped my forearms under her and lifted. In a series of heaves and tugs and scoots, I got her into a seated position, her right shoulder against my chest, her blood dripping onto my arm. Keeping her upright, I looped my arms under hers from behind, then clasped my hands white-knuckle tight around her ribs.

"Here we go. We can do this."

Heave. My legs straightened as much as her weight would allow them. Her rump lifted off the wood. Her shoulder blades pressed into my sternum, and her head flopped forward over her chest.

I would have to go down the stairs blind.

My right shoe scuffed along the landing until I found the lip. Right foot down to the tread below, pause, adjust, then the left.

Austie's limp body fought against my grip.

Next step down, taken one foot at a time. Then the next one.

Her feet clomped off the upper flight and onto the landing.

Next step. She grew heavier by the second. Her left shoe dragged through the pool of blood, smearing it over the planks.

Next step. Her shoes clomped onto the lower flight.

The farther I went, the harder she pressed against me, threatening to shove me off balance and send us both toppling to the concrete floor.

Next step. Clomp.

My grip began to slip. I dug my fingernails into my skin, clenched my teeth. I could do it. I had to do it. She needed me to do it.

Next step. Clomp.

Stars glinted in my peripheral vision. I could do it! *God, please, let me do this!*

"Jess?"

I went rigid.

From the open basement door, Ron asked, "What's going on?"

Had he seen the upstairs? Did he know? Inches from where I stood was where Austie had told me about Kyla's dad, and Ron's fortress around her.

Before I could answer, he backtracked across the threshold. "Kyla, go back to the house!"

My heart shot to my throat. I groaned and sank lower, begging God to shield the child's eyes.

Kyla protested, something about leftovers for Austie, but Ron didn't entertain it.

"Now, Kyla Jo! Go!" His anger pelted against me too. I bowed my head. My arms shook. The rest of me begged to collapse.

Footsteps rushed toward us, firm and swift. Then Ron was next to me, on the stairs, edging Austie out of my grasp.

"I've got her," he said. "Let go."

I wanted to say no. Wanted to tell him it wasn't what he thought. Instead, I flopped onto my backside, spent and shivering. Even at his age, he was stronger than me. He maneuvered

Austie up into the cradle of his arms like he carried the wounded every day of his life. The bloody side of her head nestled against his jacket. He reached the bottom of the staircase, then paused and nodded toward the door. "Make sure Kyla's gone."

The command lifted me to my feet. I hustled to the door. Across the lot, Kyla rounded into their open garage, then dipped out of sight. I nodded to him.

He trooped toward me with Austie secure in his grasp. "Open the truck."

I obeyed and waited by the opened passenger door. As he came near, I tried to speak, to explain.

"Get in," he instructed.

Unwilling and unable to argue, I cut through the headlight beams and climbed inside.

As he raised Austie into the truck, I guided her head and shoulders to rest in the middle seat. Ron's gaze avoided mine. His brow was pinched and his mouth drawn tight. Whatever the thoughts going through his head, he guided Austie's feet onto the floor mat, then handed me a handkerchief from his back pocket for her face. "I'll lock up."

Before I could find my voice to thank him, he shut the door. Austie's head jerked with the force and brushed against my leg. Her hair had splayed across her face. I smoothed it back, pulling it out of the sticky red. The light from the dash caught on the massive knot rising from her temple. I could take her to the hospital, ensure she got the medical attention she needed, but I couldn't stop the consequences from unfolding. If Ron found out what was upstairs, the impact of those consequences would not be limited to Austie.

45

UNDER THE RED ER AWNING, two men in scrubs loaded Austie onto a gurney and sped her through the sliding glass doors. I had only a moment to shut Hank's passenger door before a nurse rushed me inside behind them. She lobbed rapid-fire questions my direction. Austie's name, age, known injuries. I had time to tell her all I could before we reached the thick automated doors on the other side of the ER waiting area.

She veered into my path, bringing me to a stop. "Are you family?"

"Roommate," I said.

"We need to get her stabilized before we let anyone back. Wait out here."

"But—"

"Out here." She hurried after the men. The door sealed behind her, shutting me off from the young woman whose blood still speckled my skin and whose limp weight still haunted my arms.

"You can have a seat, ma'am."

I turned toward the new voice.

The nurse behind the check-in desk pointed at the bank of thin-framed chairs. "Someone will be out to talk to you soon."

Soon. Such an empty promise in a chaotic, friendless place.

I gestured toward the entrance. "Got to park my truck."

The nurse looked down at her computer screen as if not hearing my response at all. Maybe I hadn't said anything. Maybe my voice was only in my head, and to everyone else, I stood there dumb and gaping, with a thousand questions pounding against the inside of my skull and the inability to shake the image of my friend's crumpled body. My friend who, only hours before, had smiled the biggest of all over a Thanksgiving meal of brisket.

In a daze, I retreated through the lobby, past the handful of other waiting people—none of whom seemed to care about my movements either—and back to Hank. I secured myself inside the cab and grasped the top of the steering wheel with both hands. The firmness of it was a reassurance, the vibration of the engine a steady, even soothe. Hank could shut out the world, but not the confusion it had wormed into my mind. The fizzling adrenaline burned the muscles of my arms, buzzed the length of my legs. Every part of me ached to shut down.

I shifted into drive. My headlights swung away from the building and into the thick night. Hank filled a spot on the mostly empty front row. The illuminated red marking the ER doors was more ominous at that angle. More menacing than a bile-green sky. A stone's throw away was the wide awning under which, not so long ago, a nurse had delivered me to a waiting van. Not so long ago, I had been the patient sucked through the automated doors of the ER. The hospital had swallowed me, isolated me to a bed, angled an IV into my vein, subjected me to the cold touch of stethoscopes and strangers' hands and the terror of language I didn't understand. Austie would wake up to that, would be thrust into a sequence of events she had no say over by outsiders she was expected to trust.

I tightened my hands around the steering wheel. In the low light, the blood splatters on my forearm were inky blemishes on my pale skin. Ron's unused handkerchief lay on the floor. I grabbed it and blotted them away.

Grief and anger lashed against me in equal strength. Why would Austie shatter her promises? Who had she allowed in my house? How dare she, but also had they done something to her? How had she ended up like that on the stairs of a locked basement?

I tossed the cloth aside and pressed my forehead on the wheel between my thumbs. A dull ache crept up from my shoulder blades into my neck. There was no making sense of the day. It had begun in a home I could no longer be in and ended at the place I never wanted to return to.

Amid the tempest of questions, two answers rang clear. I needed to get back into the waiting room in case "soon" really was soon, and Reva needed to know what was going on. I pushed off the steering wheel and dug my phone out of my purse. As I pulled up Reva's name in my contacts, I tried to form some coherent way of telling her about the events over the last hour. Even as our phones connected over the distance, the explanation proved too slippery to shape.

Reva barely had out her "Hi, Jess" before the mass tumbled from my mouth. Each sentence smashed into the next one, detail stuttered into detail, about my early arrival home and the missing Beetle and the crushed cans and Austie's crumpled body and Ron's furrowed brow.

When the last words rambled out and I came up for air, Reva, in her Reva way, spoke with a calmness beyond comprehension. "Oh, Jess, what an evening you've had."

Somehow, despite my communication failures, she had collected the random pieces and put them all together in an order that made sense.

"First of all," she said, "you did exactly the right thing getting her to the ER. Second, I can't imagine what it must have been like to come home to such a situation. How are you doing?"

"Me? I'm good."

Her silence told me she didn't believe it.

I squeezed the bridge of my nose with my free hand. "Guess I'm feeling a wee bit powerless at the moment." Impotent, feeble, small. Those were even better descriptors.

"Jess, that is the first deeply honest thing you have ever said to me."

I pulled my hand away, a protest poised on my lips. But it soon withered, shrunken by the light of truth. My fingertips found the bridge of my nose again and massaged in small circles.

"If it helps," she said, "you feel powerless because you are."

That was supposed to help?

"Trust me, it's a good thing," she said, my thoughts still so obvious to her even when she couldn't see me. "It's a reminder for us all who really has the power."

I dropped my hand to my lap and let my head slump back against the seat. My eyes pointed up, but all that was there was the dim ceiling of the cab. Impotent, feeble, small. That wasn't a reassurance. It was exhausting.

"I'm guessing you have many of the same questions I do about what happened at your house," Reva said. "I suspect we will understand everything clearly once Austie is awake and can tell us. Until then, let's avoid the temptation to write any stories of our own. What she needs more right now is exactly what you're doing—a readiness to help."

That was more than a direction; it was a permission. It was okay to turn off my overextended brain and focus on taking up my watch. I closed my eyes and exhaled. "I plan to stay here until someone tells me how she's doing," I said. "Hopefully they let me see her before long."

"Yes, hopefully. And in the meantime, there is something else we can do. The most powerful 'one another': pray."

The answer seemed inevitable. It seemed to be the most popular Christian answer. It was what people claimed in social media posts that they were doing in times of tragedy. It was what members of Allelon promised to do when someone shared something hard—or used as a cover for gathering details about someone else's life. I had shot up prayers several times that week. Prayer certainly wouldn't hurt, but it also wouldn't stop the consequences from engulfing Austie.

"How about you start and I'll finish?" Reva asked.

I pushed off the headrest. "You mean pray right now?"

"Of course. What did you think I meant?"

In private. Individually. Where no one could hear my muddled heap of words. "I'm not—I mean, I'm sorry. The day is catching up to me. My mind isn't quite tracking. Do you mind praying?"

So much for deep honesty.

"Happy to," she said with no hint of disappointment.

Someday, I might be like that. Confident in faith and ready to spin a theologically rich prayer, but there under the visage of the night-draped hospital, with aching neck and drained limbs, I was a silent participant. Reva prayed for the medical staff, for Austie's healing, for mercy, and for God's will to be done. Her words were unhesitating, her thought patterns crisp, and both brimmed with belief that heaven absorbed every word.

So why did praying seem as flimsy as tossing dust to the wind?

46

"ER SOON" REMAINED as unpredictable on a holiday as it was on a normal day. Each lurch of the minute hand on the large clock over the registration desk took an entire revolution of Earth to complete. I opted for a chair against the wall, directly across from the thick automated doors so that anyone who came through them would come face-to-face with me. The only people to appear, however, came for others.

The lobby slowly emptied, until it was only me and another man who kept looking at me as if he wouldn't mind the distraction of conversation. I closed my eyes and leaned my head back against the wall to pretend to sleep. The buffer worked, but then, little by little, as every drop of adrenaline diffused, my body gave in, and I no longer pretended.

I floated out of the room with stiff chairs and slow-moving clocks to a place undefined, where Austie sneered at me over the top of an open beer can and the intensity of Ron's averted gaze and snipped replies matched the sear of my dad's. Reva appeared too, on a rise in the middle of a tallgrass pasture, hands folded, head bowed, oblivious to the swelling storm clouds behind her. I cowered low to the ground, as low as possible. Stalk heads thrashed at my bare arms. A horsefly menaced above me, zipping side to side. It dove for my exposed shoulder and thumped against it. When it backed away to reposition, I threw up my hands to block its path. But it flew toward me again, swelled to ten thousand times its size, and latched on to my right hand.

"Jess?"

My eyes flickered open. The prairie fell away. The lobby pixelated back into clarity, with Ellen's face above me. She stood to the side of my chair, leaning forward with my right hand in both of hers. I jerked upright and moaned. A bad pillow could do a number on a middle-aged neck, but sleeping against a wall was worse. I grabbed my neck with my free hand and dug my fingertips into the worst part of the knot.

"Sorry if I scared you." She lowered into the chair to my right, the soft cocoon of her palms still cradling my hand. The sling bag across her chest bumped against her arm as she settled.

"Not at all," I said, trying with each dig at the taut fibers to rub away all imaginings of her as a horsefly. "What are you doing here?"

"Reva called me. She told me what happened."

"She did?" The real question was why? I let go of my neck and rested my hand in my lap.

"After she told me you all were here, I knew I wouldn't be able to sleep," Ellen said. "I thought you would appreciate someone taking second watch so you can go home and rest."

Second watch? Sure enough, the clock's hour hand had progressed well past nine.

I slipped my hand from her grip. "That's kind of you to offer, but it's okay. I don't mind waiting."

"Actually, it wasn't an offer." The sweetness of her tone hid the meaning at first. It only took a moment for it to unveil.

"Did Reva put you up to this?"

"It was my idea. Reva agreed."

I folded my hands over my waist. "It's really not necessary."

"Jess," she said gently. "I know Austie means a great deal to you, and after everything you saw, you're anxious to know what's really going on. Answers can be hard to get in the ER and hard to wait for. That's why I came."

But I was already there, already taking care of it. Answers wouldn't come any faster with two of us waiting.

"Has anyone come out to talk to you?" she asked.

I shook my head.

"Thought that might be the case. I came prepared." She reached into her sling bag and pulled out an employee badge for Northland Memorial Senior Care. The hospital's logo sat in the lower right corner. "I could probably get someone to talk to me."

Her badge picture looked exactly like her. The bold RN next to her name declared a power I didn't and couldn't possess.

"I'll make sure Austie is taken care of," she said. "And I promise to let you know as soon as I find out anything. You can go home and sleep."

The mention of home and sleep inflamed the exhaustion seeping up from my toes. But how could I leave? I was just as much a guardian for Austie as Reva was.

Ellen lay the badge in her lap and cupped my forearm. "Remember that Austie will need you more than only tonight. It would be wise for you to rest up." In her gaze was an appeal to trust and a staunchness that could not be diminished. In that way, she reflected our Sunday school leader.

I was too weak, too feeble and small, to challenge. I sighed and unwove my hands. "Let me give you my number."

For the third time in one day, someone edged me out of responsibility. First with Dad, then twice with Austie.

After we exchanged numbers and I gave her Austie's phone, I plodded toward the sliding glass doors, knees weaker than before. The doors whooshed open before me. I paused at the threshold and turned back to Ellen in her chair. She looked up at me and smiled. It was true that Austie would be better off with a nurse holding vigil at her bedside. Ellen could give her a voice I couldn't and never had for myself in that place. But Ellen's smile plunged like a dagger into my heart, puncturing the most tender spot.

I turned away and headed for Hank.

Back at the house, I shuffled up the front walk, my head low and my neck raging. The living room light still spilled into the night. Two things, however, were different from how I left them. The cooler was gone from where I had dropped it at the top of the steps, and someone had taped a folded piece of notebook paper to the mailbox on the porch post. I tore it off and unfurled the note. One simple line: *Got your leftovers, Austie.* Kyla had signed it with a smiley face after her name.

The puncture in my heart ripped wider. Kyla had promised to save choice spoils for Austie, and she was determined to keep her promise. Like her, I had made a promise to Austie. "I got you," I had declared over her as I lifted her from the stairs, out of her helplessness. Unlike Kyla, however, I could not keep my promise.

Feeble, small, impotent. Elbowed aside by the stronger.

I balled the note and marched inside. I would not settle for being weak. My body did not determine what strength I had; I did. Resting was not an option. The lights would burn out before me. I tossed my purse on the armchair, then strode to the cabinet under the kitchen sink, where we kept the roll of trash bags.

I did not stop cleaning until even the air gleamed.

47

ELLEN'S TEXT MESSAGE arrived around two o'clock the next morning, shaking me from a loose doze. In the light of the flickering images on the television, I lifted my phone from the coffee table. Reva and I were both recipients of the update.

> Austie is going to be okay. No concussion or broken bones, but she does have dissolvable stitches on the inside of her upper lip. Finishing IV treatment for dehydration. We should be to Jess's by dawn.

Despite those answers, many questions remained. About what had happened, and about what would happen next.

My mouth had become sticky dry in my sleep. I laid my phone on the coffee table and pushed up from the futon. With just enough glow from the television to show the way, I shuffled into the kitchen for a glass of water. I drank standing over the sink. Nearby, the Daily Allelon was only a dull figure on the freezer door. Somewhere on that page was the command Reva said was the most powerful—the command to pray for one another. Though my brain wanted to remain switched off, a yes rose from the deepest interior of my core.

I lowered my cup, closed my eyes in the subdued kitchen, and relayed the only thing that came to my heavy mind. *Thank you that she'll be okay. Please, may she be honest. And please, may I be patient.*

Painfully sparse. Abundantly weak. But it was all I had to offer. Like fine dust to the wind.

I downed the rest of the water and returned to the company of the television.

Several hours later, a series of knocks woke me. A soft predawn haze coated the living room. Squinting against it, I peeled myself from the cushions. The clock on my phone showed half past six. Austie was home. On the way to answer the door, I smoothed my shirt and raked my fingers through the mad tangle of my hair, preparing to take the next watch.

When I opened the door and her eyes met mine over Ellen's shoulder, my breath caught. She really was okay. She was alive, upright, conscious, with skin washed clean though grossly miscolored. I started to smile. She quickly looked away.

"Sorry if we woke you," Ellen said. "Austie realized she didn't have a key."

The swelling of Austie's temple, nose, and lip appeared puffier with her head angled downward. "Glad you're home, Austie," I said.

Her "yeah" was almost imperceptible. The listless response stabbed at that tender place. But as Reva did the night of the kickball game, I held fast to calmness and welcomed them inside. Ellen allowed Austie to pass through first, keeping one hand near her elbow as a good nurse would.

Gaze glued to her feet, Austie entered and waited off to the side. The back of her hair was disheveled, her clothes wrinkled. A white hospital band looped around her wrist, and a bandage on the back of her hand tagged the placc where her IV must have been. She marked out the room, gazing over the pass-through window, the floor, the table, as if checking for any remaining evidence. Her attention caught on Mariah and the large crack down the side of her ceramic pot.

Ellen entered with several papers in her hand. "Austie should feel a little more like herself after some rest and pain management. The nurse gave her care instructions on these discharge papers, which she's going to follow, correct?"

Austie nodded, dipping her head once again.

Ellen gave her the papers. "First, though, you should call your manager about taking the weekend off. Doesn't your shift today start at eight?"

Another nod.

That Ellen knew about her work schedule shouldn't have been a surprise. Surely they had talked during the many hours they were together. A chill skimmed through me anyway. I crossed my arms.

"Better go make that call," Ellen told her.

Austie mumbled a thank-you. Then, without a glance or word my way, she trailed to her room and shut herself inside. Did she really not want to talk to me?

"She's pretty tired," Ellen said, pulling me back to the moment.

Austie wasn't alone in that. I nodded. "Been a long night for everyone. Thank you for all you've done."

"Happy to do it. By the way, how incredible that you came home when you did. She said you weren't due home until tomorrow. What made you come home early?"

I tightened my arms. "Just a change of plans."

"Must have been providence," she said. "Austie could have been much worse off."

Spoken as someone who didn't see fallout about to strike. I moved my hands to my hips. "What happened anyway? Did she say?"

"She's been tight-lipped about what led up to her falling down the stairs. The toxicology report showed only a small amount of alcohol in her system."

I frowned. "So, she hadn't been drinking?"

"Very little. But what is concerning is that she had a high level of diphenhydramine."

"Diphen—what's that?"

"It's a common ingredient in sleep aids. Mixed with alcohol, it can be dangerous. From what I can make out, she didn't ingest it knowingly."

My lips parted. The implications painted themselves in vivid strokes. It was something the Shuckers staff was trained to protect patrons against, particularly the females.

Seeing my reaction, Ellen held out her hand. "Not what you think, praise God. All her injuries are consistent with a fall—and only a fall—though it seems probable that fall happened because of what she ingested. We could piece together only so much based on what she was willing to share. Maybe you can get her to open up more."

"Maybe. I'll try." Though Austie may have seen me as a safe person, the way she barely acknowledged my existence when she walked into the house indicated she wasn't exactly champing at the bit to trust me with everything. Had she known what was happening to her? Did she remember being locked in a basement?

Ellen smiled and patted my arm. "I'll get going. Encourage her to drink plenty of water, and she should stick to soft food until her stitches dissolve. The doctor wants her to see a dentist about possible damage to her front teeth. Do you know if she has a dentist?"

"Doubt it."

She nodded. "There's one at Trinity. I can give him a call. I bet he'd be willing to check it out."

Inserting one more person into the mix didn't strike me as the best idea, but considering Austie's quickly mounting medical bills, I couldn't begrudge her his help.

Ellen turned to the door and paused with her hand on the

knob. "One last thing. Did Reva tell you she was working with the police to find Austie's car?"

"She didn't," I said. In fact, the car hadn't crossed my mind to worry about.

"Trinity has a police officer as well," Ellen said. "Reva told me last night when she called that she planned to reach out to him."

For a small church, Trinity had a fortuitous mix of professionals.

"You know him too," she said. "Todd Savoy? Thea's husband?"

My stomach sank. The last person who needed to know about any of this was Thea, who would undoubtedly find out from Todd. "That's . . . great."

Ellen flashed one last smile and invited me to call her if we needed anything. Soon she was back to her minivan, and I was alone in my living room.

I shut the door and pressed my forehead against the cool wood. Austie was okay, but there was a lot to figure out, a lot to unravel. Medical bills, a dentist, her work schedule, her car, Mariah's broken pot. But the biggest questions were the hardest ones to answer. What had happened in my house? What had happened to Austie? Should I be ready to kick her out or stand even firmer in the gap for her? Cut my losses or help her carry hers?

I closed my eyes.

Honesty, Lord, and patience.

48

AN ENTIRE DAY HAD PASSED, and still Austie didn't talk. At least not to me. Someone—or someones—on the other end of her texts got plenty of her words, though. In between her long stretches of sleep, she would emerge from her room, rumpled and sloughy, to use the bathroom or grab some of the soft food I had run to Cost Cutter to obtain. Each time she came out, she had her injured nose buried in her screen and her thumbs pumping away. Not a word to me, though, about the applesauce, pudding cups, bananas, gelatin—or soup. If any illusions played in my imagination about me bringing her a bowl of broth and engaging in a heart-to-heart, her avoidance made them scutter away.

At least Reva had paid me mind when she texted bright and early Saturday morning on her drive back from Chicago. She asked after Austie and me both and promised to stop by the following afternoon. Then came Ellen a few hours later, knocking on the front door shortly before nine to take Austie to the dentist.

Her warm smile cut the chill that pressed against the house. "Is Austie ready?"

"Almost." I motioned for her to step inside.

She bobbed in next to me and surveyed my home. "You have a lovely place, Jess. I love the bay window."

"That was a selling point for me too." I shut the door and craned my neck toward the hallway. The smaller bedroom remained closed. "It was nice of the dentist to open his office on Saturday for Austie."

"He was delighted to do it. How is she today?"

I shrugged. "Still looks like a boxer after a fight but doing better. Don't think she'll want to go to church tomorrow."

"Is she sleeping? Eating?"

"Yes, to both. Couldn't tell you how much water she's had, but I assume she is managing that."

"Good." She stepped closer and lowered her voice to a whisper. "Have you two had a chance to talk?"

I shook my head. "Been avoiding me."

Ellen glanced at the hall. "Could be fear. Give it time. I'll keep praying."

Fear had a way of looking a lot like pride. My own prayer for Austie's honesty had yet to bear out. The petition for patience had held, though that patience quickly wore thin.

The bedroom door clicked open. Austie ambled out with the hood of her oversized puffer coat pulled low over her brow and her head down. Her holey jeans flapped against her bare knee. The phone was lodged in her left palm.

"Hey there," Ellen said brightly. "Ready for Dr. Riggs?"

She nodded and came to a stop a few paces off. Her eyes flitted to me before returning to a spot in front of her shoes. Her swollen lip created a drag on her speech. "Reva called. Police found my car at the Fast Stop up on Barry."

My eyes widened. "You're kidding. The one a mile from here?"

"Mm-hmm."

Ellen turned to me. The confusion in her expression surely tinged mine too.

"Was it damaged?" I asked.

Staring at the floor, Austie shook her head. "Someone left the keys with the staff. I just need to pick it up."

"Weird," Ellen breathed.

"Very," I agreed. And incredibly, incredibly lucky.

Austie jiggled her leg. "Guess we better go."

At the reminder, Ellen sprang back to life and pulled open the door. "Got everything you need?"

Assuring her she did, Austie headed toward the porch.

"Good luck," I said as she passed by me.

"Thanks," she mumbled from somewhere under the low hood.

I held back a sigh and followed them outside. Snow was expected later that day, and the temperature certainly acted like it. I huddled deeper into my sweater and crossed to the top of the steps.

"Should be back within an hour," Ellen said as they tramped down the front walk.

"See you soon," I replied. Only one person responded to my farewell, and it wasn't the person I meant it for the most.

The frosty wind bit my hands. I shoved them into my pockets to keep them out of harm's way. As the ladies bundled into Ellen's minivan, the thud of a different car door sounded across the lot. I leaned around the post for a better angle. Ron stood at the driver's side of his Toyota, watching the action in my driveway.

The van engine hummed, wheels turned backward onto the street. Exhaust puffed from the muffler as they got underway. Ron watched them trace through the neighborhood, then he set his sights on my house.

"Oh boy," I whispered.

With the same brisk march as the first day we met, he aimed himself my direction. I curled my fingers inside my pockets and lowered onto the sidewalk.

Moments later, he stopped in front of me on the concrete. "Morning, Jess."

"Ron."

"Kyla's been bugging me about bringing over some leftovers for Austie."

I pulled my hands from my pockets and crossed my arms. "Found her note. That's kind of her, but Austie is on soft food for now."

He nodded, requiring no further explanation. The images of the young woman's bloodied face were likely as seared into his mind as they were in mine.

"We both owe you a debt of gratitude for your help the other night, Ron."

His brow flickered. "That's actually what I needed to talk to you about."

Specters of clouds lurked across the dull sky. I shivered against the kick of wind. "What about it?" I asked.

He hooked his thumbs into the pockets of his Carhartt jacket. "I was the one who dropped off the note from Kyla. I had come back over here to ensure the front door was locked." He glanced at me. "I saw the state of the house."

I sucked in my breath. He had seen it all. Of course he had. The blazing evidence of the things he wanted to keep his granddaughter away from.

"Seymour strictly forbids those kinds of parties on his properties," he said. "It's a violation of your rental agreement."

It had been months since I signed the lease. There had been an extensive list of clauses with requirements and prohibitions, but the one about parties hadn't resonated. Such activities were not of interest to me, so the risk had been low. At least until I got a roommate.

"I think I do recall something about that," I said. "Don't remember super well, though. Does it say I have to pay a fine or something?"

His gaze shifted away. He tapped his fingertips against his jacket. "No, Jess. It's a zero-tolerance policy. It means you broke your contract."

The cold punched through me. I fought to find my voice. "Broke? As in . . . I'd be—" The word seemed impossible. Surreal.

Flashes of my stuff shoved in the back of a truck, of me driving away, never to return. Because of something I didn't do.

"I'm sorry," Ron said. "It's policy."

My breath came quicker. "It's a little extreme, isn't it?"

"Seymour's been burned too many times."

"Not by me! Surely we can work this out. I've been a good tenant, haven't I? And nothing was damaged, I swear. Come look!" I thrust my arm toward the front door.

But his feet stayed put, and his adherence to his boss's rules, unchanged. "It's not up to me. I'm obligated to report the other night to him. I wanted you to have a heads-up."

The hands clipped to his pockets were the same ones that had helped carry my moving boxes, the ones that had guided a mower across my lawn and lifted a broken Austie from my arms. Now they were turning inward, away from me, away from anything good between us.

I clenched my fists and punched them in the air at my hips with every word. "Ron, please. I know this looks bad. I know it looks like just an irresponsible kid doing irresponsible things, but you have to understand there's more to that night than either of us saw. Much more."

He shook his head, clearly ready to check out. Only one thing could keep him from tuning me out altogether.

"Austie was drugged!"

His eyes cut to me. The hook had worked.

I took a step forward. "She was in the basement when I found her. The door was locked behind her. They took her car. Clearly something happened to her. She hasn't told us all the details yet, but we know she was a victim of something. Seymour's got to allow an exception for that, wouldn't he?"

He looked at the house, then back toward the driveway, as if piecing it together.

"I get that you need to do your job," I said. "I get that you need to tell Seymour about the other night. But please, I'm begging you, let me find out what happened. That way you can tell him all the details. And maybe—I don't know—maybe it will help."

The last of my air expelled with the final plea. I went stock-still, waited.

He worked his lower jaw back and forth and glanced over his shoulder, toward the spot where Austie's car normally sat. At last, he returned to me. "He's out of town until Monday. I'll give you until then to find out."

I drank in air. "Thank you, R—"

He thrust up his hand, bringing me to a halt. "I hope you understand that I have a policy of my own. Which is why, until further notice, Kyla is not to come over or be around her. That includes church."

I could only stand there, silent. The grace period before telling Seymour had been for my sake, not Austie's. Because he was still a grandfather who would do what he had to do.

He turned on his heel and headed back to his house.

The impact of consequences rolled, plowing through the lives of those who'd had nothing to do with the choices made. If any of the damage had a chance at being reversed, then Austie needed to start talking.

49

ELLEN HAD PROMISED they would be back by ten. Eleven came and went. I traced the same oblong path across the living room, from behind the door to the far edge of the picture window. Each step pounded on the same essential question: How would I get Austie to talk?

To the window, spin around, back to the door.

Unsettledness tremored through my hands as much as it did my feet. I moved them from my pockets to my hips to under my elbows. No position lasted long. The straight-line gaps in the floorboards directed my feet, every knot and grain serving as a mile marker. A black swirl in front of the armchair resembled a human cell. The peaked waves on the boards by the coffee table echoed the chevron pattern on Austie's curtains. She didn't understand how precariously we remained under this roof. She *must* start talking.

Finally, at ten past the hour, the purr of an engine floated through the air. I hurried to the picture window. A red Beetle reversed onto the upper reaches of the lot. Austie had returned, with a key piece of her belongings back in her possession as inexplicably as it had disappeared.

Sharp pains needled the backs of my hands. She would not

enter my house until she started explaining. I threw on my coat and stepped onto the porch.

Austie eased out of her car, hood down and face aimed toward the empty, silent lot. If Ron's policy reached far enough, the lot would remain in that state for a while.

I huddled in full view at the top of the steps. Despite me making my presence known, she didn't look my way. She turned and rummaged in the back seat.

The day hadn't warmed much. The sun, near its zenith, dribbled its rays through the thickening cloud cover. To my left, the tips of white envelopes protruded from the mailbox affixed to the post. I flipped up the lid and pulled out the deliveries. A utility bill, a credit card offer, a SuperSave magazine of coupons. At the tail end of the stack, though, with repugnant timing, was a thick envelope addressed to me from Northland Memorial Billing Office. I thrust it into the pages of the magazine and stuffed the bundle under my right arm.

Austie cut across the yard and watched her shoes tromp through the paling grass. Instead of palming a phone, her left hand curled around the handles of a plastic shopping bag from a hobby store. The sides bulged around the contents and brushed the seam of her jeans.

I descended onto the first step, slapping my shoes hard against the tread.

The noise lifted her gaze to me. She slowed.

I crossed my arms and stood dead center on the passageway, leaving no room for anyone else. As she inched closer, I jutted my chin toward the Beetle. "Got your car back."

Her voice was a wisp. "Yeah."

"No damage to it at all?"

She stopped a few strides from the steps and shook her head. The natural light underscored the nuances of the purplish-red stain on her nose and temple.

"What about your teeth? Any injury?"

Shake. "Got a cavity, though." She pointed to the lower right side of her jaw, underneath and back from the swollen lip.

"The tooth that's been bothering you?"

She nodded. "He'll fix it when my lip's healed. Won't charge me."

"That's generous of him." A lot of people had been generous to her.

She dabbed her mouth with the back of her hand and made a quiet sucking sound. Swollen lips made it hard to restrain saliva. Regardless, she was going to talk. Too much was at stake.

She glanced up at me, as if checking whether I had budged.

I tightened my arms and leveled my eyes at her.

Her feet shifted. She had to expect my patience to run out at some point. That point had almost arrived.

"Got something for you," she said and dug in the bag.

I started to reply, to tell her I didn't need peace offerings, only answers.

But then the bag crinkled away from the pot. A simple molded plastic variety. Glossy finish. Bubblegum-pink tone that harmonized with the stripes of a certain leafy diva. She held it up to me. "Think it's the same size."

The tension in my arms loosened. She had noticed Mariah. She had noticed and cared.

Our gazes connected. A wrinkle puckered the soft place between her eyebrows, the first hint at sorrow. Slowly I reached for the pot.

When it was secure in my left hand, she dipped into the bag again. "Also . . ." She pulled out a packet of beveled jewel adhesives. "For sparkle."

As the packet slid from her grip into the pot in mine, the rigidity in my neck and shoulders faded further. "Thank you," I said, hugging the gift to my hip. "That was thoughtful."

She tried to smile, couldn't, then settled her eyes on the porch steps. Her skin bore the marks of mistakes, and her posture rang with shame. That was how I was too the night Tillie Watts told me to come in from the storm. Tillie had sung truth over me, drawing me gently toward the shelter my soul intuitively sought. I didn't have a hymn to sing over Austie, but I did have facts to share that could speak louder than any angry lecture ever would. Facts that could, at last, draw her gently to honest replies. I needed to put all else aside and find a way to share them. One idea presented itself, centered on the pink plastic item resting against my side.

I nodded toward the front door. "Want to help me get Mariah switched out?"

She looked up at me. The pucker released. Nod.

It was a start.

With the mail bundle held fast under one arm and the gift under the other, I led us inside, to the table where our most pleasant and pointed moments mingled. We stripped off our coats at our respective chairs. Austie's hoodie pocket showed the perfect outline of her phone. Notes of unease lingered.

As I laid the mail in front of my chair and the new pot in the middle of the table, Austie lifted Mariah from the floor, careful to hold her ceramic home on either side of the crack. She placed her next to the pink replacement. The two containers stood side by side, one cracked, one whole, and were nearly identical in dimensions.

I picked up the packet of jewels and slid it across the wood. "You're better at decorating. Could you come up with something?"

"Me?"

I nodded.

"Um, okay."

Another small movement in the right direction.

After a moment of consideration, she retrieved the masking tape and measuring tape from the junk drawer, then returned to the spot next to her chair. She began taping off spots every inch and a half around the top edge of the new pot.

While she worked, I wet a paper towel and began to clean Mariah's top leaves, some of which retained stubborn splatters of sticky residue. A stillness soon dwelled over us. It was, at last, the ripe environment for sharing the facts that could lead to honesty.

I wet my lips and began. "Ron came over."

She smoothed a thin strip of tape onto the pot and started to pick off another from the roll. "What did he say?"

Sticking only to the facts, gentle and inviting, I shared, "He wanted to check on you. Did you know he carried you to my truck?"

Her hands paused. She shook her head before ripping off the next strip.

The facts would only get harder to hear from there. "That night, he also saw what was left in the house. The cans and bottles and whatnot."

She smoothed and resmoothed that same piece of tape.

"After seeing that, and your condition, he isn't real keen on letting Kyla come around."

Her hands drifted to the table. The roll of tape tapped against the surface. She turned to the bay window and the empty, silent lot beyond.

But it was the last fact she needed to hear the most. I finished Mariah's upper leaves and cradled one on the next level down. As tenderly as I dabbed at the grime, I said, "He also reminded me that my lease includes a zero-tolerance policy for parties. Violations result in eviction."

Austie righted. "That's a thing?"

"It is in my lease."

The wrinkle over her nose returned, deeper. Her gaze plunged to her hands.

I refolded the towel to a clean spot, then started on a new leaf. "Ron did promise, though, that he would hold off on reporting the party to Seymour so I could find out the full details of what happened."

Across from me, the person who held the answers I needed—that Kyla needed and Ron needed and her own future depended on—dug her thumbnail at the jagged end of the tape. She bent her neck forward until her nose pointed straight down and the full length of her eyelashes showed.

"This is where you come in, Austie," I nudged.

The facts had spoken and were resounding even in silence.

Suddenly, she dropped onto her chair. She clutched her discolored face with her hands. "I didn't throw a party."

The first ray of truth broke through. I lay the towel aside and came over to the chair where Reva normally sat. With the softened daylight over my shoulder, I folded my hands on the table in front of me.

"Please, Austie. Tell me what happened."

50

IT HAD STARTED with a passing comment to Demi in a conversation during their Thanksgiving morning shift. Austie told her she was alone in the house and would be for several days. With someone like Demi, that was risky information to put out there. It equated to an open invitation to come by late that afternoon with the kind of people and products that Austie wanted to avoid.

"I told them on repeat to leave, I swear!" Austie recounted as she aggravated the torn edge of the tape. "But there were, like, eight of them, mostly guys, and they were so loud and obnoxious. They were playing some ridiculous music."

The bit of tape ripped off, creating a slender tag she began to pick at. Her forehead constricted as the scenes replayed, of strangers ignoring her demands and draining more cans, of vodka being swirled into cups of my soda.

"Demi kept telling me to calm down even though she knew I could get in serious trouble with them there. At one point I told them I'd call the cops, but they only laughed in my face. That's when one guy took my phone from me and wouldn't give it back. They threw it around like a football until it was just gone. I had no idea where they put it."

"My sock drawer," I said, hands clasped on the table. "That's where I found it."

"Stupid," she muttered and wiped her mouth. Her bottom lip collected sheen every few sentences.

The more she shared, the clearer the events of the evening became. Austie begging Demi repeatedly to make everyone leave, reminding Demi it wasn't her house, but her "friend" refused every petition. Until finally, a deal was offered.

"She said if I stopped being dramatic and drank one drink, then they would leave." She huffed, ripped off the tag of tape, and smacked it onto the table. "I knew I shouldn't believe her, and I didn't want to drink. But I didn't know what else to do. Ron wasn't home. I didn't have my phone. It wasn't like I could leave with them here. I—" Her mouth flailed at the loss of words. She wiped once more, wincing when she pressed her swollen lip too hard.

I started to stand to get a napkin, but she waved me off.

She found the jagged tape edge on the roll and picked at it. "Max handed me the drink, and I chugged it. I thought it was just a rum and coke. But I guess . . ." Her tone stiffened. "Guess they had found the sleep aid stuff I had in the bathroom."

Which explained the ransacked medicine cabinet. "So it was yours?" I asked. "Didn't know you used it."

"Not as much recently."

The dark circles under her eyes had faded over the last three months, a small mercy that had gone uncelebrated.

"They had dissolved it in your drink?" I asked.

Nod. The rims of her eyes glistened.

A defenseless Austie, surrounded on all sides by guys bigger than her, telling her to drink or else—and drink something that could have easily done much more damage. Every piece of me wanted to rise from my chair and throw haymakers at their ghosts.

"I . . ." Her bottom lip trembled. "I don't remember anything after that. Demi said I went to the basement on my own, but . . ." Tears pooled. Her voice strained. "I don't remember."

I clenched my jaw. Doubtful she went to the basement on her own, and no possible way she locked the door behind her. Had she passed out on the steps? Been banging on the door before she fell?

"Demi said it was just a prank," she added.

"You talked to her?"

She pulled her phone from her hoodie pocket and flashed it to me.

A day's worth of nose to screen and thumb taps had been for a specific purpose. "That's who you've been texting."

She nodded, laid her phone next to the tape roll, then outlined the case with her fingers.

"What about your car?" I asked. "Was taking it a prank too?"

Nod. "So stupid."

And so illegal. "Austie, you can press charges."

"No!" Her eyes flew to mine. "I already told Todd no. I want to forget it and move on. And I never want to see them again."

I couldn't blame her. The wild and improbable story aligned with the observable details of that night, but it also captured the abject humiliation she'd endured alone. Someone she thought was a friend had manipulated her into a dangerous situation, allowed her to get hurt, then left her to face the consequences solo.

"Austie, why didn't you tell us before what happened? Why keep it bottled up?"

She stuffed her phone in her pocket. "A lot of it I didn't remember. And what I did remember"—she glanced at me—"I didn't think you'd believe me."

I bit my lip. Her honesty came loaded with conviction, slicing deep. Indeed, my first instinct that chaotic night had been to blame her. I started to reach out my hand, to offer an assurance that I believed every word, but her chin began to convulse. Her face scrunched tight as a fist.

"Jess, I'm so sorry! I screwed up everything!"

"No, Austie, come on." I rested my hand near her arm and leaned toward her.

She sucked at the liquid spilling over her lip but couldn't quite catch it. It blended into the streams that angled down her cheeks and into the corners of her mouth. Cords strained in her neck. "If I move out, will they let you stay?"

The question seared me. Spoken by a defeated young woman so used to being the one cast aside, so conditioned to believe she was always the problem.

I grabbed her forearm. "We're not going to think like that. I don't want either one of us to leave. Seymour is a good man. We'll pray for mercy." That was a prayer I intended to speak in earnest. "We'll be eating pizza and drinking frozen sodas for many weekends to come."

Austie snuffled and wiped her face and mouth with the sleeve of her free arm. The cotton caught the moisture in dark streaks.

I squeezed tighter. "Yes?"

Unable to blink fast enough to stem the pools, she nodded.

Did God see? Was he stirred by the sorrow of his young daughter? Would he move hearts and policies on her behalf? Not to mention mine.

I patted her arm, then drew back my hand. "You should go call Reva. She'll want to know everything that happened too. We can finish with Mariah's pot later."

Austie dabbed her eyes with her sleeve cuff, then started to stand.

I quickly added, "Ask her if she has any advice on how to talk to Ron."

Agreeing, she grabbed her coat and trudged to her room.

When her door tapped shut, I stood and scooted in our chairs. My hands lingered on the back of Austie's. Scattered on the table was evidence of our harmony being repaired. A bubblegum-pink pot bought in love and hope that I would forgive her, hear her.

Fake jewels for sparkle. If God really was stirred by her sorrow, then a bigger reunion could happen there at that table, one in which all four of us sat in our chairs once more. Together, we'd help Austie continue to bear up, even if it meant personal sacrifice. Because we wanted what was best for her.

Lying in front of my chair, concealed among the pages of a coupon magazine like a water mug hidden in the cabinet or folded notes secreted away under my socks, was the wild, humiliating story I held back. After everything that had transpired the past three days, that was where it needed to stay.

51

DAYBREAK STRETCHED a colorless band across the expanse outside my bedroom window the next morning. The brute wind knocked against the windowpanes, rousing creaks from their bones, but it could not move the trees. They resisted its whip, holding their limbs rigid, their leaves cast in snow that had fallen overnight. In the basement, the furnace clicked on and churned warmth up through the vents. It would take a while for that relief to reach the back part of the house. I kept the blanket pulled tight against my chin to trap in as much heat as possible. No part of me wanted to break the delicate shell between sleep and wakefulness.

A noise rolled from somewhere in the distance, too soft to be anything but a fleeting thought. I dozed only to wake up to the periodic noise having grown louder, like it approached my house in stages. Each round was more distinguishable than the last, until it was crystal clear: a thump, followed by a long, steady scrape. Someone was shoveling snow.

Bracing for a chilly assault, I peeled back the covers. The air stung my skin, prodding my sluggish feet to my closet. I grabbed my favorite sweatshirt, a tan cotton number with the words "Tell your plants I said hello" embroidered on the front. Its weight staved off the worst of the sting, but my body ached for bed and protested every movement. Cold had the same effect on middle-aged bodies as extreme heat, apparently.

By the time I entered the hallway, another round of thump-scrape had begun. I crept by Austie's shut door, avoiding the worst of the floorboard squeaks, and made it to the picture window in time to see Ron scoop the last of the snow from the front walk. He flung the shovel load into the yard by the steps. Behind him, the driveway asphalt peeked through streaks of white. He had cleared the entire thing, from the street to Hank's front end and around Austie's Beetle parked at the top of the lot. Both vehicles' windshields were scraped clean too.

"Goodness," I breathed. That much work completed meant he had started before dawn.

Finished with the sidewalk, Ron stowed his shovel on his shoulder and marched toward the driveway. I knocked on the glass, but the buffer of the stocking cap pulled low to his eyes and the hood of his Carhartt proved too effective.

I lifted my coat off the armchair, my makeshift outerwear rack, and attempted to walk and dress at the same time. My arms were heavy and uncooperative, causing so much trepidation that I almost tripped over my own toes. Finally, with one and a half arms in my coat and shoes most of the way on my feet, I twisted the dead bolt and opened the door. The icy blast nearly skinned me alive, and Ron was already two strides past Hank. I was too late.

"What's going on?"

I turned toward Austie's voice. She ambled down the hall in a hoodie paired with flannel pajama pants.

Quickly shutting the door to the tundra temperatures, I gestured toward the Torres house. "I was trying to catch Ron. He cleared the snow for us. Even cleaned our windshields."

"Really?" She crossed to the bay window. Her gaze must have caught on his retreating frame because she stood and watched. A lonesomeness tinted her words. "He's a good man too."

That was the kind of hope we both needed to retain. Time dwindled to tell him about what had happened.

Shrugging off my coat took far less time and energy. I tossed it on the armchair as I shook off my shoes. If I was allowed to stay in the house, a coat rack was first on the list of items to buy, after curtains.

I headed to the table. "I can tell him we both said thanks when I go over to talk to him later today. You coming to church this morning?"

She shook her head, still watching across the distance. "If it's all right, I'd like to be the one to talk to Ron."

"You would?"

"Well, not talk, really." Turning from the window, she reached into her hoodie pocket and pulled out a piece of notebook paper folded into thirds.

"What's that?" I asked, sidling up to the back of her chair.

"Reva said I should tell him everything I told you all. I'm not good with that stuff, so I figured I'd write it down."

"You wrote him a letter?"

"It's for both of them, Ron and Seymour." She looked at the letter, then at me. "Would you read it and tell me if it's any good?"

"I can if you want me to."

She held out the paper.

Moving my hands in space was like moving through water. My limbs simply refused to accept it was time to be awake and active. I took the letter and sat to read.

Meanwhile, Austie stepped over to Mariah, who now proudly bore the jewels Austie had finished affixing the night before—a crown around the rim and an outline of a lion's head on the side, an echo of her own tattoo, as if she wanted to mark Mariah with the same symbol of strength and spirit. Because they had both been tossed and broken, then redeemed. The jewels glinted like the covered ground outside. Austie petted Mariah's largest top leaf as softly as stroking a baby's hair. She had done the same thing several times in the last few months. No one had ever been that gentle with the divas besides me.

The letter took up most of the page. In simple language full of misspellings and grammatical neglect, Austie explained what had happened in the unseen hours on Thanksgiving night. The wild, fantastical story explained all the weirdness in such a way that it had to be true. She capped it off with a humble admission:

> *I don't say all this because I espect anything . . . I know how bad I messed up. I am sorry. I want a safe home too, its the only thing I've ever wanted. I didn't know how much I didn't have until I got what I have here. Please forgive me, even if I can't live here anymore. Thank you for considering.*
>
> *—Austie Russell*

In front of me, the author continued to caress the leaf and waited patiently for my response. The degradation of that night was still fresh on her body, marks she could not hide and chose to accept as discipline.

I smoothed the paper along its folds. "Those are moving words, Austie."

She came over and retrieved the letter from my extended hand. "Think it will help?"

"I don't know, but it's worth them knowing the truth."

Shoveling my driveway may have been part of Ron's job, but the clearing of our windshields was not. Maybe mercy stirred under the surface of that protective grandfather and loyal employee. Though he wouldn't have the final say over what became of us, he would have influence. Austie's case would be stronger with his endorsement.

"Might take it to him now," she said. "Before I overthink it too much."

"Want me to walk over with you?"

She shook her head and glided the letter into her hoodie pocket, careful not to bend it. "Probably should face him on my own."

That, too, would speak to Ron. It lauded the character she was trying to build. That had to count for something.

She moved to the front door and the row of our footwear by the frame. "By the way," she said as she wriggled her left foot into her shoe without untying it, "I have a question for you about that night. Something that didn't make sense to me."

"What's that?"

She stomped her shoe into place and started on the right one. "Why did you come home so early?"

When Ellen asked me that question, a vague answer had sufficed. The same answer would not work with Austie. What little I had shared with anyone about moving my dad in with me had fallen on her ears.

I ran my fingers through my hair. "Dad and I got into a fight. Basically, he has a girlfriend in his house now, and that's where his commitment is." It was an experience Austie understood well.

She took it all in, standing with her hands in her pocket. "Does that mean he's not moving up here with you?"

A flash of his curt tone, the cut of his rejection. An ache seeped up my chest. I shook my head. "Don't think it's meant to be."

"I'm sorry, Jess."

I shrugged. "He snores anyway."

The jest didn't erase the empathy from her expression. "Be back soon," she said, reaching for the doorknob.

"Austie?"

"Yes?"

"Please use my coat."

She harrumphed, but grinned. "Fine."

When the door shut behind her, I sighed and propped my head in my hands. Surely Ron would be kinder in his reaction to her than Dad had been to me. He would consider the evidence she presented and remember how good she had been for Kyla.

Maybe he would remember how good I had been for her too. He would realize that those who stood to lose from a nullified rental agreement included his granddaughter.

God, may it be the most persuasive letter he and Seymour have ever read.

I prayed the words over and over, my head and heart bent under the weight of worry.

Suddenly, I jerked awake. When had I fallen asleep? I sat upright, tried to shake away the grogginess. Rising from the chair took far more effort than it should have. Allelon began in less than two hours, but my body cried to stay snuggled up and warm. I never liked driving in winter weather anyway.

I pushed away from the table, my feet sliding more than stepping, and mentally formulated a "don't worry" text message to Reva as I headed for my phone on my nightstand. She would understand why I needed to stay home—the roads, Austie. Besides, she was due over that afternoon, if the roads were better by then. She could catch me up on anything I missed.

I flipped on my bedroom light and shuffled over to my nightstand. There, next to my phone, was the folded SuperSave magazine. I paused. A letter of my own waited inside.

Alone in the house for the first time since it had arrived, I sat on my bed and brought the magazine to my lap. The pages fell open to the envelope from Northland Memorial Billing Office.

"Just get it over with," I whispered. Like Austie was doing.

The sealed flap tore unevenly from the force of my finger. I tugged out the stack of folded papers and tossed the envelope on the nightstand. Holding my breath, I unfolded the stack. Five pages in all. Five pages to detail the charges of my hospital stay. The invoice was almost as overwhelming as the experience itself. The grand total owed, out of pocket, had four digits before the period. That bill was only the beginning.

The brute wind smacked against the windowpanes. My hands slumped to my lap, crushing the edge of the stack against my thigh. I turned to the window and the bleary ether doming over me.

What am I supposed to do?

Would there ever be a return answer? Would anything ever make sense? Kansas City was supposed to have been the restart. Had I misunderstood? All those things that had fallen into place at precisely the right time in the right way to bring me to that little house—were they only me assuming that heavenly favor existed where it didn't? Was it selfish ambition? The rules of Christianity were as perplexing as the five-page bill crumpled against my leg.

How amazing it would have been to vault under the covers and never resurface. But I couldn't. Not with Austie in need and the threadlike hope we both clung to about the landlord's decision. I was still on watch for her as she healed, and I had to be there for her, for us. Despite what tiredness beset me.

I thrust the bill and its envelope under my pillow, an incentive to stay away from my bed. After sending the text to Reva, I left my room to wait for Austie. We could camp out on the futon and watch movies and eat toaster pastries straight from their foil packets. We could take the opportunity to relish the little house while it was yet ours. Together. In harmony.

52

SCARCITY AMPLIFIES a thing's value, makes its preciousness more radiant. Even a simple thing, like a shared bowl of white cheddar cheese puffs and a mug on either end of the coffee table. That morning, as Austie and I lounged on the futon and watched movies from my collection, distracting ourselves from the agony of winter weather and a looming judgment, the details of her being in my house shone brightest. I leaned back on the throw pillow wedged behind my neck and soaked in them. The way she tilted her chin up and to the side as she watched a movie. The way she hugged the other throw pillow to her stomach and sat with her legs crisscrossed. She ate her cereal like that too sometimes, with her legs tucked up on her chair, one angled over the other. Only the young and slim could pull off such a position.

Kyla could too. And match Austie chew for chew as they inhaled their pizza. And beat her nearly every time in Crazy Eights. Of the handful of times that Reva full-on smiled in my presence, one of them had been over a Kyla victory, and the other four had also happened somewhere in that little house on the narrow street. Reva, the genteel bear fighter, with a scar under her eye holding a tale she hadn't yet told. Kyla, on her way to high school soccer legend status, thanks to the tutelage of the most unexpected teacher. Austie, a compassionate soul learning to come out of hiding.

Why couldn't there be more? Why would the home we had created be knocked over and cracked down the side, leaving the delicate roots to dangle?

The moments, the faces started to drift away from me. I tried to grab at them, but they fizzled into the unreachable place beyond the bend of the earth. Until they were gone, and I zapped back to the futon.

I blinked, lifted my head from the pillow. Despite the unplanned nap, tiredness pressed in on me. The television was dark. The cheese puffs bowl was gone, as were the two mugs.

"Austie?"

Behind me, a cabinet door padded shut. "Making lunch."

Lunch? How long had I been asleep?

Something tapped against the counter. The faucet kicked on.

Burying my fists into the cushion for leverage, I bent at the waist and pushed myself onto my feet. Halfway up, a wave of exhaustion stormed through me. I teetered and flopped back onto the cushion. My legs and arms begged to be still. My heartbeat thundered in my ears. But I had to get up, had to be there for Austie. That was my only job for the day: Austie. I sucked in my breath, willed my strength to revive, and fought my way to standing. Once upright, I paused to breathe, in and out, until I could command my feet to move. I shuffled forward. Every step was like walking headlong into a high Kansas wind.

On the other side of the pass-through window into the kitchen, Austie stood with her back to me, attention focused on whatever she was doing over the counter.

I dragged myself to the kitchen doorway. "Sorry I fell asleep. I must be more wiped than I thought."

She looked at me as she stirred a powdered cheese packet into a single-serve mac and cheese cup. "You were out. I didn't want to wake you."

The stove clock confirmed it was nearly one o'clock. Reva was due at three. Austie had changed into jeans and styled her hair. I hadn't even put on underwear yet. The other pieces of her soft-food lunch waited on a plate nearby—a dollop of applesauce and a small heap of leftover scrambled eggs from the night before. My stomach twisted away from the food. I leaned against the doorframe and crossed my arms.

"Want me to make you something?" she asked.

"Not super hungry at the moment."

She peeked at me. "Feeling okay? You didn't eat any of the puffs either."

"I'm fine. Just a bit draggy today." And achy with a touch of nausea. Like the flu. It would be my luck that I had come down with the flu at the most inopportune time.

Austie eyed me a moment longer, then set the spoon aside and took her mac-and-cheese cup to the microwave. "Reva said she'd order us dinner tonight."

"That's nice of her."

While the microwave ran, she scooped a spoonful of eggs to her mouth.

I averted my gaze. "Think I'll go take a shower. Maybe that will help perk me up."

"Sure you don't want something?" she asked around the bite.

"No thanks. Maybe later." I started off down the hallway.

Five steps in, a second wave of exhaustion stirred up. I paused, pressed my hand against the wall, took deep breaths. It passed, a blip compared to the first one, but the rest of the way to my bedroom, I traced my fingertips along the wall.

Once inside, I shut the door and slogged to my dresser. Underthings first. My leaden arms struggled to rise to the drawer handles. I managed to work an opening and reach inside for the necessities. When it came to socks, my hand danced with several balled pairs before trapping a fuzzy, thick-soled set that would be much warmer than the thin athletic ones I had on. As I retrieved the ball, my fingertips dragged against the papers lining the bottom of the drawer. Echoes of the words printed across the discharge papers and pre-appointment notes rang up my arm. Warnings about symptoms. About fatigue and dizziness and vertigo and weakness. Sudden or slow build. Fleeting or lasting for days. Stress could be a trigger. Every patient experience was different. Unpredictable.

Was I having an attack? What if I was? What if it was not simply the start of the flu or the fallout from several high-octane days in a row? What if, in the middle of everything else being upended, my body had decided to have a go too?

I shut the drawer with my shoulder. There was no point thinking like that. No point dwelling, only doing. We had company coming. We had unity to continue to repair and unknowns to pray over.

Planting one hand on the front of the dresser for support, I leaned and opened the lowest drawer for a pair of joggers. Pants slung over my shoulder, I pushed the drawer shut and started to swing myself upright.

Another wave. Fierce.

The underthings slipped to the floor. I latched on to a drawer handle, but it did nothing to keep me on my feet. My knees hit the floor first. Then my hands. Pound, pound, pound. I sank to my belly, prostrating my entire length on the floor. Cold, solid wood pressed against my cheek, pressed into the chaos churning inside me.

Breathe in, breathe out. Over and over.

The pounding mellowed, enough for me to open my eyes. I turned my head toward my bed, my nose dragging across the floorboards. Grizzled light from the window pooled on my comforter. My limbs shook, my face wore an invisible mask of heavy plaster, but I rose to my hands and knees. I let the joggers crumple to the floor and crawled the vast seven feet to my bed.

From my knees, I rolled back the covers. Then I heaved myself into bed and wrapped my achy, unpredictable body.

Later, when Austie knocked and asked through the door if I was still going to take a shower, I told her I wasn't feeling well after all.

A while later, she knocked again and asked to come in. She brought me water in a plastic Red Rooster tumbler and a bottle of ibuprofen. She folded my abandoned clothes and stacked them on top of the dresser. Ensuring I had my phone, she told me to text her if I needed anything.

"We'll try to keep it down for you," she added.

We. Because Reva came soon after. There were murmured words and clanks of silverware and sprinkles of laughter. An evening of simple, precious things unfolded. Things only they knew the radiance of.

As for me, I dreamed of red Beetles and soccer balls and turquoise earrings and diet sodas. Then I dreamed it was all a dream.

53

THE PLAN WAS SIMPLE: Fill the Red Rooster tumbler with more water and get back to bed. A refill at three o'clock in the morning was no need to text Austie. I eased up from the bed, measuring out each movement before I made it. Outside my window, snowflakes dashed through the open air, glinting in the moonbeams like white static on a screen.

My legs were languid but stable—and fully sensitized. I palmed the empty cup and followed the silvery light to the door. The jerky swing of my gait evoked the Claymation shows of my childhood Saturday mornings. As hushed as possible, I opened my door and slid my feet along the floorboards into the hallway. More pale light angled through the bay window, illuminating the turn into the kitchen.

I slid forward, left foot, right foot, quiet as the white blanket over the house.

Then the cup fell from my hand.

One second it was in my palm, secured by all five fingers, and the next it sailed down. The bottom edge struck first. *Clank!* The force flipped it in the air and brought it down on its side, bouncing it several times. *Clack, clack, clack!* Then it rolled to the frame of Austie's door.

My breath stuck in my throat. So much for stealth.

But after several beats and no sounds, I exhaled and shuffled toward the wayward cup. I crouched, reached. Almost there. My head was too heavy, limbs too onerous. I sagged to my hands and knees. I paused there, mustering my control.

Get the cup. Get up. Get out.

Gritting my teeth, I lifted one hand. No sooner did my fingertips raise from the wood than a band of light popped through the gap under Austie's door.

No!

The door opened. Full light pounded into my eyes. I abandoned the cup, sank against my heels, and turned my face away.

"Jess?"

No chance to hide. No redeeming the mission. And no use trying to convince her I was fine. So I said nothing and kept my profile masked by the mayhem of my hair.

She knelt in front of me and cupped my upper left arm. My muscles went taut.

"Come on. Let's get you back to bed." She tugged me upward.

"I can do it." I wriggled in her grasp, but she only fastened harder. Even I couldn't deny the rag-doll quality of my ascent to a standing position. At one point on the way up, my head nearly touched her shoulder. The cup stayed where it was, and she guided me back to my room, latched to my arm the whole way.

My legs began to fade, ready to drop any and all weight they held aloft. We reached the nightstand. I leaned toward the bed. In the dim light, the edges of the hospital bill peeked out from under my pillow. I had forgotten it. Blocking Austie's view as best I could, I tapped the papers back into their hiding spot before ebbing back into my own.

With me safely supine, Austie began to retrace her steps. "I'll get you more water in a fresh cup."

Her energy awoke; mine drained. How pathetic that getting

my own cup of water would be too much. Was it an illness? Or was it another taste of the reality of a diseased brain? I loathed the not knowing. But either way, I needed it to go away. I lugged the covers to my chest and let my head loll to the right, to the darker side of my room.

In the kitchen, cabinets opened, water poured. Soon she returned, and the tone in her voice was different. "Jess, were you in the hospital?"

My eyes popped open. I rolled my head toward her. The moonlight seeping through the window outlined the large plastic mug with a flexible straw in her grip. Another mission failed. I should have thrown out the mug the same day I arrived home with it from Northland Memorial.

"They tried to give me one of these too," she said. "When were you there?"

Of all the times my hospital stay could have come up before, especially from Kyla's lips, it never had. I had fooled myself into believing it never would. "September," I said, my voice fading under the heft of words.

"September?" She paused. "You mean, that's where you were when I came looking for you? Labor Day?"

"Mm-hmm."

"You never said anything."

"'s okay." The back of my head pressed deeper into the pillow. My eyes closed.

Maybe it was my waning interaction, but she let it go. A scooch and tap on the nightstand indicated she had found a place for the mug to roost.

"You should call out of work today," she said.

"Mmm."

"Or can you text your boss?"

"Mm-hmm."

"I could do it if you want."

On my next exhale, I pushed out a "'kay." Because lifting a

thousand-pound barbell over my head sounded easier than finding the brain power to peck out a message.

Another scooting sound. "Okay, I've got your phone." She narrated every action she took, from waking it up to navigating to my text messages. "Searching for the new-message icon. Oh, wait." She paused again. Several seconds passed. "Sorry, here it is. I'm ready. What's your boss's name?"

Thankfully it required only one easy syllable. "Paul."

"Got it." Her thumbnails occasionally clicked against the screen as she prepared the message. "Don't worry, I'll read it to you before I send."

That wasn't the worry. It was the second sick day I had taken in less than four months of working at HML. If whatever it was holding me to bed didn't pass quickly, I'd need more. Paul knew I was an efficient worker, but he had limits too.

"Here's what I've got," she said at last. "'Paul, feeling sick. Need to take the day off. Thanks.'"

If it were me writing, I would have promised to make up all my work when I was back. I would have started with "Sorry." And I would have waited until a more reasonable hour to send it.

"Sound good?" Austie asked.

"Mmm."

"All right. Sent."

Couldn't get my own water. Couldn't send my own texts. If I'd had the energy, I would have cried. The tap against my nightstand told me she had replaced my phone in its spot.

"I work six to one today. I'll try to keep my phone on me in case you need something." Her footfalls tracked across the room. Then a moment of silence, followed by her voice, carrying a sullen note. "Jess, if there is something you need—ever—I hope you know that I'd help."

I wanted to tell her not to be so worried, that it was nothing to concern herself about. But I didn't have the juice, and that likely only added to her chafe. It certainly did to mine.

The door shut softly behind her. My cheek soon fell against my pillow.

For the next many hours, I drifted in and out of sleep, deep into other worlds, then surfacing again in the one that wouldn't let me go. I came back first to Austie moving about the bathroom before work. Then to Paul's return message that I found a moment of energy to read. He encouraged me to feel better. Then to the daylight wresting the snowy caps off the trees. And last to more sounds from the kitchen. Glass clinked against glass. Beeps of the microwave buttons. A whir. A drawer opening. Silverware against counter.

I pulled the covers to my forehead. Life carried on for Austie despite all that loomed, despite the many questions yet to be answered.

The microwave dinged.

I rolled onto my right side, away from the door, and tucked my bottom hand under my pillow. The edges of the paper stack poked into my skin. I pushed it deeper into its hiding spot.

Footsteps came down the hallway. But they didn't stop at the bathroom, nor at Austie's room. They bore straight for my door and stopped outside. A knock.

How did I get her to stop fretting over me? I dipped the covers under my chin and coughed to wake up my vocal cords. "Yeah," I called.

The doorknob creaked, followed by a faint whoosh of air and pats of soft-soled shoes. But the voice did not belong to Austie.

"Good morning, Jess."

A burst of cold flooded me. I twisted my upper body toward the door, bringing my attention to the speaker standing there.

Reva's turquoise earrings still swayed from her trek. The end of her Bible stuck out from under her arm. At the waist of her long brown skirt, she held either end of a large plastic plate. A few saltines leaned against the bowl in the middle.

"W-what . . . ?"

"What am I doing here?"

I nodded.

She pointed her eyes to the Bible, then back at me. "Being the bigger ox."

54

"SIT UP AND HAVE some food." Reva carried the plate closer to the bed, careful not to disturb the bowl in the middle. A savory aroma fanned through the air and roused a twinge of nausea. According to the alarm clock, it was still breakfast time.

"Not feeling well," I rasped.

Unmoved by my pitiful reply, she landed the same hawklike stare on me that she had the first time we met, when I tried to escape from under the church awning. "In that case," she said, "let me put this down, and I'll help you sit up." She strode toward my workstation with evident determination.

"Okay," I said, bringing her to a halt. With much effort, I flopped my lower half flat to the mattress. As she returned to my bedside with the plate, I labored to a seated position. My backside pushed the pillow up on end, then came to rest on top of the hospital bill. The papers would remain well hidden there. I leaned my head against the wall behind the bed. My arms throbbed with exhaustion and drooped at my sides.

None of it deterred my visitor, however. She placed the plate on my wide lap. "Have something to eat."

A saltine cracker shifted against the bowl of soup. Chicken noodle, the kind with carrot slices and doughy pasta in golden broth. The noodles' irregular shape indicated they were homemade. The twinge sharpened.

I shook my head. "Not too—"

She leveled her gaze at me.

I sighed and reached for the spoon. With the strength of a feather rolling a stone, I scooped a bit of broth and a short, fat noodle, then lifted it toward my lips. I hunched forward, inflaming the weariness, but somehow managed to get the contents into my mouth without losing a drop. The seasoned broth woke every taste bud, and its heat rippled through my chest on the way down. Beyond a doubt, it was the best soup of my life. I laid the spoon in the bowl and started to lean back.

Reva cleared her throat, then jutted her chin at the food.

Protesting had proven futile. I took a second bite that included a softened carrot slice. It warmed my entire core and surprisingly tempered the nausea. For good-behavior points, I slurped a third spoonful as well. The warmth seeped down to my legs and up to the tips of my ears. I set the spoon on the plate, then chose a cracker and nibbled off the corner as I leaned my head against the wall. My hand holding the cracker sank to the comforter.

Reva rolled my office chair into the space between the rag rug and the foot of my bed. She lay her Bible in her lap and crossed her hands on the cover. "Austie called and asked me to come check on you. She's worried about you." Reva tilted her head. "Should she be?"

The mushed saltine stuck to my teeth. A slurp of broth or a sip of water would have loosened it. Instead of reaching for either liquid, I let my hands rest where they were. "Just got a little bug or something."

Quiet lingered. Reva's stare pierced through my meager shield and straight into my chest.

Then her eyes swiveled to the nightstand. "Need some water?"

Heat poured into my face. She had spotted the hospital mug.

Austie had probably told her about it and the unexplained medical care it represented. I shook my head and deposited the cracker next to the bowl.

Reva's voice was steady, not forceful, not singsong, but stalwart and as rhythmic as the Wood River current. "Yesterday in Allelon we talked about speaking truthfully to one another. In the spirit of that, I have a few questions I'd like to ask you."

I gathered the surface of the comforter in both hands.

"My first question is this: What do you see when you look at me?"

I blinked.

"It's an odd question, I know," she said. "But it's an important one. Tell me what you think of when you look at me. What words come to mind?"

In other contexts, such a question from a woman could be a minefield. But that wasn't how Reva played. I bobbed one shoulder. "Wise?"

She waited, clearly wanting more.

I rubbed the comforter with my thumbs. "Strong . . . compassionate . . . observant."

The corner of her mouth slanted up, as if even she knew how eerily accurate her observations could be. "I'm glad that's how you see me," she said.

Something in that reply hinted she was about to lean into all four descriptions.

"My next question, Jess, is what do you think I see when I look at you?"

My lips reflexively puckered. For a Becker, sentimentality was as natural as a dog's meow. "Cringe," Kyla would have called it. I would have given anything to submerge myself alongside the carrots. But I wasn't going anywhere. Neither was Reva. So I shook my head.

She unstacked her hands and spread them flush to the Bible's cover. "I see someone I care about deeply. Someone Austie cares about deeply, enough to give up her home to protect that someone. I see a woman who modeled that kind of self-sacrifice for her young Christian sister."

The heat rekindled and spread through my stomach. I pulled my gaze to the bowl.

"I see an inclination to the least of these," she said, "and a faith big enough to grow into."

I clinched the comforter.

"And the more I get to know you, Jess, the more one thing becomes clearer. I see a child shivering under storm clouds that she doesn't yet recognize contain blessing."

A hush enveloped the room. What did she mean?

Reva locked onto me and scooted her chair closer. The wheels caught against the rug. "That brings me to my next question. It may not seem related, but it is. And it's a question I'm guessing has crossed your mind a time or two." She pointed to the scar under her left eye. "Have you ever wondered how I got this?"

I nodded.

"Good, because it's time you knew." She reclined, then crossed one knee over the other, perching her Bible on top. "Not long after the second time Gio and I separated, I made the foolish decision to drive when I wasn't in the proper condition. The accident left me in the hospital for months, and in physical and occupational therapy much longer. I had to relearn how to walk and talk and regain the use of my hands."

It was hard to imagine. Those hands on her Bible, which moved with a beautiful fluidity and produced pitch-perfect blue marks on a whiteboard, had once been fruitless. Her feet, on which she sailed across sidewalks to greet newcomers, had once been inert. And her tongue, which produced such insight, had been stilled. The gash that had created her scar must have been one of many.

"It was frustrating being in a body I couldn't control," she said. "Even the most basic functions were out of reach for me for a long time. I was heavily reliant on others, and I hated it. I hated feeling useless."

I swallowed and focused on the bowl.

"But the worst part of it," she continued, "was that I was convinced Gio wouldn't want someone as foolish and shattered as me. No one would, I thought, so I pushed him and everyone away."

The bill burned through the seat of my pajamas. Across the room, in the top drawer of my dresser, the buried papers clattered like dry bones.

"Gio wouldn't settle for that, though. He came to the hospital when he could and sent others when he couldn't. One of them was my coworker at the time, Jackie. She showed up three times a week, always with her Bible. She read every Gospel book to me at least twice. Initially, I resented it, but she came so consistently, with such joy, that I began to look forward to her visits. It was there, laid up in a hospital bed, that I first understood my need for Jesus—and for his church."

That last part snagged against me. My attention moved to her.

She flipped open her Bible and turned to a page marked by a note card. "Jackie loved to sing old hymns with me. One of her favorites was 'God Moves in a Mysterious Way.' It came to mean so much to me that a lyric from it was among the first things I learned to write." She lifted the note card and passed it to me. "Would you read this, please? Aloud."

The card's surface was worn smooth with age and use. The edges were crinkled. Wobbly black-ink writing crawled across the plain white background. I held it over the plate, called up what power I could, and read, "'Ye fearful saints, fresh courage take; the clouds ye so much dread are big with mercy—'" The image stopped me cold, the words caught on my tongue. With constricted voice, I finished, "'And shall break in blessings on your head.'"

Tingles fired up my arms. Clouds, dread. Mercy. Blessings.

"Many believe it's based on a verse from Ezekiel." Reva traced a line on the page in front of her and read, "'I will send down the showers in their season; they shall be showers of blessing.'" She leaned forward, fixed me with her stare. "In my experience, Jess, the showers of blessing were not necessarily healing or miracles, though those are certainly included. Often the blessings arrived in the form of his people being his people."

My hand began to shake. I laid it on the comforter, note card still in my grip.

"They were the ones bringing a meal to my family or praying for me or reading the Gospels to me or helping me understand what the doctors said."

The rattle shot to my chin. I clamped my teeth on my lip, but it did little good.

"And I almost missed them, Jess. I almost missed the beautiful hands and feet of Christ right in front of me on earth because I was too fearful of the clouds overhead. If I had rejected their love, whose love really would I have rejected? Who really would I have held at arm's length?"

Fiery pressure built in my chest, my head, my eyes.

"God takes his one anothers seriously. Because through them, he grows our maturity and lets us know that he hasn't forgotten us in our trials. He sends his people as an assurance that he doesn't look away."

The flames flared. He had sent his people. Under a church awning. With a pizza box. To an ER waiting room. In a laugh, a smile, a touch. In a text, a prayer, a new pot. With a bowl of soup to my bedside, a vision and desire only he knew about. He had heard, seen, and come contained in the beautiful hands and feet that had been right in front of me. The hands and feet I had not counted trustworthy.

Tears blurred everything. I squeezed my eyes shut.

Reva's tone softened. "Jess."

I shook my head.

Her hand grasped my arm. The shock of her touch snapped my gaze to hers. The drops teetering on her lashes harmonized with mine.

She searched my face. "Will you tell me what's going on?"

In our first full conversation on her back porch, with the bird skimming and the ice cubes melting, she vowed to let me tell my own story in my own time. The time had arrived, and she had guided me there not with guilt or expectation but with gentle candor and an earnest willingness to stay in the ugly. With a relentless commitment to the high call of sisterhood.

Pouring out with the sobs came every truthful detail.

55

AUSTIE SAT WITH HER LEGS crisscrossed in the office chair, Cost Cutter polo untucked, bruised face scrunching tighter with every new bit I shared. Reva perched on the foot of my bed and nodded me onward through the hardest parts. She had heard them herself only hours before. Though the fatigue still encased me, the full bowl of soup and morning nap had given me enough spark for this little conference. Reva showed her the discharge papers and my handwritten notes as I talked about my hospital stay, the upcoming neurologist appointment, and the vast unpredictability of my body. Austie looked between us, as if reading our cues for how to feel. Reva's strong, squared posture lent calm.

When all of it was out in the open, Austie stared down at the stack in her hands, quiet.

"It's a lot to take in, isn't it?" Reva asked.

She nodded. "But I knew it had to be serious."

I frowned at the response. "How?"

The two of them exchanged a look. Reva tipped her head in encouragement for Austie to continue.

She shifted in the chair. "I happened to see the texts from the neurology place in your message history. That's what shook me enough to call Reva."

The moment from early that morning resurfaced, of the odd pause when she'd prepared to contact Paul. The clinic's messages had been a dim memory. So many weeks had passed since Dr. Levan's team had sent me the appointment reminder and the link to the patient forms.

"Guess I didn't cover my tracks as well as I thought," I said.

"Glad you didn't," Reva replied.

And maybe there was a reason for that. If Austie had not come across those text messages, had not seen the plastic mug and put the clues together, then my plan to keep them in the dark would have held. Someone more powerful had had other ideas, though, the way he did at the entrance of Trinity. God didn't send his people on fruitless missions.

Reva gathered the papers from Austie and leaned over the end of the bed to toss them onto my workstation. They landed next to the invoice, which she had put there as a reminder for me to call the billing office and inquire about a payment plan.

She resettled and trailed her palms down her thighs. "Jess, how much does your dad know about this?"

I leaned my head against the wall. "Not much. Told him I had MS on Thanksgiving. Conversation fell apart after that. The whole visit did."

Her brow narrowed as she, too, put together clues. "That's why you came home early."

I nodded.

Sympathy pooled in her expression. "Could it be that he's scared? I can imagine it's hard for him to know what to do with the news."

Dad had yelled, cursed, turned away from me. It still needled days later. But he had done the same after Mom's funeral, when people had tried to bring food. Fear and pride so often looked the same. I shrugged. "It's possible."

Austie eased her feet to the floor. "But what do *we* do with the news?"

Her question contained a vow. Though we might end up living in separate homes, she wanted to stay with me in a way that mattered, like Reva. That alone told me everything I ever needed to remember about them both.

"One practical thing we can do is research MS together," Reva said. "That way we all understand it better."

Both nodded, eyes firmly on me. The last time I lay in a bed with people paying such close attention to me, I was a puzzle to be solved, a case to be charted, a source of fluid to be studied. To these two women, however, I wasn't something to understand within the parameters of impersonal medical science. I was a soul to bolster, a sister to hold. And whose hands were they ultimately? An ember ignited in my chest.

My phone's ringtone cut through the room. Our gazes pivoted to my nightstand.

The name on the screen pulled me upright.

"Who is it?" Austie asked. "Your boss?"

I shook my head. "My dad."

Reva chuckled. "God really does hear everything, doesn't he?"

I gnawed my lip. What would I say to him? Did I even want to talk to him right then? He wasn't the only one who was scared.

"We'll give you some privacy," Reva said. She stood and motioned for Austie to follow suit. As they strode out, Reva looked at me and smiled. The scar under her eye contorted with the lift of her cheek. One small gesture spoke a dozen encouragements of what to do in the face of fear. Be kind, be at peace, live in harmony, speak truthfully, be humble, outdo in honoring, forgive. It was the kind of love we were called to give each other, and to model to anyone who may have been watching, including those who hurt us.

When the door thumped shut, I took an anchoring breath, then answered on speakerphone. "Hey, Dad."

His tone was guarded. "This a good time?" The familiar creak of his office chair punctuated his words.

I lay the phone on my thigh and rested against the wall. "Yeah. What's up?"

"Bonnie wants to know what you're doing for Christmas. She's trying to plan some things."

Straight to business. No inquiry as to how I was doing or apology for how our Thanksgiving ended. But I couldn't expect anything else. I let my arms go slack next to my legs. With both my health and my living arrangements so undefined, the holidays had not been in my top five concerns. "I'm not sure yet. Can I let you know in a few days?"

"That's fine." He cleared his throat directly into the phone.

Some things about Kevin Becker never changed.

"Her family's trying to get together for dinner again," he explained. "Not that I'm eager to get back to that mess."

"Know what you mean." Her family celebrations were a far cry from the ones he and I shared in front of the television. He had probably endured off-key karaoke at some point, and certainly some animated exchanges about each other's shortcomings before they moved on to those of people who were not in the room. Which begged a question.

"Dad, did you tell Bonnie about my diagnosis?"

In the distant background, one of the boys hammered on metal, the noise too thundering to be stopped by his office door. Dad's reply layered over top of it. "Figured it was up to you to tell whoever you wanted."

I exhaled. At least his favor for privacy remained intact.

"By the way," he said, "found a box of things in the closet I thought you might want."

"What kind of things?"

"From your mom."

I lifted my head from the wall. "From Mom?" I'd never had reason or welcome to go into their closet. He had cleaned out the house after I graduated, and my assumption had been that process included the most private spaces.

"Yearbooks, photo albums, an old watch, stuff like that," he said. "Also a locket I gave her for our wedding. Chain's broke. Pendant's silver and has her birthstone in the middle."

Though he said so little, a picture began to form of a young bride opening a velvet box from her groom. Him smiling with satisfaction. Her tearing up. Such a sweet, intimate moment. Those were the kinds of moments, stories, my daughter's heart had always craved.

"Anyway," he said, "I can mail it to you if you want."

Another scene formed. Of him and me on the couch, the box of Mom's belongings between us, each item tenderly ushering in questions and memories. Stories. The help I could get only from him, the help he finally seemed ready to give. The sun brightened outside the window.

"Or I'll get it at Christmas," I said.

More hammering pounded in the background, a reminder of the hardened world to which he clung. A world that was antithetical to mine, with a cold, ragged chasm in between. But his tone loosened, and his reach was evident. "That works too."

He had been close to saying he missed me before; that whole conversation was closer still. For the moment, it would be enough. A place to start.

Door hinges whined, and a male voice poured into the background. Long strings of muffled words. Dad mumbled a response about "idiots," then returned to me. "Gotta run, Jess."

"Thanks for calling, Dad."

Off he went, out of his chair to tend to whatever the boys had done.

Some things with Dad, with our relationship, might never change. But some things, in important ways, were poised to shift.

Outside, a rich sapphire accentuated the snow that stuck to the leaves like puffs of cotton. Many things in my life, in important ways, had already started to transform.

As I was about to lay down my phone, a text message popped

onto the screen. The words from Austie quickened my heartbeat.

When ur ready Ron wants to talk to us

The answer from the landlord had come. The proverbial fork in the road had been reached. Soon, she and I would both know which way we were to go. But no matter which way it was, one thing remained certain.

I turned to the window. A chunk of snow slid from its loft, broke apart on the descent, and fell to the ground in a gentle, gleaming shower.

"I don't go alone," I whispered.

56

THE MINUTE HAND on the clock over Gio's head inched closer to the top of the hour that marked the end of class. It was almost the end of 2023 as well, almost time for my first appointment with Dr. Levan. In four days, I would be sitting in the neurologist's exam room, once again trusting a stranger in a white coat to decipher the behavior of my body. The research Reva and Austie helped me do could tell us only so much. I would leave Dr. Levan's with a plan, a few more answers, and maybe a few sobering reality checks.

Austie sat next to me in the back row of the classroom, Bible open in her lap, pointer finger fanning the top corners of the pages. She glanced at the clock, as if she, too, counted the drumbeat of time. Her week also contained a momentous occasion. She would start her job as a receptionist at Dr. Riggs's dental practice. Higher pay, better hours, more professional coworkers. Applying had been one of her best decisions to date, aside from meeting with a community college admissions counselor.

Gio continued with the last strains of the lesson, encouraging us to take the reminder to "spur one another on" into the week. The soft "amens" trickling across the room were interrupted by the click of the door opening. Kyla poked her head into the room and scanned the faces. I started to stand so she could see me better, but she zoomed onto Reva in the front row and scampered to the seat next to her.

"What's Kyla doing here?" I whispered to Austie.

She only grinned and closed her Bible.

At the lectern, Gio closed his as well. "We're going to end class a little bit differently today," he said. "You may recall that this is an important week for one of our members. Not too long ago, she shared some difficult health news with us."

He zeroed in on me. The heat of a hundred summer days burned my cheeks.

"Jess, would you please join me up here for a moment?"

Every pair of eyes zipped to the back row. Even the roots of my hair began to burn. Austie patted my arm, encouraging me to go. She clearly knew it had been coming. So had Kyla. Reva caught my attention and gently tipped her head toward the front of the room.

Slowly I rose and laid my Bible and notebook on my chair. My classmates' stares followed me up the center aisle and stuck to me as I turned to face the room. Kyla smiled and waved. Reva's squared posture lent peace. Beyond them were the people of Allelon, some of whose names I had said multiple times—Ellen, Thea, Todd—and some whose names were newer to my repertoire—Joan, Jenny, Ben, Erika, Jake, Anne, Jordan, Rachel, Alice, Becky, Kurt, Linda, Dan, Laura, and others. A replenishment of the community I once had and lost. But they were different. They were the kind who received the news of my diagnosis with offers to understand it better and connect me with others they knew who had experience with MS. It was stunning how many people were only a few degrees separated from the disease.

"This Thursday," Gio said to the class, "Jess has her first neurology appointment. It is the start of a long journey for her. First Corinthians 12 tells us that as one member goes, we all go, whether in suffering or rejoicing. Let's live that out right now. Everyone, please stand and gather around our sister."

Instantly, I tensed. Chair legs scooted. Bibles patted cushioned seats. Shoe soles squeaked. They were coming toward me, for me, swirling into a single cell that sucked me into its core. So close, they filled in the gaps. So near, the tallest men partially blocked the fluorescent lights. I dipped my head, hunched away. But Reva, in her earthy brown flats, came to rest at my left side, her shoulder pressed against mine. Austie's sneakers shuffled into place on my right. Kyla's crew socks in Birkenstocks rested in front of me, toes pointed to mine.

Gio called for everyone to bow their heads. All other noise fell away—the tick of the clock, the voices from the next room—and all movement stilled.

"Heavenly Father," he began, "with the same hands that hung every star, you hold Jess. You know the number of hairs on her head and can discern every question that clouds her mind. May your mercy flow through her this week, as gentle as a stream, calming every fear and whispering your promises to be with her."

God would not look away, nor would he push me away. He knew what to do with what befell me.

I reached for the locket dangling over the collar of my sweater. My left thumb traced back and forth over the amethyst in the middle. The jewel had twinkled at me from the velvet box Dad had set in my hands on Christmas Day. I hadn't taken the necklace off since then.

I returned my hand to my side as the prayer popcorned from Gio to others, each person advocating on my behalf in full belief that heaven absorbed every word. Todd prayed for God to defend me, a true-to-form ask of a police officer. Joan prayed for patience to abound. Others spoke of wisdom for the doctors, grace from my employer, provision for expenses. Thea ended her portion with a plea for "any unspoken burdens" I might be carrying. Based on what I had seen of her, perhaps she shouldered more than a few unspoken burdens of her own. Perhaps I needed to be better at offering her a holy greeting.

Ellen prayed for the medical staff to have empathy and for me to have the presence of mind to seek, ask, and understand. Even so, I was thankful she would be with me at Dr. Levan's to listen and understand with more ability than I possessed.

Kyla took a turn, asking that I "would be strong and recover quickly from any relapses," a sign she had learned the lingo of my world the way I had amassed a vocabulary for hers. She suddenly latched on to my hand, causing me to stiffen. But as her next words came, laced with gratitude for me and my willingness to bring her to church and welcome her to my table, I relaxed in her grip.

"And thank you, God, that Jess and Austie are still my neighbors. I hope they will be for a long time."

My chest hitched. I squeezed her hand, and she squeezed back.

Then Austie's trembling voice spread through the hushed room. "I pray for Jess. I pray she has a good appointment and gets good information. Thank you for the way she is so kind to others and for how she sees the best even in the worst of us. God, whatever I can do for her, please show me."

Like her young counterpart, Austie reached for me. She hooked her arm around mine. This young woman who had overcome so much stood ready to help me conquer too. I did not deserve such support. I did not deserve such prayers. I sniffed back the pressure building behind my eyes.

But then came Reva.

"Mighty God," she prayed, "indeed, whatever we can do for one another, please show us. Stir us to unity and good works. May we never grow weary in pursuing either. Help us remain faithful to Jesus's instruction to love one another, bending to your sovereignty and being a witness to a watching world. May the testimony of Jess's journey with MS be a brilliant light that others in her life cannot ignore or turn away from."

The tears began to seep onto my lashes. Would Dad see? Was he watching? Could it be that the journey given to me would be, in part, a reason for him to lean closer to that brilliant, unignorable light? I bowed lower.

Reva stretched her arm across my shoulders. Her strength coursed into me.

"You have told us to expect the road to be hard, but you do not send us where you have not already treaded, and you do not send us alone. Grant each of us, in increasing measure, the perseverance and compassion required. May the heavy clouds ahead not fill us with dread, but an expectation for your blessings to break upon our heads in their season. Guide us as we walk together, side by side, shoulder to shoulder, life against life, as you have designed your church to do. In Jesus's name . . ."

The entire group joined together to finish. "Amen."

The prayer had concluded. The class had ended. The new hour had come, drawing people to the next part of the morning. But the four of us stayed where we were, bowed and linked, hearts full and sore. Even if I wanted to wipe my eyes, I couldn't. Austie had one arm locked in place. Kyla had the other. Reva had yoked herself to me. Each of them bore pieces of my burden that I did not have to coax them to take. I didn't have to try to convince them to follow me into this new chapter; they already strode next to me.

After a moment, Kyla took a step back and loosened her grip. "Jess?"

I lifted my head and blinked against the blur. "Yes?"

She puckered her brow. "Can we get frozen sodas on the way home?"

Reva was the first to laugh, the sound as sweet as light rain dancing on a river's surface. Then Austie, bold and free.

Then me. I held out my fist to Kyla, who bumped it in response.

"Kyla," I said, "I can think of nothing better."

AUTHOR NOTE and RESOURCES

Having community is one thing we all crave yet struggle with on some level. For Christians, forming and nurturing community with fellow believers is not only important for us to stay focused on Jesus in every dimension of life, but it's also a command.

The initial idea for this book came from an adult Sunday school series at my church. The series centered on the "one another" verses of the New Testament, and the goal was to help the church understand why God takes Christian community so seriously, for our good and his glory. My family and I were new to the church at the time. We were in the thick of finding new community after a difficult goodbye to our previous church. I was in the thick of wondering how much to reveal about myself and to whom. The series was both emotional and eye-opening.

Of the many perspective changes that resulted for me, chief among them was an acknowledgment that we as people tend to be inclined to *do* the one-anothering but shudder at the thought of *being* one-anothered.

Around the same time, I became more aware of multiple sclerosis. Chances are good that you, too, know or will know someone living with MS. According to the MS International Federation, more than 2.9 million people worldwide have been diagnosed as of 2023.* MS has also come more into the spotlight thanks to celebrities such as Selma Blair and Christina Applegate sharing their experiences.

I was drawn to studying MS and the stories of people affected by it. The more I learned, the more I understood how the disease could be known yet unknown, have typical symptoms yet also be so wildly unpredictable, possess a universal quality yet be completely individualized.

What struck me the most was a certain dichotomy about this disease: Those who have a strong support system are generally better equipped to navigate life with MS, but people diagnosed with it often feel reticent to share this part of their lives with others, mostly out of fear. Fear of how they will be perceived, fear of losing their jobs, fear of being a burden, fear of not being understood as their symptoms form a new reality for them that looks so different than "normal." The thing they are wired to desire—community—is something that can feel so far out of reach.

Isolation, loneliness, and fear are relatable emotions, and they are all the opposite of what God wants for us.

My hope is that you will come away from this book inspired to nurture healthy, biblical community, especially when it comes to trusting others to help carry the most delicate parts of your life, as godly discernment leads.

Because God tells us it is worth it. So very worth it.

*MS International Federation, "Atlas of MS," accessed November 1, 2025, https://atlasofms.org/map/global/epidemiology/number-of-people-with-ms#about.

RESOURCES

Among the many resources I used in the research and development of this story were the following:

Up the Down Escalator: Medicine, Motherhood, and Multiple Sclerosis by Dr. Lisa Doggett (memoir)

A Sundog Moment by Sharon Baldacci (fiction)

31 Ways to Be a "One Another" Christian: Loving Others with the Love of Jesus by Dr. Stuart Scott (nonfiction)

Living Out the One Anothers of Scripture: A 30-Day Devotional by Revive Our Hearts Ministries (nonfiction)

ACKNOWLEDGMENTS

Acknowledgments are a time capsule of sorts. They not only allow me to capture the names and contributions of people who had influence over this story, but they also stand as a reminder for years to come how God has worked through so many people to get this book to the audience for whom it was intended.

My deepest gratitude goes to:

Stacy Kroeker, Kristie Brinkley, Dr. Anne Jacobsen, and Dr. Julie Kostreva, who helped me write about the MS experience with accuracy and sensitivity.

Jackie Wilson for opening up the world of radiological science.

Rachel Rice for sharing her professional experience in the legal field.

Ruthie Burrell and Bekki Diefendorf for insightful comments and feedback on the earliest draft.

Angela Bell, Heather Kaufman, and Jamie Ogle for a timely brainstorming and encouragement session when the biggest hurdles to finishing this book pressed in on me.

The pastors and elders at my local church, whose Sunday school series based on the "one another" verses of the New Testament planted the seed for this book—and changed my mindset.

My local church, whose members unfailingly give their support and prayers in all the ways that matter.

Cynthia Ruchti, who keeps my attention on the One who deserves it most. Thank you for being more than an agent.

Rachel McRae, for your compassionate editorial guidance. You allowed me to lean on you in the drafting of this book and never wavered from your belief that this was a story worth telling. To me, you are always Editor of the Year.

Jessica English, in whose hands I trust everything I write. Thank you for catching the vision of my stories and ensuring no thing, big or small, hinders that vision from taking full shape.

The entire Revell and Baker Publishing Group team, who patiently field my many questions and ideas, see things I cannot, and do things I cannot.

My daughters, who served as cheerleaders, coffee break companions, and subject matter experts on the teenager world. Thank you for not cringing (too hard) when I asked you to verify usage of generational vernacular.

My husband, Robert, who has learned far more about the "one another" verses, MS, and the inner workings of my mind than he ever saw coming. Thank you for receiving the windfall of my musings, questions, and tears with gentleness.

Above all, Almighty God, who faithfully provides stories to tell and the grace to tell them, especially when the telling is beyond what I think I can handle. Each book leaves behind evidence of change and growth in me, and I pray the same is true in these precious readers you have brought to this story. May they see you on every page.

READ ON FOR AN EXCERPT

FROM SARA BRUNSVOLD'S

The ATLAS of UNTOLD STORIES

AVAILABLE NOW

WHEREVER BOOKS ARE SOLD

1

STRANGE HOW AN EMPTY ROOM could be haunted by sound, especially a sound as whispery and distant as the *shiff* of sand between the bowls of an hourglass. Tendrils of the memory prickled Edie Vance's skin. She hugged her arms to her stomach. The Persian rug under her feet still bore the indents from the weight of her mother's grand mahogany desk. Her spirit zapped back to those afternoons decades prior.

Her eight-year-old form in the wingback chair in the corner, in the room but out of the way, the chair far too big for her body, and the book open on her lap far too dense for her comprehension. Across the room, in the soft touch of light from the bay window, her only remaining parent sat bent over an English major's research paper, red pen scratching across it. Between them was the antique hourglass, enthroned on the corner of the imposing desk. She could not see her mother without first seeing it. Every grain that fell was one second less of her time allotted in her mother's presence. The sand ran faster than her eyes across the page. The page could never hold her attention for long anyway. None of the books in her mother's ample collection lining the walls ever had pictures.

And none of those minutes measured out by the hourglass included a glance from her mother, not until the last grain had slipped to the bottom bowl.

"Did you enjoy your book, Edith?" her mother would ask. *Your book*, as if Edie had any rights to it.

Edie took her time answering. The longer the wait, the longer her mother's eyes had rested upon her.

Many decades removed from those afternoons, Edie stood freely in the middle of the study and breathed in what once was so real in that space. The desk, the books, the wingback chair, the silent cascade of sand were all gone. The last grain had fallen, for good. Still she waited for her mother's eyes to fall upon her. Could her mother see her now, through the veil between eternity and present?

A knock on the open door drew her attention.

"Me," Grant said. "It's quarter to two. Don't want to be late."

"Coming, dear."

He adjusted his bifocals on the bridge of his nose and swept his gaze across the room. "Seems bigger now that it's empty."

"Bigger in so many ways," she murmured.

"Want me to take the rug downstairs, put it with everything else?"

The plush piling cushioned the soles of her flats. She curled her toes as if attempting to root herself in deeper. The ornate gold and burgundy paisley had elevated the richness of the wood furniture with which her mother once surrounded herself with pride, a victory statement after being left with nothing when her husband abandoned her and their two small children. The rug was all that remained of the Moria Mondell dynasty. The walls bore scars from the dismantled bookshelves. The books, once so prized, faced an unknown fate at the estate sale.

"I'll bring it down later," she replied to his offer.

"Meet you downstairs." Promise given, he headed back toward the stairs.

His occasional habit of shortening sentences, leaving off the subject and sometimes the predicate, had been the first hash mark against him on her mother's mental scorecard. The second, his openness to any financial advice other than Warren Buffett's.

She squeezed her arms tighter, traced her fingertips along her sides. If given the choice between her husband and her mother, she would always choose her husband.

So why did she still dream of those afternoons?

2

CHLOE VANCE TRACED her Pitt pen along the penciled sketch marks she had made earlier on the page, angling the ultra-fine point down and to the left. She then carefully crosshatched over the dark line to convey the softness of the jawline she had known all of her twenty-six years. The softness of her mom's jaw complemented the delicate nature of her fingertips, which always bore some dainty shade of pink or red. Maybe only artists noticed such details.

The framed photo of her mom sat to the right of her sketch-book. Without question, the photo was the best Chloe had ever taken of her. It provided the perfect reference for what she had tried three times so far to bring to the page as a surprise parting gift for her mom. She needed something of great value to demonstrate that her talents and gifting could be a blessing to others, a way to help them notice the world, and themselves, in richer ways.

If only she could get her mom's eyes right. She could never quite capture all the nuance they possessed. The eyes contained the light of a person, a collision of past and future, with soul secrets that couldn't stay hidden entirely. Where words failed, drawings spoke. They could speak a language all their own. They held the striking tension of whimsy and reverence, hope and fear, longing and duty. To express all that required the right combinations of forms and shadows.

Maybe the fourth attempt would be different.

She sang along to the praise music rising from her phone. She worshiped with her voice as well as her pen, pouring out the talents her Creator had entrusted to her, believing that someday others would see it as wise stewardship as well. Others including those who shared her last name.

Her bearded dragon supervised from under his terrarium lights.

"What do you think so far, Jeremy?" She kept her eyes on the paper, guiding the pen with a loose wrist. "This time will be different," she said, more in a prayer of assurance than in conversation.

It had to be different. Because *everything* was about to be different.

A chime cut into the song, bringing her sketching to a momentary halt. The final of the three reminders she had set blazed across the screen of her phone, in all caps: FOR REAL THIS TIME: LEAVE.

She sighed. Time bore down on two o'clock, and getting to the Kansas City Central Library down Main Street would take more minutes than she had before her mom arrived, promptly as always. Of all the times not to ruffle her mom, the day she told her she was leaving the country was it.

She slipped her pen back among its cohorts in the Gates Bar-B-Q cup at the top of her desk, then tapped pause on her playlist. "She's going to be mad, Jeremy."

He flicked his tongue, wishing her luck.

"Thank you, bud." She stepped over to his abode and stroked her fingertips down his spiny back. "I think I'm ready. But probably not."

In the week she'd had to prepare for their Friday afternoon coffee date, she had tried on several potential ways to break the news of her acceptance of the elementary art instructor job at the Redeemer International School of Prague, even practiced a few with her dad, but none of them had held up against the imagined scrutiny of Edie Vance. Her mom hadn't traveled farther than the other side of Missouri. It was one thing to tell her mom she was going halfway around the world. It was another to tell her she would be gone for two years. Still another to reveal she had to raise her own salary to be on mission at RISP.

All the things she needed to say bucked her mom's idea of what Chloe's life should be like "by this point." That seemed to be one of Edie Vance's most-repeated phrases—"by this point"—a constant reminder to Chloe that she was in some way always missing a mark she'd never agreed to meet.

"I had been married for four years by this point"—said on Chloe's last birthday. "All the girls your age have an advanced degree by this point"—said the previous Thanksgiving. "Aren't you tired of being a barista by this point?"—said more than once. Her mom's measure of an adult had nothing to do with mastering the art of conveying a magnificent collision in another's eyes or the ability to teach others how to do it.

Chloe stopped in her kitchen before heading out the door. Two containers of protein balls waited on the counter. So simple and easy to make, and a runaway bestseller with her coworker Sori's MBA classmates, especially as spring finals approached. Thanks to Sori, she had learned that her customers' wallets opened widest when presented with a healthy, filling snack in the most stressful points of the semester. Two protein balls huddled together in adorable little cellophane bags, and each bag was adorned with a sticker featuring an inspirational quote. The added touch made the treats all the more sellable, Sori said. After two years, the joint endeavor had given Sori real-world business experience and Chloe a savings surplus that would cover her flight to Prague, with some to spare.

She tucked the containers into her backpack and paused at the small mirror by the front door. Red curls as gregarious as ever. Freckles a little darker after spending more time in the embrace of the outdoors. But her eyes—those eyes. Emerald glinting from a dream so close the taste never left her tongue.

So close, yet one giant mom-shaped step away.

My boldness is in you, God.

She pulled open the door, then trooped down the stairs of her fourplex.

Out on the porch, her landlord, Seymour Bove, looked up from his usual chair where he worked on his afternoon crossword puzzle. Thick-frame glasses dominated his face. His short white hair offset his deep bronze complexion.

"Afternoon, Seymour!"

"Purse," he reminded her.

Her shoe scuffed against the concrete as she came to a halt. "Right." She set down her backpack against the brick facade and hustled back up the stairs. Her purse hung on the hook Seymour had installed by that little mirror specifically to help her remember to take her purse. Most days, it worked. Other days, it took a village.

By the time she arrived back on the porch, Seymour had helped himself to a treat. He stood by the door holding her backpack, crumbs on his lips.

"You're eating my fundraising," she playfully reprimanded him.

"This batch is better," he replied as if not hearing. "What's that I taste?"

She turned toward her bike in the opposite corner of the porch. "Almond extract. Like it?"

"Not bad. You late for work again?"

"Late, yes, but to meet my mom at the library. Figured I'd drop off more product with Sori while I'm there. She's working the coffee shop today."

"You're late meeting your mom?" He gave a low whistle.

"I question my choices too." She unlocked her bike and wheeled it toward him.

"You have a car, you know." He nodded toward the bright yellow Xterra in the driveway, wedged between their fourplex and the neighboring one. "Four wheels're better'n two when you're late. Not to mention an engine."

"Goldie and I have an agreement. I only drive her on the weekends. Gotta make her last."

"Junkyard don't care if a car runs or not."

"She's got plenty of life left, Seymour. Something I'm sure you can appreciate."

He looked up at her over the rims of his glasses. "Just for that, I'm taking another package." He swiped a cellophane-wrapped treat, then handed her the backpack.

She chuckled and zipped the bag. If her mom had been there to witness his act, she would have been incredulous. But a ten-dollar bill would "somehow" appear under Chloe's door before she got home, more than three times the value of the snacks.

Chloe strapped on her backpack and lifted her bike down the stairs. "See you later, Seymour. Keep everyone in line while I'm gone."

"Don't have to tell me twice."

Sara Brunsvold is the Christy Award–winning author of *The Extraordinary Deaths of Mrs. Kip*, *The Divine Proverb of Streusel*, and *The Atlas of Untold Stories*. She creates stories that engage contemporary issues through the lens of hope and unshakable faith. Her passion is to connect with readers first through books, then through meaningful conversation. She lives with her family in Kansas. Learn more at SaraBrunsvold.com.

CONNECT WITH

SARA

SARABRUNSVOLD.COM

SHARE STORIES THAT SPEAK

SaraBrunsvoldAuthor

Sara_Brunsvold